# THE BRIDE'S SECRET

BOOKS BY ROSIE WALKER

*The Baby Monitor*
*My Husband's Ex*

*Secrets of a Serial Killer*
*The House Fire*

# ROSIE WALKER

# THE BRIDE'S SECRET

bookouture

Published by Bookouture in 2025

An imprint of Storyfire Ltd.
Carmelite House
50 Victoria Embankment
London EC4Y 0DZ

www.bookouture.com

The authorised representative in the EEA is Hachette Ireland
8 Castlecourt Centre
Dublin 15 D15 XTP3
Ireland
(email: info@hbgi.ie)

ISBN: 978-1-83618-079-1
eBook ISBN: 978-1-83618-081-4

*For Suzy Pope,*
*excellent BFF, writer, editor and first reader*

*And for Charlotte Robertson,*
*brilliant literary agent and friend*

PART ONE

1

## MAEVE

'Tomorrow marks the first day of the rest of my life. And I can't wait for it to begin,' I say in a quavering voice as I look around the table at my closest friends and family.

They gaze back at me with expectant smiles. I wink at Ella, a client-turned-friend who encouraged me to stand up tonight, pressing a fresh glass of champagne and orange juice into my hand and chanting, 'Speech, speech, speech!' She nods back, a huge grin on her face as she smiles at Robert and me. So many weddings have men talking *about* the bride, she'd argued: the best man's speech, the groom's speech, the father of the bride... so today with Ella's encouragement I decided to buck tradition. And because it's such a tight-knit group of close friends and family here at the rehearsal dinner, I have the courage to stand up and speak.

I glance up at my fiancé Robert, who stands next to me, a glass in his hand and his other arm wrapped around my waist, pulling me close.

He smells of home, and I want to nuzzle into the space between his neck and his shoulder. His hazel eyes twinkle in the candlelight, and I think I detect a sparkle of an unshed tear. I suppress a giggle and remind myself to tease him later. But I wouldn't change a thing. We're perfect opposites, always: I'm rough, he's smooth. I'm rigid, he's soft. And somehow, it works.

We made it.

I clear my throat, knowing what I'm going to say even without preparing. I'm going to tell the truth, from my heart. Even if I feel a bit ridiculous doing it.

'I hadn't been looking to fall in love. I was perfectly fine on my own, I'd tell myself. And anyone else who'd listen.' A knowing laugh echoes around the restaurant from my closest friends.

A few seats away down the table, Mum and Dad exchange a smile and I see Mum grab Dad's arthritic hand under the table and squeeze, their shoulders touching. They coordinated their outfits: the baby blue of his tie matching the sash on her dress.

Next to them, Robert's mother Hilda takes a pinch-mouthed sip from her glass before setting it down, her trade-mark brown lipstick leaving a perfect half-moon on the rim. She's staring at the tablecloth in front of her, not looking up to meet my eyes as I speak. She's never liked me – I put it down to typical reservations about my look: my short red wavy bob, muscular physique, and stacked ear piercings. But she's here for Robert and that's what matters.

'I had my friends, my classes and clients, my little flat, my cat Napoleon. I'd been intentionally on my own for years and wasn't looking for a man. I was tough and spiky and independent, and quite content. Until one day two years ago I met my best friend Sarah's older brother at her thirtieth birthday party. It's a bonus that our marriage will transform Sarah into my sister-in-law, too.'

I glance at her empty seat halfway down the table and a twinge of disappointment squeezes my chest. But she's a high-flying data technology lawyer and she'd already warned me that a big meeting with New York clients might mean she misses the dinner tonight.

I see a frown cross Robert's brow at the mention of his sister, too. I know he was disappointed when she phoned to say she wouldn't make it tonight. Even though they're adults, they sometimes bicker like children and I could hear from Robert's whispered admonitions down the phone that he wasn't pleased with her, and I suspect the feeling was mutual. Still, tomorrow's the most important part and she'll be here for that. Sarah's always come through for me in the end.

I take a breath and continue with the speech.

'Within just a few dates my armour fell away and my heart opened up to this tall, skinny and slightly awkward artist with kind eyes that crinkle in the corners.' I feel my cheeks growing hot at this uncharacteristic openness, and Robert tightens his grip around my waist, planting a kiss on the top of my head. I look up at him in silent thanks for his solidarity. He's always right next to me when I need him.

'I fell in love fast and hard, and when Robert proposed on our one-year anniversary, I didn't hesitate for a moment before I said "yes". "When you know, you know," they say – and I did know. I'm in my mid-thirties and I've had enough dysfunctional relationships, flings, situationships and heartbreak to know a good man when I find one. And Robert is a good man. The best.'

I lean into Robert and embrace the moment, feeling so lucky to be loved and accepted for exactly who I am by all these wonderful people who wanted to celebrate with Robert and me today. To be able to stand up and open my heart in front of them without fear.

I tighten my grip around the chilled glass and raise it into the air, tiny bubbles floating up, up, up past the restaurant's chandelier. I can see a waiter hovering in the doorway, wanting to come in and clear the dessert plates and napkins. Time to finish up and let everyone mingle until the restaurant stops replenishing our glasses and waiters begin stacking chairs around us.

'So please raise your glass to my lovely husband-to-be, Robert, and to a happy future, together for ever. Happily ever after.'

'Until death do you part,' shouts someone, and a few people 'whoop' in agreement.

I look around the room as everyone repeats my final sentiment and sips from their champagne flutes in unison.

And then Robert takes my glass, places it down on the table beside his own, and pulls me into a kiss.

A smile tugs at the corners of my mouth as I open my eyes the next morning and stare at the ceiling, lit blue-black like a bruise in the dawn light as the day creeps around the edge of the bedroom curtains. I'm careful not to move so I don't wake Robert; he's a light sleeper and it's a big day today. *Our* big day.

I can see the silhouette of my dress hanging on the back of our bedroom door. It looks ghostly in the half-light, the beautiful lace details and scalloped edges not yet visible. It must be about 4 a.m., reckoning by the lack of daylight, but the thrum of excitement and anxiety in my chest tells me I won't be able to get back to sleep, even though I want to. I'm too wired. But it's nice to take a moment to lie here in the silence, savouring these last moments before my life changes into another phase. A new start. A new name. A new identity: from single woman to wife.

Still groggy, I close my eyes again and stretch out my sleepy limbs, pointing my toes and easing out my spine. I must have slept very heavily – it feels like I barely moved all night. My muscles ache to move. Ordinarily if I'm awake this early I'll slip out of bed and pull on my running gear and go for a quick jog, stopping in the park to do squats, lunges and tricep dips on the edge of a bench. My legs twitch just thinking about it; they want to move. My body is strong and lean, my best asset and my most powerful tool. I put a lot of work into being strong. Strong enough to run, to jump, to climb, to fight. But today's not a day for exercise. Today's a day for make-up, a pretty dress, a demure smile. Hiding my muscles under lace and tulle. Fitting into a mould that no one – not even me – ever thought I'd fit into.

The day is planned down to the last detail, which is Robert's doing, not mine. I would have been happy to elope and get married just the two of us on a beach in the Caribbean somewhere, but Robert wanted the rehearsal dinner and the big day, the bride in the white dress, our families and friends celebrating with us. And why not? We only do this once, right?

I mentally run through the day we've planned together: a leisurely breakfast with Robert, eggs Benedict and fresh coffee in the sun-filled living room – although right now my nerves make my stomach churn at the thought of food. Then it'll be time for me to shower and start the beauty routine with the help of Sarah, who's coming round after breakfast to wrestle my unruly curls into order and apply all the concealer, foundation, eyeshadow and whatever else she keeps in that enormous make-up bag of hers. She'll make it fun, too: pouring us drinks, cracking jokes, pressing play on a cheesy Spotify playlist and reminding me of long-forgotten dance routines.

Then we'll head to the venue in separate cars: Sarah and me in a rented Bentley – a nod to tradition that Robert insisted on – and Robert in his own battered Lexus. Our friends will all be waiting for us in the amazing, arty venue Robert picked out for us: an old Victorian vaulted hall in an art gallery, in the centre of one of Glasgow's leafy parks. It's airy and stylish, just like the rest of my life since I met Robert. The congregation will be a striking mix of quirky artists (Robert's guests) and ravers and martial artists (mine). A perfect mishmash, just like our relationship. I can't wait.

I open my eyes again and see that the sun has crept up past the horizon, and the room's blue-black has lightened to a pink hue on the walls and carpet, although my wedding dress is still in shadow.

A smile creeps across my face and I turn over to face my fiancé; my soon-to-be husband, and reach out to wrap my arm around his sleeping form. He won't mind being woken up early on our wedding day, by his excitable fiancée and a kiss, surely?

I snuggle up to him and pull him closer, but something feels wrong. His body is rigid, unyielding. And my hand is wet where I touch his abdomen.

I push myself up onto my elbows, frowning. Even before my brain catches up, my body senses that something is wrong. My breath snags in my throat and my heart judders in my chest.

Robert's face is grey, his mouth slack, his cheeks and eyes sunken and the lids firmly closed. The crinkles around his eyes are gone – there's no ready smile about to cross his face. He looks alien, like a badly-sculpted wax figure of himself.

'Wake up, Robert,' I croak, my voice grainy and unused from hours of heavy sleep.

I lift my shaking hand to my eyes, the hand which touched Robert's sodden abdomen just moments before. My fingers are covered in blood.

The room is silent except for my own ragged breaths. *I am the only one here.* The only one alive.

My love is dead. Murdered next to me in our bed, my hand coated in his blood. And on the bed next to me is the knife that killed him.

I have no idea what to do.

## 2

### GILLY

Gilly knows exactly what to do. As much as she's ever sure of anything.

She's gone through extensive training for calls exactly like this, and it's actually a relief to speak to a caller who might genuinely need her help, instead of a teenager giggling down the phone on an elaborate prank call, or an old lady who refuses to read the local bus timetable and wants her to google the next bus into town for her.

Not that Gilly's judging anyone, of course. That would be against the principles of the helpline. Well, even if she does judge, it's only inside her mind. And that's harmless, surely?

The heavy breathing continues, punctuated by the occasional sob and wet-sounding snuffle. The caller – Gilly thinks it's a woman, but she's learned not to assume; not to judge – must be incredibly upset. Or scared. She's not sure which.

'I'm here when you're ready to talk,' Gilly says, in her most pressure-free, gentle voice. It's OK if this caller never says anything, she reminds herself.

As expected, the caller doesn't respond, their juddering

breaths continuing as if Gilly hasn't said a word. She can't help but wonder what's going on in this person's life. Have they been assaulted? Are they hurt?

There are some situations in which Gilly can call the emergency services, but she was surprised to learn during her training that it's only a very small number of circumstances. In general, the caller's anonymity takes precedence over everything else, and it's only really if they seem like they're about to kill themselves that she can ask them for an address so she can send an ambulance. And if they don't provide an address, there's nothing Gilly can do. Except listen.

Callum was the most concerned about that rule, when Gilly came home from her first training day and told him how powerless the call handlers were.

'But you can't really help, then?' he'd said, his brow furrowing with concern as he ignored Polly squirting too much ketchup onto her plate and Jake whining for a sweet treat before he'd even finished his first bite of dinner. 'You just have to absorb all that pain and suffering and you can't do anything? What about you? You're just a volunteer with anxiety issues. Do the helpline care about your welfare at all?'

At the time, Gilly had brushed him off with a very breezy assurance that she was sure the helpline had systems in place to help their call handlers if they'd had to deal with a distressing call. Even if she'd known the lack of welfare support on offer, Gilly would still have continued with the training. She was so desperate for a change in her life now that both kids were at school full-time and her days stretched out ahead of her endlessly. It was like an itch: an itch to make an impact on the world somehow, for her life to feel important again. To work out who she was and where she fitted in this universe, as someone other than a mother.

But six months into the role, Gilly knows how rare it is to

receive a call where she feels she's actually made a difference to a person's life.

Now, her whole world narrows to a pinpoint as she homes in on the individual on the phone, tries to work out what they need, what might help. As she listens to the despair and sorrow on the other end of the line, she feels alive and alert.

She clears her throat, hesitates a moment, and then adds, 'I'm listening. I'm right here.'

The caller draws a shaky breath and then their breathing settles into a steady rhythm again.

Gilly closes her eyes and rolls her head from left to right, easing out the tension in her neck. She glances at the display on the phone on the desk in front of her: 00:53:37. Almost an hour of this.

She opens her eyes, the narrow pinpoint of focus widening to take in the room around her, the handful of other volunteers on shift, separated by Plexiglas barriers for privacy. The low hum of conversations and calls, Henry the coordinator across the room in his office, visible behind a glass partition so he can see the volunteers. Across the desk, her colleague Vivian waves a hand at her and gives her a thumbs-up, switching to a thumbs-down, her head tilted quizzically. She's asking if everything's OK.

Gilly purses her lips sideways and gives a half-shrug. *Not sure.*

Vivian nods and mimes to ask if Gilly wants a cup of tea.

Gilly nods enthusiastically and gives a grateful smile. She's parched, she realises now.

Calls like this are exhausting, but she won't fully tune in to how much this has taken out of her until she hangs up the phone at the end of the call. And she can't be the one to do it – it has to be the caller who decides when the phone call is finished. Her record is four hours, one weekday afternoon when someone phoned from a bridge, but wouldn't tell her which one so she couldn't summon help. She tries not to think about that call, and how she'll never know what happened to that caller in the end. She hopes they hung up because someone came to help. But she'll never know. There's no way to find out.

She'd not been able to sleep properly for weeks after that one. There was only so much that Holland and Barrett's valerian root capsules and ashwagandha supplements could do to calm her down after that, especially when she's got pretty high anxiety levels anyway. Callum had tried to make her see the GP to get something stronger, but she just couldn't face it.

That can't happen again, she vows, although she knows really that she has no control over that. It's one of the things that Callum really doesn't like about her coming here three days a week. The emotional impact of everyone else's problems, and no way to follow up, to know that you've actually made a difference. He just doesn't get it.

Since she joined the helpline, she's felt so much happier, more fulfilled. Perhaps someone like Callum can't be happy without a tangible result at the end of a project, but Gilly gets a lot out of the work she does here, and mostly she's OK with the anonymity, the not knowing. And it works both ways, too: there's a comfort in being a disembodied voice at the end of a phone line, not having a name or an identity. She's just a voice, her identity boiled down to what she chooses to say or not say. It's refreshing, slipping out of her skin and leaving her life behind for a few hours. She feels powerful. She feels like she has a purpose.

Vivian returns and puts down a cup of strong tea in front of Gilly, along with a Penguin biscuit, placed on the desk with a wink. Gilly rolls her eyes at her, but she smiles too. Vivian knows that Gilly's trying to lose a few pounds, but phone calls like this need sugar to get through. She'll park further away from the supermarket later to add some steps in and make up for it. Maybe she'll be able to persuade the kids away from

CBeebies and into the garden for a game of football before dinner, too.

'Thank you,' Gilly mouths at Vivian, as Vivian takes her seat back at the desk opposite and pulls her headset on with a grin.

Vivian pushes a button on her phone and through the Plexiglas between their desks Gilly sees her mouth move. She can make out the words that have now become so ingrained in her consciousness that sometimes she almost answers her own mobile phone with them too: 'Hello, you've reached Safeline. How can I help?'

On her own call, the caller's breathing seems to have calmed down and they haven't sobbed or howled for at least five minutes. Perhaps she's helped. Sometimes people just need to know that there's a person who *could* listen if they wanted to talk. Maybe that's enough for this person today. Gilly will have to tell herself that, if this is all that happens in today's call. That'll be how she justifies it to herself; how she'll make herself feel good about today.

'I'm still here,' she says in her soft voice. 'We're open twenty-four hours a day, so if you need—'

A heart-wrenching scream pierces her eardrum down the line, but it's quickly muffled as soon as it began.

Gilly's mouth drops open and her hand flies to the headset, as if by holding the earpiece against her ear she can somehow offer more comfort to the caller, or let them know that she's there.

'Is everything OK? What happened? Hello?' She drops the soft tone and reverts to her ordinary voice, the one she uses when one of her kids falls down and is lying on the floor and she's rushing over, still waiting to know if this is an antiseptic-and-a-plaster injury or a rush-to-A&E situation.

Her ears are still ringing from the blood-curdling scream,

but now there's just sobbing again, muffled as if the caller has their hands over their mouth as if to stop the noise.

'I'd really like to help you,' Gilly starts to say, but the line goes dead, replaced by a throbbing dial tone in her ear.

The caller has hung up.

Gilly hasn't helped anyone.

## 3

## MAEVE

My throat is raw from screaming.

At some point, I scrambled out of bed, away from the body. I sit curled up against the wall, my naked body huddled and shivering against the wall, as far away as I can get. The sun's fully up now, and in the golden dawn I can see the speckles of Robert's blood splattered across the bottom of my once-white wedding dress. And a smear on the bodice: a bloody handprint.

I'll never wear my wedding dress. My fiancé is dead.

My own hands are covered in his blood, and my body, too. I don't know how, but perhaps I touched him in my sleep and didn't realise. I've always been an odd sleeper: talking in my sleep, sleepwalking as a child, night terrors. Weird things that get worse when I'm under stress, like the night before my wedding. In my uncharacteristically heavy sleep last night I probably wrapped my arms around his corpse without realising. The thought makes bile rise up in my throat and I force myself to swallow it down.

At my feet is the knife, thrown across the room as soon as I realised my fingers were wrapped around it. One of our kitchen knives, from a Sabatier set given to us as an early wedding present from Ella. It's covered in Robert's blood. And my fingerprints.

I look at my shaking hands, Robert's blood already drying and turning the colour of rust. Even if I wash my hands, scrub them with a nail brush, there'll be dried blood in the crevices of my palms, under my fingernails. Even if I wash the knife, there'll still be evidence tying me to the murder weapon. There's no washing this away. And how can I explain to the police that I slept through a murder?

I pull myself to my feet, my legs shaking uncontrollably. I grip the edge of the bed to steady myself and force myself to look at the body. Robert's body.

He looks so normal, yet entirely different. Like returning in adulthood to a once-familiar childhood place and wandering through the mixture of lost memories and long-held ones. Like a dreamscape. His hair is still the same, a caramel, salt-and-pepper mix I've always loved. His nose still has the little bump on the bridge, from an old hockey accident in his school days. It gives his features – *gave* his features – a nice jauntiness, I always thought. But beside these comforting familiarities there's a haunting, stark newness to him. Unfamiliarity. Like he's a stranger.

He's so still, his chest not rising and falling with his breath. Without blood pumping through his veins there's a grey waxi-ness to his skin. He's Robert but not Robert at all.

A wide spread of blood has pooled underneath his body. Soaked into our once-white sheets and down into the mattress, creeping over to my side where I lay asleep, no idea of what was happening next to me as his life slipped away. So much blood. More than I could even imagine a body could hold.

Perhaps the police will ask me why I didn't call for an ambulance straight away. Why I didn't perform CPR on his lifeless body. But lifeless is the word so clearly imprinted across every element of this person in front of me: he's lifeless. He's dead. There's no hope of coming back from this. CPR would do nothing. He's been dead for a long time. Hours, probably. I can see a darkness where his body touches the bedsheet underneath him: the blood pooling in his corpse.

My fingers gripping the edge of the bed, I steel myself to pull back the sodden quilt and look where my eyes have avoided until now: the wounds that killed him. I've looked anywhere but there, taking in the details of Robert for the final time before his body is taken away, but it's time.

Because despite my avoidance, a part of me has known the truth since the moment I realised I had his blood on my hands. I ball my hands into fists, gripping the bedsheets tighter, and I breathe out with a huge shudder.

The quilt is heavy with his blood as I lift it away from his abdomen, and all my instincts tell me not to look at his injuries. At what his attacker has done to my fiancé, the love of my life. How they took his life.

What I see causes the blood to drain from my head and my vision to darken in shock and fear. I can't get enough air into my lungs. I'm going to faint.

I have to look away.

I bend over, my head between my knees, willing myself not to lose consciousness. Not now. I can't. I need to think, to plan. I need to get out of here. NOW.

I'm naked and covered in blood, but I need—

The landline starts to ring, the handset next to Robert's side of the bed filling the air with a shrill tone that jangles my brain. I straighten up.

It's my wedding day. The best day of my life. The first day of the rest of my life. Family and friends are waking up, dressing ready to celebrate with Robert and me, to watch us pledge the rest of our lives to each other and to drink and dance and cele-brate. Sarah's probably packing her make-up and her dress; sending a last-minute work email (she can't ever switch off); tying a scarf around the rollers in her hair.

No one knows the nightmare I've woken up in today. The person on the other end of that phone is probably calling to talk about some tiny, insignificant detail about today: what time are the flowers being collected, or how many vegetarians are attending the reception. It's laughable, what felt important just a couple of hours ago.

Everything has changed. The life I thought I would lead is over.

The ringing stops, the caller giving up when no one answers. Robert's phone starts to buzz on the nightstand next to his body.

Soon, someone will arrive at our house and knock on our door. The chauffeur, come to take us to the wedding. My dad, to ride in the car to the ceremony and walk me up the aisle. Sarah, ready to help with my make-up. Sarah, whose only brother lies dead in front of me.

Will she blame me? Have I lost my best friend, as well as my fiancé, today? Will she believe I did it? Will everyone? The knife was in my bed. I'm covered in his blood. I didn't wake up when it happened. I couldn't protect him. And I'm still alive.

I let go of the bed, a new resolve straightening my spine and balling my hands into fists. Purposeful, now.

I need to leave. When anyone arrives at my house today, I need to be gone. I need to disappear, even if it makes me look guilty.

I take another look at those gaping wounds on my fiancé's body, no longer bleeding since his heart stopped. Those telltale markings that might as well be my name carved into his flesh. The killer left a calling card and it says *Maeve*.

The person who killed my husband knows me very well. They know how my mind works. They know how I would kill a man, if I had to. And that's how they killed Robert.

I need help, but I have no idea who I can trust. I've been framed.

# 4

## GILLY

The empty Penguin bar wrapper lies crumpled next to her mobile on the desk, the photo on her lock screen lit up as a text from Callum arrives.

*Will head to Morrisons at lunch. Want me to get anything for dinner?* Callum's asking.

He's planning his break: a small half-hour window in his day that his receptionist guards with her life and makes sure no patients are scheduled so he has time to choke down a sandwich while catching up on his texts.

She can't think about dinner. She stares at the lock screen picture as if it could neutralise the swirling, panicked feeling after that call.

It's a lovely photo, one which makes her smile every time her phone lights up: it's her and the kids – a rare photo of the three of them, since she's normally the one taking the photo. They're all grinning widely and both children have ice cream around their mouths. A gust of wind has blown a blonde tendril of wavy hair across her face and she was just reaching up with a hand to move it out of the way when Callum took the picture. She's wearing sunglasses and her face doesn't look as chubby as it sometimes does nowadays. A day out last July at the beach on one of those gloriously sunny Scottish summer days which feel like a day in the Caribbean.

Of course, in the minutes after the photo was taken, Polly fell on her bum in a rock pool and cried all the way back to the car because her pants were wet and sandy. And Jake whined as they passed the ice-cream van because he wanted a second Twister. But, childhood complaints aside, it was a beautiful day, and Callum had held her hand while the children played in the waves.

She shakes herself back to the present, feeling a little better after the palate cleanser moment of reminiscing. Her shift is nearly over; she'll be home in time to collect the children from school. Around her there's the low mumble of chatter from the handful of other volunteers on the early shift with her.

She revisits some mindfulness techniques she always uses when she's feeling overwhelmed and anxious. Focusing on something she can smell (stale coffee), taste (the Penguin she just finished), hear (the low hum of Vivian's conversation), feel (the rough wool of the desk chair through her thin trousers), and see. She looks up.

Henry's watching from his office window while he talks on the phone, his headset flashing a little Bluetooth connection light. Sometimes he listens to their calls, checks they're following protocol. But today his mouth is moving, his hands gesticulating, his earring glinting as he moves. He's not eavesdropping, she notices with relief. It makes her uncomfortable to know that he could listen into a call at any point, even though she's careful to follow the rules and refer back to her training. It's just the invasiveness that bothers her. Like she can't 100 per cent be herself if she knows she's being observed.

At the desk opposite, Vivian's hunched over her keyboard, researching something for a caller on the line. 'Here, I've got the number for your local Citizens Advice branch,' Gilly hears her say, Vivian's voice carrying over the partition. The Plexiglas partitions aren't soundproof, but they do muffle sound enough that the callers can't hear other conversations around the office, which feels important. They need to feel like their call is the only important one.

She picks up her mobile, about to reply to Callum's text, when her desk phone rings, the shrill, melodic ringtone which all the phones in this office are set to. It's a ringtone that's replicated on business phones around the country, and occasionally Gilly will be sitting in the hairdresser's or in a local takeaway when their phone rings in exactly the same tone. Every time this happens, her whole body freezes and her stomach flips and fizzes like she's immediately on alert. She's like one of Pavlov's dogs, but instead of a bell meaning food, this ringtone brings a little dread of what might wait for her on the other end of the line.

She pulls her headset back on and hovers her finger over the 'answer' button. What will it be this time? An immediate hang-up? The rhythmic breathing of a telephone masturbator? Someone she might genuinely be able to help? *Helpline roulette*, she thinks to herself, and answers the phone.

'Hello, you've reached Safeline. How can I help?'

She closes her eyes in resignation as she hears the now-familiar distressed breathing on the other end of the line. Ragged breaths in and out, as if the person has been running, or having a panic attack. Perhaps both.

She feels a flash of frustration. Why couldn't someone else have answered this call? They're randomly assigned by the phone system as they come in, and it feels unfair that this caller has come through to her desk twice in one day. And her shift finishes soon – she can't be late to pick up the kids, but she also wouldn't know how to cut a call short if the caller wants to stay on the line.

She leans down to one of the lower drawers of her desk and

with trembling fingers she pulls out the Safeline Training Manual, a thick document about the size of a phone book. If this caller isn't going to speak, she can at least take the time to look up their policies on what to do if a call is running over the end of your shift.

The breathing continues, feeling curiously intimate in her ear, like this person is a lover who has fallen asleep unable to face the wrench of saying goodnight.

Without consulting the manual, she knows that the non-judgemental and anonymity principles of the helpline mean that unless the caller tells her they've already spoken to her today, she can't assume it's the same person as before. Unless told otherwise, each call has to be treated on its own merits, as an independent and separate conversation. If a caller wants a regular, ongoing therapeutic relationship with a call handler, the volunteers are instructed to direct callers elsewhere.

'How can I help you today?' she asks again. And then, feigning ignorance, she says 'Can you hear me? I'm not sure the line is working. I can hear you, though.'

The breathing continues.

She tries to slow her own, focusing on the rise and fall of her belly. 'Whatever you want to tell me is confidential. I'm here when you're ready.'

Nothing.

Frustrated, Gilly picks up her phone and opens up a reply to Callum, starting to type:

*We've got chilli ingredients. Maybe some tortilla chips? Thx xx*

Before she can press send, though, the caller clears their throat. 'Erm...'

She drops her mobile to the desk with a clatter. She wasn't expecting them to talk. She thought it was going to be the same as the previous call: an hour of breathing and crying and then a dramatic hang-up. She'd made an assumption and a judgement – big no-nos in the world of Safeline.

Like before, her world narrows to a pinprick as she focuses on the voice at the other end of the line. She holds her breath, listening.

'I just wanted to call back and say...' a quiet voice quivers, punctuated with a sniff. 'Thank you for being here for me.'

Gilly opens her mouth to respond, but the caller continues.

'I feel like I can trust you. Can we talk again?'

Gilly smiles and glances up at Henry's window, wondering if he's listening in. For once, she almost wishes he is. But he's not visible, his window dark. He must have stepped away from his desk. Damn. This feels like a landmark moment for her. She's not new to the helpline – she's been here for at least six months, and because she doesn't work full-time she's able to cover a lot of shifts. She's started to get a reputation among the other volunteers for being a good person to call if they need shift cover, because Gilly tends to say 'yes' if there's nothing else going on that day. And there's very rarely anything else going on in her life, if the kids are at school and Callum is at work. But she still feels new, still finding her feet and getting to know people, and she's also still familiarising herself with the many policies and approaches, and getting her head around what anonymity and confidentiality really mean when it comes to things like this.

So for a caller to give her such great feedback for a call where Gilly followed the rules to the letter, it's a real achievement. A smile tugs at the corner of her mouth and she sits up straighter at her desk.

Perhaps this is it. She's finally, after all this time, found something she's good at. A calling, perhaps.

Maybe this is the start of something. First she's a volunteer, and then maybe next she could retrain; become a counsellor or therapist or something.

She's proud of herself, she realises. She's helped someone just by offering a listening ear and showing them that she's there for them if they need her. She shifts in her seat. 'Yes, of course we can talk again. Our lines are open—'

'No,' the caller interrupts. It's a woman's voice, as she'd suspected from the sobs on the earlier call. She has a steely tone, determined and clear. Gilly imagines that she's the kind of woman who gets things done in her day-to-day life. Perhaps she's a CEO or runs her own business.

Gilly shakes her head, stopping her speculation. Judgement is against the rules, even if she's ascribing great success to a person's life in her imagination. It's still making a judgement based on nothing but the tone of a voice.

'No,' the caller says again. 'I want to talk to you. Not someone else. When can we speak again?'

She bites her lip. How can she say this gently and kindly, without making the caller feel rejected? 'All our volunteers are trained the same way. They'll all approach your call with the same values that I did. I'm so glad you found this helpf—'

'I don't want to start again with someone new. You were so patient, so kind. You sat there for an hour with me, like you were holding my hand through the line. Please.' Gilly hears the tears in her voice, the now-familiar sob in the back of the caller's throat. 'What's your name? At least tell me your name.'

The smile leaves Gilly's lips. 'I'm afraid I can't give you my name. This is an anonymous service, from both sides. To protect you. So you feel safe to tell us anything.' A sweat breaks out on her forehead as she glances at the time on her mobile and her heart rate picks up again. Nearly time to go. She needs to get the kids. It's their half-day on Fridays and it'll take her at least half an hour to get across town in the lunchtime traffic.

The crying starts again, a soft despair in every murmur. Gilly's heart breaks for her. What has happened to this poor woman? Is she afraid? Has she lost someone? What does she need?

Henry's office window is still dark.

She imagines Jake and Polly standing alone outside their school, all their classmates already collected by their parents. At nine years old, Jake in particular would find this traumatic: he feels things deeply, thinks about things a lot. She sometimes worries he's picked up her anxious nature; inherited it or somehow absorbed her stress hormones while in the womb. In his mind, a late pickup could mean Mum's abandoned him or died in a car crash on her way there. By the time she arrived, he'd be inconsolable and therefore so would Polly, who is just six and looks to her older brother for everything.

She can't do that to them.

'Look,' Gilly finds herself saying, her voice hushed and urgent. 'I can't tell you my name. But if you call back next Tuesday, you might be able to get through to me again.' Her cheeks heat up as she knows she's broken the rules. But what harm can it do, really? This caller spent an hour sobbing her heart out to Gilly today, why should she have to start again with a new volunteer?

The quiet sobs on the other end of the line pause, and there's a grateful sigh. 'Next Tuesday. Thank you so much. I'll find you.'

The line goes dead.

As Gilly grabs her handbag and picks up her mug to return it to the kitchen, a movement in Henry's office window catches her eye. She freezes and glances up. It's him, his face at the window, a frown across his brow as he looks out at her.

Was he listening? Did he hear her break the rules?

But then the caller's final words echo through her mind and her skin prickles with the horrifying realisation that she's made a mistake. *I'll find you.*

## 5

## MAEVE

I turn off my phone and slide it into my bedside drawer, next to my notebook and pen, earplugs, hand cream – all the detritus of everyday life. I can't take it with me. I can't take any of this with me. The things I thought were necessities in my previous life are luxuries from now on. Unnecessary ones. I can only take with me what I can shove in a bag and carry on my back out of here before Sarah arrives and finds her brother's dead body in our bed.

I flinch, hating that I have to do that to my best friend. She's protected me from so much, held my hand in the worst moments of my life, and I'm abandoning her for what is sure to be the worst of hers. I wish there was another way. I wish I could see her, could sob into her arms and grieve with her, and comfort her like she would comfort me.

It's just until I work out what happened to Robert. Until I have something concrete about what happened that I can take to the police. Then I'll come back, be there for Sarah like the friend she deserves. Her ride or die.

I grab the old camping backpack from the back of the

wardrobe and shove a few possessions into it: hiking socks, thermals, underwear, first aid kit... I don't know where I'm going and even though it's summer, I know that the nights are cold in Scotland. I can't guarantee I'll find some shelter to sleep every night. I need to be realistic.

After combing through my drawers, I scan the room, checking if there's anything else in here I might need. My eyes alight on my wedding dress hanging on the back of the door, splattered with Robert's blood. I can't look directly at the hump of Robert's body in the bed, and I gingerly pull the bedsheet up and over his body so I don't have to look at him again. There's no ceremony or goodbye here. It's not Robert any more.

I think back to other cases I've read about in the news – the press speculating that covering a body is a feminine act, a nod to contrition and regret. It implies the person was killed by a woman. Total rubbish. Whereas covering him now was just self-preservation, mourning and devastation. I can't bear to look at my dead fiancé's corpse. That doesn't make me a murderer. It makes me human.

I hesitate as I look at the landline phone on Robert's bedside table, the handset covered in splatters of his blood. It's not too late. I could call the police, demonstrate my innocence. Running will definitely make me look guilty.

My mind skips ahead to what the next minutes, hours, days, weeks, months will look like. They'll pretend they believe I'm the grieving fiancée at first. They might even believe it, but not for long. As soon as the forensic evidence comes in and the murder weapon has my fingerprints all over it, and they learn about my past, my job, me... Within hours my family liaison officer will have been replaced with a police officer, the sympathetic looks replaced with a steely glare. My reactions will be observed: do I seem upset enough? Traumatised enough? Or am I too calm?

I'll be cautioned and left alone for hours in a small room at a rickety table with cold tea in a plastic cup. They won't let me sleep. Testing my limits, seeing if I crack under pressure. My voice will be recorded whenever I speak and very soon they'll tell me I can get a lawyer if I want one. It'll seem like a generous and friendly offer, phrased to imply that it's not necessary. But it will be.

No. I can't call the police.

Today should be my wedding day. Soon, our friends will be gathering with anticipation in the beautiful venue, chattering excitedly. Robert's artist friends will be introducing themselves to my friends from various places: people like Ella, May and Leonard who've attended my self-defence classes every week for years, or Tilly and Tosh who lived across the hall in the flat I had before I moved in with Robert. They'll be dressed up beautifully, facing an altar adorned with flowers, waiting for me and Robert to walk down the aisle. But we'll never come. We're not getting married. We're never getting married. And I so wanted to marry him.

Robert. Lovely, kind, gentle Robert who loved me wholeheartedly right from the start. And I loved him too, in just the same way. There was no drama or conflict in our relationship, it was easy and calm right from the first date. With him I felt safe and looked after for the first time in my adult life. I could fall apart and I knew he'd be right there to help me put myself back together.

And now he's gone.

I know that if I let the grief in for more than a moment, I'll collapse under the weight of it and I won't be able to move. I won't be able to run.

And I have to run, I know that now. The one person in the world who could have helped me is gone. He's dead. There's only me, and the way I need to take care of myself is by running.

I hoist the backpack onto my shoulder and take one last look around the room. My eyes land again on Robert's body on the bed and I reach out to touch him one final time. My hands make contact with the bedsheet and I recoil. He's cold, his body stiff. It's not Robert. I can never touch Robert again.

As I descend the stairs on shaky legs, I hear sirens in the distance. They're far away, but they sound like they're getting closer. Whoever did this planned for me to be caught and charged, I just know it.

There's no more time. Whatever I have in my bag is all I can take.

With a pang of guilt, I pour biscuits into Napoleon's bowl and make sure his water is topped up to the brim. It won't be long until someone arrives to investigate the missing bride and groom. And he may not even notice my absence, as he's probably out wandering the nearby back alleys, hunting for mice. I wish I could bury my nose in the soft fur between his ears, one last time.

I check both the front and back doors and all the windows but they're secure, just as they were when Robert and I headed to bed last night. No sign of forced entry. No shred of evidence of an intruder to show to the police. Nothing to support my claims of innocence. No reason to stay. A sob bubbles up in my throat and I swallow it down hard.

I grab my hiking boots and waterproof jacket from the coat cupboard and rush into the kitchen. I unlock the back door, pocketing Robert's keys – I've no idea where my handbag is, or my own keys. Just as I'm about to pull the door closed behind me, I notice Robert's wallet sitting next to the microwave. In a quick glance I see that it's full of cash: a huge wad of it stacked inside.

Money for the photographer, I remember now. And tips for the catering staff. There must be nearly £500 in his wallet, I think as I shove it into my own pocket. At least two cash machine trips.

*Thank God.* No. No god would let any of this happen. If I ever had any belief, it's gone now. I offer up my thanks to Robert, instead: the prepared and thoughtful man who should have become my husband today. Who could have wanted him dead?

# 6

## MAEVE

I pull a baseball cap low down on my brow, obscuring my bobbed hair. The sun is bright and I don't stand out in a hat and sunglasses, a backpack on my back. I cut through Kelvingrove Park so CCTV can't track me, the dew coating the toes of my hiking boots as I leave a trail across the grass.

It's only a couple of miles from our house to the city centre, and my backpack isn't too heavy. I stride past cafés, the smell of coffee and fresh bread making my stomach lurch. I feel like I'll never be able to eat again. The people in those coffee shops are living their ordinary lives; walking their dogs; heading to work; meeting a friend. I feel a flash of anger and jealousy that I can't be there, too, living my ordinary life. That my life has turned upside down so instantaneously.

Soon the little artisan cafés, antique shops and independent shops of our quirky neighbourhood transform into the wide Victorian tenement-lined streets of Glasgow city centre, buildings stained dark with decades of exhaust fumes and rain. As I pass tanning salons, kebab shops and new builds I blend into the crowds of office workers and tourists, and as I approach

Buchanan bus station a little band of tension I had held around my chest starts to loosen.

No one is chasing me. I hear no sirens. Perhaps that siren I heard from our house wasn't even heading there. Maybe no one has found out the awful truth in our bed.

I'm going to be able to get away, to regroup, to think. To work out what's happened and why. Just because I'm on the run doesn't mean I'm a criminal. But I need space and time, and then I'll come back with the answers.

I glance at the clock sculpture outside the bus station, a giant silver pair of running legs with a square clock on top. It's likely none of our wedding guests know yet. They're all still blissfully unaware, thinking this is a normal day. For them it's still to come: the earth-shattering moment where their lives change and someone wonderful is wrenched from them. Robert was their brother, their friend, their confidant, their support. Soon they'll learn he's gone. And they'll think I did it.

I close my eyes and flinch away from the wave of grief. There's no time.

The boxy brick 1970s bus station stands ahead of me, streams of commuters pouring in and out. I pull my hat down lower on my brow and join the throng, my backpack jostling alongside briefcases and messenger bags.

Inside the echoing, airy station, I scan the departures board. London, Aberdeen, Perth... I spot it halfway down: final destination Inverness, a bus leaving in half an hour. Enough time to buy a ticket in cash and grab a coffee and a sandwich from the stall across the bustling concourse. Even though the thought of food disgusts me, this will be a long journey and I might need something later.

I choose a seat near the back of the bus and soon I watch through the window as we pull out of the station and the grey stone of Glasgow's traffic-choked streets shifts to the wide lanes of motorway. I pull Robert's keys from my pocket and check what's on the keyring. Our front door, his bike lock, his studio, and there: the old-fashioned mortise key, slight rust on its corners. And suddenly I'm back in our living room a few weeks ago, and my heart aches with love and loss.

# 7

## MAEVE

'So, these pesky vows,' Robert had said that night, placing two large glasses of red wine on the coffee table. Outside, a spring storm rattled the windows and rain pebbled against the glass. Ordinarily I hated Glasgow's wet weather, but tonight I felt cosy cuddled up inside with Robert. He picked up his notebook and fountain pen and sat next to me.

I'd leaned forward to clink my wine against his glass. We'd decided tonight was the night to write them – separately, so they remained a lovely surprise for each other on our wedding day. But we'd agreed that it'd be nice if we both wrote them simultaneously, so they somehow shared a tone and a feeling.

I smiled at him from my curled-up position on the sofa, my legs wrapped up in a blanket. In the corner of the room, quiet classical music floated from the radio: Robert liked to tune in to the BBC concerts, and tonight's was Elgar's 'Enigma Variations', a beautiful orchestral piece which made me feel like I was a seagull flying on the wind, watching the sea crash onto the shore.

I'd been staring at the blank piece of paper for the last half-hour. I had lots to say about how much I loved Robert, about my hopes for our life together after our wedding and about how I wanted to treat him for the rest of our lives. I just didn't know where to start.

Robert looked similarly perplexed, his tall slender figure hunched over a fresh page in his notebook.

'Are you struggling with what to say?' I asked, hoping to distract us both and prevent this feeling like a chore, like homework.

He put his pen down and nodded, his hair falling over his forehead and making him look much younger and more boyish than his thirty-eight years.

'Let's talk for a bit, then, see what inspiration we can get.'

He leaned back on the sofa and curled an arm around my shoulders as the radio concert paused and the audience descended into rapturous applause. One of my favourite things about Robert was that he didn't need to fill a silence. His words were considered, and never wasted. And in turn, he calmed me down from a frenetic worrier into a more measured version of myself. I felt safe when he was near. Less pressured to perform.

We listened as the announcer introduced the next concerto, and then I cleared my throat. 'I haven't told you this, but I think part of me always knew I would marry you. Even on the day we met.'

He pulled me in closer and kissed my forehead. 'That's very romantic. But... I can't imagine what you saw in me at Sarah's thirtieth that signalled "potential life partner". I was tipsy on champagne and dancing like an idiot.'

I laughed, remembering his lanky figure waving across the dance floor like one of those American car-wash flappy men. 'That was exactly what I saw. Sarah had always told me about her sensible, staid older brother with the successful art career and the mortgage, and suddenly there you were being someone much more complex than that. And I wanted to be up there, dancing like a loon right next to you.'

Robert gave me another kiss – this time on the corner of my mouth – and then he released me and pointed at my blank piece of paper with an elegant finger. 'That's good. You should write that down.'

'And spoil the surprise of my vows? No way. I need fresh material.'

He rolled his eyes indulgently and leaned forward for his wine. 'Actually,' he said after taking a sip, 'I wanted to talk to you about something to do with our marriage. Not our wedding, but the long-term bit.'

I blanched at the tone shift and tried to wrench it back to jovial fun. 'You're already married?' I filled in for him, an eyebrow raised and laughter bubbling in my throat. 'No, wait. I've got it. You want to live in separate houses, like Helena Bonham-Carter and Tim Burton? I've always thought that sounded pretty idyllic actually, popping round for a bit of you-know-what and then going to your separate living quarters to starfish-sleep...' My voice faded as I realised Robert wasn't smiling alongside me. His expression was serious, a little hurt.

'I'm sorry,' I said, reaching out a hand onto his firm thigh. 'Don't let me interrupt. Tell me what you were going to say.' I mentally chided myself, reminding myself to leave space for my gentle fiancé, not to trample him with my own forceful personality.

His expression cleared and he put his hand on top of mine, enveloping my fingers in his own. 'I know we're spending a lot of money on the wedding and that we agreed not to have a honeymoon yet, but...' He stopped himself, shrugged his shoulders like he was resetting. 'And while we're talking about vows, what we're promising, I thought we could also lay out what we're bringing into the marriage, you know?'

I shook my head, trying to be patient with Robert's habit of starting and stopping sentences, of introducing multiple concepts and not tying them together well enough for me to follow. 'I'm not following. Honeymoon and promises?'

'Maeve, there's something I haven't told you.' He removed his hand from my thigh and sat forward, both hands clasped together.

My body clenched, preparing for the worst. I was used to it. I'd been through a lot, and I should have known that things couldn't be just totally great. You couldn't meet the man of your dreams, build a life with him, move in together, and prepare to get married without something going wrong and taking it all away. That didn't happen to me, to Maeve. I got the short straw every time. Even when it seemed for a moment like I might get a brief reprieve.

Robert didn't notice my ashen face, my immobile muscles as I waited for him to drop the axe. He stared at his large hands, the fingers ingrained with ink from his printmaking in the studio earlier that day.

'I own a cottage in the Highlands,' he said.

Breath whooshed out from my pursed lips. So many disastrous scenarios had flashed across my mind, but I couldn't have predicted this.

I stared at him, open-mouthed, as he explained that when he was first starting out as an artist he'd had a mentor who'd fallen ill. Robert had cared for him in his final days and in return the artist had left him a little cottage in a remote village a few miles from Inverness. Robert had had no idea that the artist was planning to leave him anything at all, but the bequest changed his life and his career. At the time, Robert still lived at home with his family and he'd kept the inheritance a secret from them – he'd wanted somewhere he could go to work. Somewhere peaceful with space to paint and draw. That cottage opened the floodgates of his creativity, and was the catalyst for some of his most successful works.

'In the spirit of sharing things about our lives before we get married, I wanted to tell you about it. It's my little secret getaway and now it'll be yours, too.'

He'd got out an old Ordnance Survey map, then, and pointed to the village. Then he'd shown me a photograph of the cottage, one in a line of small stone buildings huddled against the landscape, and a church slightly set back from the main road. Robert's had a red door, freshly painted before the picture was taken. It looked adorable. 'And that's what the old key is, on my keyring,' he explained, clearing up a mystery I'd interrogated him about a few times since we'd met.

'I wondered if you would like to go there for our honeymoon?' he asked, a shy smile on his face. 'There's an open fire and lots of hiking nearby. Not much else but that's the point of a honeymoon, right? Just time to be alone and cosy. None of the locals know me so they won't be popping in to say hi. In fact, the village is pretty quiet since a lot of the cottages became holiday lets. It'll be just the two of us and the countryside.'

I leaned into him and nuzzled my nose into the crook of his neck, inhaling his earthy scent and then kissing the smooth skin. 'That sounds perfect,' I said, and I meant it. I didn't need an expensive beach holiday in the Caribbean, or whatever everyone else did after their wedding. I just needed him.

'That's settled, then,' he said, standing up and striding across the living room to look out of our window into the Glasgow street. 'I'll go up after our wedding and sort some things out, and then you can join me.'

Alone on the sofa, I frown in confusion. 'By yourself? Why?'

He turned and leaned against the window sill, his long legs stretched in front of him. 'It's a bachelor pad at the moment. A double bachelor pad, as some of McLeod's things are still there too. I'd like a head start to clean it up a bit and make sure it's all in working order for you. You know, get the bedsheets clean and the fires laid, ensure the electric is working and the water's running. By the time you get there it'll be perfect.'

He talked me through the route, then, showing me how to get there by public transport. At the time I was annoyed, didn't understand why we couldn't just go up together and sort the place out the two of us.

It wouldn't be until two months later, as I stood frozen in fear on our wedding day, that I realised what a lifeline he'd given me.

# 8

GILLY

It's the end of Gilly's shift and she's packing up her bag and tidying her desk as quickly as she can. She straightens the framed photo on her desk, taking a brief moment to smile at the faces of her family behind the glass: Jake with his gappy grin as he'd just lost a tooth; Polly with two skinned knees from a recent tumble. And Callum standing tall between them, a gentle hand on each child's shoulder. Her whole world in one photo.

The sooner she gets in the car, the better the traffic will be to reach Polly and Jake's school on time for pickup. It's a tricky and stressful juggle, but one which she only has to do a few days a week when she's at Safeline. Other people – families where both parents work full-time – have to do this every single day.

She knows she's privileged, not having to work. Callum is very proud that he can support his family on one income, that his wife doesn't have to contribute to the finances. But it has always made Gilly feel uncomfortable and itchy, somehow. So much so that she has become adept at keeping busy, feeling useful: keeping their life and home life smooth, helping out with school events, fundraising, running her own yoga class from the village hall, and now volunteering for Safeline. Out of all of it, Safeline is the most rewarding, the most fulfilling.

'There's something special about the people,' she remembers telling Callum over dinner at the end of her first week of shifts. 'The other volunteers. We don't have interests in common and we're all of different ages and backgrounds, and yet there's a similarity inside all of them – the type of people who'd donate their time to help others in this completely thankless task. You can't even tell callers your real name. They get nothing back, and yet they keep showing up and giving their time. I like that I get to spend time with people like that.'

'You're one of those people, too, Gilly,' Callum had said, with a loving smile.

But Gilly had shaken her head at that. She doesn't feel like a good person. She doesn't think her motivations for joining Safeline are as pure and good as the others. She's a bored housewife wanting to pass the time, stop herself overthinking and driving herself insane. She gets something out of this.

She shoulders her bag and mouths 'bye' to Vivian, who's still on the phone talking about last night's episode of *Coronation Street* with a caller Gilly assumes to be a lonely elderly person in need of a chat.

She's almost to the door when Henry steps out of his office, his brow furrowed. 'Gilly,' he says, his voice low. 'Can I have a word?'

Without waiting for an answer, he steps aside and gestures for her to enter his office. The lights are still off, she sees with a lurch, but the lamp on his desk is lit. He's been in here all the time.

She sits down in the chair across from Henry's desk, her handbag in her lap. 'I can't stay too long, I have to go get—'

'This will only take a minute.' He closes the office door and strides to his desk to sit. He's a strange candidate to run a helpline, Gilly has always thought, with his earring, goatee and slightly superior air. He doesn't have the same drive to help people that the other volunteers have, but Gilly knows his is a paid position. Not well-paid, though, like any charity job. So there must be something magnanimous keeping him here, even when he looks miserable and fed up most days, and very much seems like his passions are elsewhere.

She glances over her shoulder and out of the window over the rows of desks, four of which are occupied. Her own desk is right there, across the room, in her eyeline. Henry can glance up at any time and see her on calls, and it must be tempting to listen in, even just for a minute. With a sinking feeling she knows that's what's happened.

And sure enough, Henry clears his throat and clicks a few buttons on his computer until her own voice comes crackling out of his computer speakers.

'Look, I can't tell you my name. But if you call back next Tuesday, you might be able to get through to me again.'

He clicks the mouse and the recording stops.

She hangs her head, her cheeks hot. She feels like a child caught stealing from the sweet shop, reeling with shame and dread.

When Henry doesn't say anything for a moment, she looks up. He's frowning at her across the desk. 'I know you had a challenging shift. That caller was intense and I'd seen how long you were on the first call, so I tuned in to check if you were coping OK.'

She winces. She'd been so proud of how she'd handled both of those calls. She could have panicked, or lost her patience with the caller's refusal to engage, but instead she'd stuck with all the policies. It was an exemplary call, right up until those last moments when she faltered.

'I shouldn't have—'

Henry holds out a hand to stop her. 'You followed our policies perfectly all the way through. Even when the caller was pushing you to provide personal details, you politely and clearly resisted.'

'I know I shouldn't have told them when I was next at work.'

He nods, running a hand across his stubbled jaw. 'You're still relatively new to Safeline, and I know you're still learning the ropes. You're not in trouble for what happened.'

Gilly's shoulders loosen and she fights back tears of relief. Until this moment she hadn't realised how much she relies on this position for her sanity. It's her routine, her way of feeling useful. When she thought it might be taken away, the pain was real.

Henry leans forward on his desk, his fingers laced together and his weight resting on his elbows. He must be around her age, she thinks. She wonders how he ended up working here, when he doesn't seem the type to relish scheduling volunteer rotas and listening in on calls.

He clears his throat, looking uncomfortable. 'I know that you are very familiar with our principles and you've done the training, you've read the handbook.' His tone is gentle, and Gilly knows he's trying to be on her side, trying to be kind. 'In your training we focus a lot on the principle of anonymity, and how it benefits the caller. They feel safe to talk if they know they're anonymous. I've been revisiting the training lately, trying to redesign it a little because I think we are missing an important element here, and today's call highlighted that it's urgent we address this. The anonymity principle is also in place to protect our call handlers. It works both ways. We don't ask for details about our callers, and we don't give details about ourselves.'

Gilly feels a flush creep its way up her chest and onto her cheeks. Her palms begin to sweat. She tries to look calm, to breathe carefully and mindfully. She fails.

He shifts in his seat and takes a drink from the faded Sports Direct mug on his desk. 'About ten years ago, some Safeline locations also operated as drop-in centres. A bit like the Citizens Advice Bureau, you know. Callers could pop by for a face-to-face chat. Then one day, a call handler received an abusive call. She enacted the policies perfectly and ended the call, but what she didn't know was that the caller was phoning from a phone box outside, and he had a machete.'

Gilly reels. She knows there are some incredibly difficult callers, and she's even experienced some of them herself in the past few months, but she's never felt like her life was in danger. 'What happened?'

'Luckily the doors were locked and the attacker couldn't get in. But that was the end of our drop-in centres, and we moved our offices to unpublicised locations to protect our volunteers.'

Her face is hot and she's sticky all over with a slick of panic sweat. No longer panic that she'll be let go from the position, but panic that she's put herself in danger somehow. An echo of the fear she felt long ago when she was younger, in a different life. But it's not the same, surely? This caller needed help, they were upset, not dangerous. She's safe. She didn't give away any information about herself, only when she was next volunteering. They may not even know what town she's in, here in Scotland's central belt surrounded by business parks and roundabouts. It's the perfect hiding place.

'Anyway, I don't mean to scare you,' Henry is saying, his back straight as he comes to the end of his admonishment. 'I just wanted you to understand that we can't predict our callers. That some of them feel like they have some kind of right to you... and it's strange and unhealthy. The policies are in place to protect callers, yes, but they're also there to protect you. But not only that, you've made a promise to a very distressed person. What if you're ill on Tuesday? What if they call and you're unavailable? We don't know what they're dealing with and we can't make promises we may not be able to keep. We don't know what that might do.'

She nods, her arms wrapped around her handbag on her lap. It's the worst feeling, that plummet from a belief that you did a great job right down into the gutter to find you made a mistake. She'd been so proud of that call. And instead... She shakes the thought away. Enough. Enough recriminations.

She always says to her kids when they make a mistake that it's OK, they're still learning. And whenever she tells them that she can feel the relief coming off them in waves. Why can't she be as forgiving of herself? She's still learning. Always. Every day. She's a volunteer here, and she's giving her time for free.

Henry stands up and gives her a kind smile as he leads her out of his office. She doesn't look over at Vivian on her way out, knowing full well that Vivian will be peering at her curiously through her transparent partition, looking for the gossip.

She sidles out into the grey skies and the grey car park of the industrial estate, and she sits in the driver's seat of her car taking deep breaths. A wave of frustration flows through her mind as she remembers the shaky breathing of the caller, their sobs and wails. How helpless she felt, and then how relieved and proud when they said, 'Thank you for being here for me. I feel like I can trust you. Can we talk again?'

'Screw it,' she mumbles to herself as she starts the engine and swings the car out of the car park. She doesn't have enough energy left to admonish herself more. Henry's just overcautious and bored. He doesn't suit this job and he knows it. That person needed help and Gilly provided it. That was just a slip-up, and no one's coming for her with a machete. She's done no harm today, and no one could find this office even if they wanted to. The address is a secret.

She's safe. She's hidden. And she helped.

## 9

## MAEVE

I ring the bell and the bus stops in the middle of hills and glens and fields and sheep, and the bus driver gives me a quizzical glance in the mirror as I ease my way down the aisle towards the exit. I'm grateful Robert took the time to explain. He's given me somewhere to hide.

'You safe here, love? It's a few miles to the nearest town.'

I nod and don't reply, keeping my head down and my cap low on my brow. When my hiking boots land on the grass verge, my lungs fill with the fresh Highland air. It's much colder up here than it was in the city, the air chilling the insides of my nostrils. Above my head a kestrel circles and then swoops down fast to grab its prey.

The bus hisses and pulls away, the sound of the engine fading until all I can hear is the wind in my ears and the birds.

The bus driver's question still rings in my ears, his concern for my safety grating on my nerves. I'm safe. I can take care of myself.

.   .   .

I recognise the cottage by its red door, which is faded now compared to the picture Robert showed me. A few Scottish winters have stripped away its vivid shine, and I can understand how: even though it's summer, there's a brisk breeze and a chill in the air. The sun will remain in the sky for hours yet – those long Scottish summer nights are legendary – but the light is pathetic, the sun hidden behind layers of cloud.

My feet are sore and my shoulders ache under the weight of my backpack as I trudge the last few feet to the door and retrieve Robert's keys from my pocket. I glance over my shoulder but there's no one around: the little street is deserted.

The road is barely two cars wide, with small whitewashed cottages lining the pavements on both sides, and a little post office with a handwritten chalk sign outside which reads 'ICE CREAM / FRESH BREAD / NEWSPAPERS'. A few cars are lined up along one side, parked nose to tail. None of these cottages has a driveway or a garage. They're huddled together in a little clump in the middle of the vast countryside, as if sheltering from the elements.

Further down the road I can see the shell of a derelict church, its lopsided spire looming over the village and surrounded by weathered gravestones sticking out of the long grass at odd angles.

Robert's cottage is set back from the road, behind an iron gate and beyond a front garden, which is covered in gravel, little weeds poking through the stones.

Behind the cottage are the hills, rising into the clouds on this murky day so I can't see their peaks. I wonder why this village developed, in the middle of nowhere in the Highlands. What was here that motivated people to settle? Farmland? Industry? The now-derelict church? Something else?

I've never understood why people settled in Scotland in the first place, when the weather here is so grim most of the time. The nomadic tribes which once wandered the earth would surely want to settle somewhere warmer, with a kinder climate. Why here?

I feel the weight of Robert's keys in my hand and force myself back to the present moment. I can't avoid this any more. I can't hover on the street, waiting for someone to see me. I don't know if I'm on the news, my face plastered across newspapers and online stories. I don't know if the police are looking for me already.

I push open the iron gate, which squeals and screams on its hinges like no one has stepped inside for months, years.

I wonder how long it's been since Robert came here last. He would occasionally go on overnight trips for work or with friends, but I can't think of a time when I didn't know where he was, or who he was with.

The key sticks in the lock and my brain plays out a situation where I can't open the door and I'm stuck in the middle of the Highlands with nowhere to go. But then I jostle the door in its frame, pushing and pulling until finally the key gives and the door swings open to reveal a dark corridor and a dusty, musty damp smell of an uninhabited house.

I close my eyes for a moment and step inside, closing the door on the outside world. I got here safely. Robert is still caring for me, even in death.

I've held it together for so many hours, from finding Robert's body and packing, to walking through the city, sitting still on a coach, a hike through the hills. All the while thinking *I should be with him. He should be here. I would be married by now. We'd be kissing. Dancing. Smiling. Laughing. Holding each other. His fingers entwined around mine. In love. Till death do us part.*

Without warning, a visceral image of Robert's wounds flashes behind my eyes and my legs almost collapse from under me. I fall to the floor, the scratchy carpet against my cheek, silent sobs wracking my body.

I've managed to keep the images at bay since the moment I left the house, but now I've made it to my destination it's like I can't repress them any more. Or my fear.

Because every single one of Robert's injuries – the slice to the jugular, the slash at the carotid artery, the severed cephalic vein – are attacks that I teach in my self-defence class, using an outlined illustration of a man's body, with red pen lines to show where to cut if you absolutely need to. If your life is in danger and it's kill or be killed.

And whoever killed him emulated my illustration perfectly on Robert's sleeping body.

## 10

## MAEVE

The light has faded further by the time I peel myself off the hall carpet and wipe the tears and snot from my face with my sleeve. Enough self-pity. That's not me. I'm a strong person; a self-sufficient person. It's time to start functioning.

I stand and flick the light switch. Nothing. No electricity.

'Of course,' I say out loud, my voice echoing around the tiny entrance hall. In my former life – the Maeve of yesterday – I'd have sworn or raged at this inconvenience. Now I'm numb. Too much has happened, too much trauma, for the lack of electricity to feel like a crisis. I now know what true horror is. Anything else washes over me like waves against a rock.

But I do need to solve the electricity problem before the sun sets fully, while there's still a cold, grey light filtering through the windows.

I find a torch under the kitchen sink and shine its flickery, golden light around the ground floor until I find what I'm looking for above the front door: an old, grey fuse box. Inside, it's all incomprehensible knobs and little boxes except for one clear switch, set to 'OFF'.

I flick it to the 'ON' position and relief floods my body as the overhead light bathes the hallway in gold. The first positive thing to happen all day.

Finally able to look around, I scan the ground floor: the hallway opens into a small living room with bare stone walls and an open fire, logs stacked high on the hearth and the fire already laid. My eyes fill with tears when I see that, as if Robert's looking out for me even now.

There's an overstuffed and sagging sofa with a sheepskin blanket hanging over the back, and a little wooden dining table with three chairs by the back window. The living room has a window at each end, the room spanning the depth of the house. Then there's a door at the back, leading to the kitchen, which is tacked on the back of the cottage as an extension.

With relief I see that there's an electric oven, a fridge, a kettle and a microwave, all looking fairly new. Although there are rustic and traditional touches here in the rough white-washed walls and the stone hearth around the fireplace, Robert clearly wanted this place to feel comfortable and he upgraded it from the previous owner, who he'd said kept everything very traditional, including only cooking on an old wood-fired stove.

With even more relief, I find there's UHT milk, teabags and biscuits in the cupboard. Even better, there's at least three dusty bottles of wine in the tiny wine rack, not that I could stomach it.

Upstairs I open the first door to find a minuscule bathroom with a shower. The next reveals a double bedroom, bed made with starched white sheets, and then I find a single bedroom with bare floorboards and no furniture at all: the bed removed to make space for Robert's art supplies. Canvases are stacked against the wall, facing away, and an easel is set up by the window, looking out over the hills. I hover in the doorway, my eyes on the stool and easel, imagining Robert sitting there gazing out over the landscape while he painted his abstract masterpieces, all bold shapes and industrial figures. I don't know if I'll ever find the strength to turn those canvases, to see the art my fiancé created that no one's eyes have seen but his.

Suddenly weak with fatigue, I stumble back downstairs. I light the fire and sit in front of the dancing flames, the warmth of the fire and the events of the day lulling me until my eyelids begin to drift closed, exhaustion taking over.

But as soon as sleep begins to overtake my senses, I wrench myself awake, my heart pounding and my breath catching in my throat. The feeling of losing control, of leaving my body strikes fear deep into my soul.

Don't sleep.

In my half-awake state, a thought crosses my mind and I shake my head violently. I can't face it.

Don't sleep. But the thought won't go away.

'No,' I say out loud, my voice echoing around the empty room.

As if I can outrun myself, I stand and go to the kitchen. Trying to distract myself, I contemplate the wine rack, but the thought of wine turns my stomach and for a moment I retch.

There's a tang in my mouth, a memory. Robert and I clinked glasses together just last night, a lifetime ago. Celebrating our upcoming wedding. We didn't even finish the bottle; we were both so tired and I didn't have more than a few sips anyway. We were both exhausted from the rehearsal dinner, worn out with excitement. But now I remember the depth of my sleep last night. My eyes closed the moment my head hit the pillow, and I don't remember waking until the dawn light crept into the room, after Robert was dead.

I rarely sleep like that, I realise now, a scream bubbling in my throat. I'm a fitful, restless sleeper, I always have been. I have trouble falling asleep, wake at the slightest sound, and recently I get up at least once during the night for a pee.

But there are exceptions.

When I sleepwalk.

I've never been conscious of it, but my parents would laugh about it when I still lived at home: how they'd find me standing in the hallway, swaying and staring straight ahead, not moving, unresponsive. They'd be unable to wake me no matter how loud they spoke or how much they shook me, and all they could do was walk me back to bed and tuck me in. The next morning I'd have no memory of what I'd done, and the only reason I knew I'd been out of bed was if someone had seen me, or sometimes I'd have mud on the soles of my feet and leaves in my bed. It always happened at times of stress: the week before a school play, or the night before an important exam.

Or the night before my wedding?

I struggle to catch my breath, shaking my head as I clutch both sides of the sink with my hands and lean forward in case I vomit.

To my knowledge it's rarely happened to me in adulthood. I've told boyfriends about it – warned them with a laugh in my voice. Robert included. It's a funny quirk of mine, I'd tell them, and apparently I'm harmless, just dopey and strange. A bit creepy, Mum used to say. Sometimes she'd find me holding things and she'd have no idea how I'd got them: a flower plucked from a neighbour's garden, a half-defrosted chicken nugget with a bite out of it. Just put me back to bed if you find me wandering, I'd tell each new boyfriend, knowing I'd probably grown out of it.

I retch again over the sink, the taste of stomach acid entering my mouth. But still nothing comes up.

I almost wish I could vomit, to rid myself of this feeling. This horror and dread creeping up my spine.

I left my home – left Robert's body – knowing the scene looked bad. Knowing I was probably in the frame for his death, but also intending to return as soon as I'd gathered my thoughts. As soon as I knew who could have done this. I was going to help the police find his killer.

When I was young I used to sleepwalk when I was stressed. The night before a wedding is as high-stress as things get. And sure, I just wandered around as a child, didn't do anything. Certainly nothing violent. But that was then.

This is now. I'm a martial artist. A self-defence expert. It's my literal job to hurt people and stop people hurting me. I've been trained to kill.

Maybe I haven't been framed. Maybe I killed Robert after all.

# 11

---

## MAEVE

Terrified to fall asleep, I try to stay awake all night, stoking the fire and sitting upright in the armchair next to the window. I watch as the light fades a little before 11 p.m., and soon thousands of stars emerge. I could never see this many stars over Glasgow, and I wish I could share it with Robert. It's one of the things he mentioned about this place – how amazing the sky looked at night. I wish I could tell him I've seen it too. I wish he was here next to me.

With the feeling of nausea swirling and whirling into the early hours, I contemplate my potential role in my fiancé's death. His murder.

Did I do it?

I remember the knife in my hand, his blood drying on my body.

I've read news stories about people killing their partners during sleep. I never looked it up, but knowing my history with sleepwalking I did pay attention when stories like that crossed the news: the once happily married renowned surgeon serving life in prison for stabbing and drowning his wife; the son in a psychiatric institution after acquittal for killing his own father;

the man who turned himself in to police after waking to discover he'd killed his in-laws... their stories lodged in my brain because I was once a sleepwalker, too.

And now maybe I'm just like them.

My body shivering with dread, I wonder whether I should turn myself in. There's a phone in the cottage; I could call the police any time and tell them where I am. They'd be here within an hour. Could I pick up that phone? After all, this changes things; maybe I'd get a shorter sentence if I could prove I didn't kill Robert on purpose. That it was a horrific sleepwalking accident, not cold-blooded murder.

My heart feels like it might burst with grief, shame and guilt. I don't know if I fall asleep, but it feels like the sky is dark for only minutes before a faint blue glow starts to appear on the horizon. My eyes are gritty and my face feels dry and sore to the touch.

I make myself a cup of tea and, mug in shaking hand, I wander through the cottage's rooms, imagining Robert spending his days here for weeks on end while preparing for an exhibition, painting and singing to himself as he often does. *Did*.

I hover in the doorway of Robert's art room, yearning to move the painted canvases and look at his art – to see these pieces of my fiancé's soul that he shared with no one else. But I don't touch them. I can't – I've lost too much. I'll never learn anything new about Robert now he's gone. Every thought he had has disappeared. He'll never surprise me. All I have is my memories of him, and these paintings. Little treats still to come. I need to savour them, look at them only when it feels right, when my head's in the right place. Not while I'm a sleep-deprived, grieving zombie holding a lukewarm cup of Tetley and UHT. Not yet.

As I turn to leave the art room, I see a large cupboard door recessed into the wall, which must be over-the-stairs storage. But when I try to open it, the door won't budge. It's locked.

I make a note to look for a key soon and wander on, discovering lost corners of Robert's cottage like I'm uncovering parts of him I'll now never know any other way.

As I'm at the top of the stairs, a shrill sound forces me to a stop, my hand gripping the banister and my knees almost buckle beneath me.

Somewhere close by, a phone is ringing.

Bile rising in my throat, I descend a few stairs and stare at a landline handset, mounted on the wall at the bottom of the stairs. Its black old-fashioned shine seems to glint at me, like the threatening eye of a wild animal eyeing its prey.

Who could be calling Robert's cottage? What do they want?

I move down a couple more stairs, towards the phone. It's probably just a scam caller. No one knows I'm here. No one even knew Robert was here, most of the time. I don't know who has this number.

Perhaps he did tell someone about the cottage. Maybe it's his family. Maybe they know where I am.

Or the police. I swallow hard, and feel a nervous lump descending through my chest.

The ringing fills my ears, rattling my eardrums. I wish it would stop. But I can't pick it up. Of course I'm not going to pick it up. Never.

I can't let anyone know that someone can hear this ringing phone.

After what feels like minutes of standing frozen halfway down the stairs, the caller finally gives up and the ringing stops, although there's an echo in my ears for long afterwards.

Gingerly I pick up the receiver, holding my breath. Its dial tone hums in my ear. No one there.

I could just unplug it. But then would they know someone was here?

I put the receiver back down in its cradle and stumble into the living room on shaky legs, slumping into the armchair where

I spent most of the night. I wait for my heart rate and breathing to return to normal, for my shaking to subside.

As I glance around the room, I see the corner of a picture frame, just out of sight behind a vase on the mantelpiece. I stand and pull it out, my heart breaking anew as I see a photograph of Robert and me inside the frame. A fresh wave of grief, as this picture is the physical evidence that he truly loved me: that he brought a photograph of the two of us here and framed it, so even while we weren't together, I was still with him.

It's a photograph from a year or so ago, taken at a barbecue at our house one sunny afternoon. I remember this day.

When the picture was taken we'd all finished eating and I'd stood up from the table to clear the plates when Robert grabbed my hand and kissed my knuckles.

'A wonderful spread,' he'd said, rubbing his thumb on the back of my hand before he released it. That's when someone – Pablo or Ella, I guess – snapped the photo.

I remember blushing at this moment of public intimacy, especially in front of our friends. Ella, always loud and a little brash, hooted and teased Robert for his chivalry. In the picture, my cheeks are flushed, a semi-embarrassed grin across my face as I gaze at Robert while he holds my hand and smiles up into my eyes from his seat at the table.

If I could go back, I wouldn't blush. I wouldn't pull my hand away or bustle about clearing plates. I'd sink into his lap, bury my face in the warm crook of his shoulder, breathe in the natural scent of his skin, run my hands through his hair. Who cares who saw, or that they thought we were soppy together? I'd cherish every moment knowing it wouldn't last. Knowing something would take him away from me.

I remember Ella and Pablo at that barbecue. Ella, a no-nonsense nurse who'd started taking my self-defence classes years ago and quickly became enough of a friend that we invited her to our rehearsal dinner. And Pablo, one of Robert's artist friends from years back. They'd drunk three bottles of wine between them and left together, and Robert and I speculated on the future of their relationship late into the night, talking about how wonderful it would be if two of our friends found love because of our Sunday afternoon barbecue.

They would have been at our wedding yesterday, I realise with a jolt. Not together – whatever burgeoning attraction that appeared that sunny Sunday afternoon didn't blossom into a relationship – but they were friendly. They might have even sat together in the congregation.

They'll know, now. His family will know he's dead. They'll be grieving. One of them will have seen his body, would have had to identify it lying on a slab in a morgue or police station somewhere. Would they have seen his injuries? Those gaping, red slashes.

Would they think it was me who did it?

And again, the thought flashes through my mind and my stomach lurches: *Did I?*

Did I slice my fiancé open and cause him to bleed to death? Did I hold the knife in my hand? Did I watch as the life slipped from his eyes?

Did he open his eyes, look at me while he died? Did he ask me why?

Tears pour down my face, snot from my nose as my body is wracked with sobs.

Throughout my life, I've frequently experienced what some call 'high place phenomenon'. The call of the void. Standing at the edge of a building or a cliff, and wondering 'What if I jump?' Or holding a knife and thinking, 'What if I push it into my own eye?' Driving down the motorway and imagining wrenching the wheel into oncoming traffic, or standing on a railway platform as a train rushes through the station... imagining stepping forward. I know these thoughts are common, and they don't mean I *wanted* to do any of those things. It's just my brain warning me, telling me that to do those things means death.

But there's always been another, quieter thought alongside that. A similar flash of disaster which feels different, somehow. More true, and more terrifying. It also feels unique to me: I don't think others experience it in the same way. An echo. A premonition. A little voice from the future, which tells me *One day you're going to ruin your life. One day you'll do something big, something you can't undo.*

What terrible, un-fixable thing might I one day do to wreck my life? I'd ask myself in quiet moments.

Maybe a child would one day run out in front of my car while I glanced down to change the radio station. Maybe I'd trip while carrying a knife and plunge it into another person's stomach. Maybe I'd misjudge a move in a self-defence class and accidentally administer a killing blow on a pupil.

I'd always hoped I was experiencing an extension of the high place phenomenon when these thoughts crossed my mind. That they didn't mean anything except 'be careful'. But now, sitting here in this cottage alone while my fiancé's body rests in a morgue, I wonder:

Did I destroy my own life? Did I do this?

After all, I know first-hand how one moment can alter the course of someone's life for ever. This isn't the first time my life has changed course because of one tiny decision.

This isn't the first time someone has died because of me.

# 12

## GILLY

'Can Tim come round after school tonight, Mum?' Jake asks from the back seat. 'We could have pizza.'

'Yay, pizza!' Polly yells, clapping her hands. 'That's my third favourite. Can we, Mum?'

With a flash of irritation, Gilly flicks her eyes up into the rear-view mirror, catching sight of Polly and her big expectant eyes. Next to her, Jake is grinning mischievously, his new adult teeth too large for his face. He knows what he just did.

'Mum?'

Gilly suppresses a groan and tries to focus on the road ahead, negotiating the early morning traffic to get the kids to school on time. She mumbles something non-committal, but even as part of her brain runs through the contents of the fridge and whether she has Tim's mum's mobile number, she can't engage properly. She's too distracted.

Today is Tuesday, and there's a low-level feeling of dread bubbling low in her stomach.

That caller is going to ring back today. And Gilly knows Henry is going to be listening in his office when they do.

Taking deep breaths to slow her thumping heart, she grips

the steering wheel harder while Jake tries different tactics of persuasion and bribery, outlining his commitment to his home-work and assuring her that Tim won't unplug all the cables from the back of their TV this time or once again find a way to get around the parental controls on Jake's tablet.

But Gilly barely hears him, her mind whirring too fast, the worries crowding out Jake and Polly's chatter. Even though she felt defiant when leaving at the end of her last shift, the feeling faded fast. She thought telling that caller about her next shift was harmless, that she was helping. And now she has to face the consequences of her mistake, the reality of momentarily breaking free of the life she has chosen: walking the line, keeping her head down, not standing out, all to keep calm and feel safe. She shouldn't have broken the rules.

When she pulls into the Safeline car park, kids safely dropped off at school and no after-school promises made, Gilly sits in the driver's seat, listening to the quiet ticking of the car engine as it cools. Usually she'd gather her stuff and get out immediately, trotting across the tarmac towards the faceless, anonymous Safeline office with urgency, as always.

She's a textbook anxious overachiever, according to her googling: trying to do everything perfectly and never letting herself pause because stopping means she would have to face her fears. She doesn't give herself breaks. She doesn't feel like she deserves them. And that way she can often outrun the anxi-ety. But today the dread and fear just won't shift.

She opens her eyes and grabs her car keys from the ignition and her handbag from the passenger seat footwell. Her feet are heavy as she walks to the office door, punches in the security code, scans her pass, and makes her way to her desk.

Vivian is already there, sipping a coffee and mumbling 'mmhm' into the phone. She gives a friendly wink as Gilly sits down and logs into the PC.

She's spent the long weekend distracted from her family,

gazing into space as she thought about the caller, the ragged breaths and keening sobs echoing in her ears even as Polly demanded her attention on the playground, and Jake pestered her with questions about her job for a school project, or as Callum squeezed her hand in concern. She'd passed it off as a head cold making her spaced out and tired, but instead of falling straight to sleep when she climbed into bed like she would if she were genuinely ill, she lay awake staring into the dark, feigning sleep while she wondered what happened to that person; if they'll ever tell her what devastation happened in their life. Wondering if she can help. Wondering if she *should*.

No call has ever affected her like this, she thinks as she opens up the Safeline call logging software and reviews the call categories. They have to assign each call a category, from 00 – silent call; through 016 – loneliness; and 076 – suicide. Last week's caller was 083 – unknown. Maybe today she'll be able to give it a more specific call category. Maybe today she can feel like she made a difference.

But the day rolls on and she fields call after call without hearing the familiar ragged breaths. To her relief, her first call is someone asking about what day the new issue of *Radio Times* comes out, and the next one is a teenager worried about her upcoming biology exam, and the one after that is a new mum at the end of her tether with a colicky newborn.

By noon, Gilly is alive with enthusiasm for Safeline again, galvanised in the knowledge that she's helping people who really need help, that this is where she should be.

Lunch break with Vivian, sitting on a picnic table at the edge of the car park talking about how Vivian's team almost won the pub quiz at the weekend but were stumped by a question about 1980s cricket. Vivian is a chatterbox, and Gilly's grateful for it – she doesn't have a very exciting life, and her anxiety calms down when conversation flows and the other person can chatter away while Gilly listens. Then it's back into the office for more calls: money worries, exam stress, eating disorder, two silent callers, and it's nearly time for the end of her shift.

The dread has faded as the day progressed. Maybe the caller won't call back today. Perhaps whatever awful thing was causing them so much upset has been resolved, and they're back to their normal life.

She's just filling in some final admin details onto the call log and gathering her stuff into her handbag when her phone rings. She pauses, unsure whether she should answer or whether she could transfer through to someone else. There's ten minutes left of her shift, and answering is always a bit of a risk. But as she glances around the room, she sees that all her colleagues are busy. Even Henry: through the glass window she can see him pacing around his office, moving his hands as he chats on his headset.

That decides it. Henry's busy so she can answer without the risk he'll be eavesdropping. She's more helpful and able to give real advice when she isn't worrying she might say something wrong or accidentally break a Safeline rule. She pulls on her headset and presses 'answer'.

'Hello, you've reached Safeline. How can I help?'

She holds her breath, listening. Who's going to be on the other end? Someone lonely wanting to share good news with a listening ear? Or someone teetering on the edge of a motorway overpass, ready to let go and plunge?

A cold feeling creeps across Gilly's body as she hears the now-familiar rattle of breath at the other end of the line. A little sob, muffled, as if the caller has placed a hand over her own mouth to suppress her emotion.

She waits, holding her breath until her hands are shaking and she's forced to draw air into her lungs. Saliva pools in her mouth and she swallows, trying to think about what to say next. Trying to remember to breathe.

*Get it together,* she chides herself. *You've been trained for this and you're good at it.* She forces her back to straighten and her shoulders to unfurl.

One advantage of being an anxious person is that she's always prepared for anything. No matter what life throws at her, there's always an elaborate worst-case-scenario her brain's already tortured her with. And even if there's something about this particular caller which unsettles her, she'll be okay. She's decided.

'Hello?' she says in a cheerful voice, deciding to stick to the anonymity policies as closely as possible. She'll pretend she doesn't know this person, that she didn't listen to them sob down the line to her for hours on end last week. 'I can't hear you. Are you there?'

There's an intake of breath at the end of the line, and Gilly's stomach twists with anxiety again. *Anxiety is just an emotion,* she tells herself. *Nothing here can hurt me.*

And then the caller starts to speak.

## 13

### MAEVE

Some days I can pretend this is just my normal life. I get the local bus into town and wander the aisles at Lidl, flinching when I consider putting items into my basket that were Robert's favourites. A certain brand of cream cheese, the really vinegary crisps... There's a moment when I reach out to pick something up and then I remember. He's gone. He's been gone for a week, maybe more. I've lost track of the days.

Whenever I have to talk to another person, my voice comes out in a croak from disuse, until I cough and try again.

'Two ba—' I clear my throat. The cashier barely looks at me. 'Two bags, please. Paying by cash.'

It's like my brain zooms out from the present moment and I'm suddenly aware of the big picture, of why I'm here and what brought me to be standing in a supermarket miles away from home, surrounded by strangers with a baseball cap obscuring my hair.

I'm not on holiday. I'm not just picking up our weekly shop. He's not waiting for me at home. He can't eat those crisps.

Robert is dead and I'm wanted by the police for his murder.

There's always a moment where I almost fall to the ground,

the weight of it too much to bear. But as the days pass, the moments move further apart and although the feeling doesn't get any more bearable, I learn how to breathe through them, to steady myself and focus on what's in front of me until my brain zooms back in and I can continue.

And then other moments I can't escape the reality. I can't even pretend. Like later when I'm leaving Lidl, a heavy bag of groceries in each hand, and I pass the entrance to Currys and glance inside. There among the stacked computers, speakers, and fridges is a wall of televisions, all showing my friend Ella's face.

I freeze, watching as my friend talks into a proffered microphone, the news interviewer just out of shot. Along the bottom of the screen, a little red ribbon unfurls: 'ELLA PRIESTLEY, FRIEND OF ALLEGED "KILLER BRIDE" MAEVE ROSS.' My stomach squeezing, I squint and I can just make out the subtitles as Ella's mouth moves on the screen, forming the words:

'She gave this amazing speech about how much she loved him... and then she goes home and slices his throat. It's inhuman. No one's seen her since the night of the rehearsal dinner, but everyone's looking. We need justice for Robert.'

Tears prick my eyes and I almost double over on the pavement, my shopping bags slipping from my grip. I thought Ella was my friend. Despite everything I thought that some people would believe in me, would know I was innocent. But there's someone who I thought of as one of my best friends, denouncing me to a new reporter.

Around me, afternoon shoppers jostle past, chatting and laughing like it's a normal day. I hear one old lady tut to herself as she has to wheel her shopping trolley around me where I stand frozen on the pavement.

I watch her familiar face on the TV – the concerned tilt of her eyebrows, the slight dimple in her left cheek – and I try to understand. What would I think, if our roles were reversed and

Ella had fled, leaving her fiancé dead in their bed? I can't blame her, not really.

And then the screens change, and it's a picture of me on the screen. A picture I haven't seen before: from my rehearsal dinner. Someone must have given it to the media. My hair curled and pinned back, my make-up flawless, my eyes sparkling as I raise my glass and gaze into Robert's eyes.

Another world. Another lifetime.

I want to curl up in a ball and die.

But I need to move. I need to be far, far away from the bank of televisions with my face on them. And I can't cry. I have to look like a normal person, out for their groceries. Not a wanted criminal without a friend in the world.


The air smells cleaner than the city. Sheep wander through the village sometimes, and I've seen deer running across the mist-strewn hills above the cottage at dawn. Sometimes, when I haven't been able to sleep, I'll wander through the old graveyard reading the faded names carved into the moss-covered stones. Generations of families now gone from this almost-abandoned village. I've seen only a couple of other people since I moved here: an elderly lady, the postman and the man who owns the village shop. It's a beautiful place, and I understand why Robert kept this cottage so secret, just for himself. And I also feel so grateful that he chose to share it with me when we were about to get married. Like he was inviting me into his special club, that no one else knew about.

He would want me to be here, I think to myself as the little bus winds through the lanes back in the direction of the village. If someone had presented him with this scenario as a hypothetical, Robert would have wanted me to use his cottage for this very purpose: recovery and planning. A refuge to save myself.

He was a caring, kind man who loved me. And he gave a lot to me, to help me.

A memory of Robert's kindness flashes across my consciousness. As well as childhood sleepwalking, for most of my adult life, I've suffered from occasional bouts of insomnia. I've never understood what triggered them or what solved them when they finally ended – until the next time – but when I'm deep in the throes of sleepless nights, I always feel like they'll never end. I fear that this is me forever, and that eventually the lack of sleep will drive me insane or I'll kill myself from despair.

'Wake me up,' Robert would say to me, his eyes roaming my grey miserable face with sympathy and love.

I'd shake my head, in my sleepless state completely unable to imagine a reversal where I gave Robert permission to curtail precious sleep when I got so little. But Robert would give that to me.

He'd nod and smile. 'It must be so lonely. And everything feels worse in the middle of the night when you're not sleeping. So wake me up. We'll make hot chocolate and snuggle up together. Maybe listen to the radio. Even if you don't go back to sleep, at least we'll be doing something nice.'

So that's how I know he'd be happy I'm here, using his cottage as a refuge while I work out what to do next. He was generous to a fault. Self-sacrificial, almost. I wonder what he'd say if he knew that now when I wake up in the mornings, there's dirt on the soles of my feet and I don't remember where I've been. That things move around in the night. And sometimes the back door is standing open, flooding the kitchen with the chill dawn air. Maybe he shouldn't have been so accepting of my sleep issues after all. After years of lying dormant, my sleepwalking has returned, as frequent and unpredictable as when I was a child.

I'm off the bus now, carrying my two Lidl carrier bags one in each hand through the quiet village. It's always quiet. I barely see anyone walking down the lane, except the occasional hiker with their big backpacks and muddy boots. Perhaps most of these houses are holiday homes like Robert mentioned, the residents visiting occasionally and renting to tourists the rest of the time. In which case, it's the perfect place to hide out.

Inside the house, I lock the door behind me and hang my keys on the key hook by the door, but for some reason this time they slip off the hook and fall behind the little shoe cabinet. I swear under my breath and slump my bags to the kitchen with the groceries, the palms of my hands stinging from the straps. I could have gone to the village shop, but I can't risk being recognised. And it's not like I have anything else to do.

I leave the bags on the counter and head back to the front door, knowing I'll forget to retrieve the keys if I don't find them straight away. My memory has been terrible lately. Trauma will do that.

I shift the cabinet away from the wall and slide my hand down the back to grab the keys. I'm about to push the cabinet back into the little divots in the carpet where its weight has sunk down the pile, when I see something glinting between the carpet and the skirting board.

I pull the cabinet right back and kneel down. A key.

And I know what it opens.

# 14

## MAEVE

Groceries forgotten, I rush up the stairs and into the spare room. I don't really understand why I'm so fixated on this locked cupboard. Perhaps because the cottage is so impersonal, and I miss Robert so much. I want more pieces of him. I want clothes that smell of him; I want papers with his handwriting all over them. It's all I have left.

And there are some pieces of Robert around the cottage as things are. But it's not enough. Nothing will ever be enough.

Logically I know that this cupboard will not have what I'm looking for. I can never have what I'm looking for again. I'm like a former smoker, craving nicotine every day for the rest of my life. Only the thing I'm craving can't be assuaged by a clandestine trip to the corner shop and disguised with breath mints. I can never see Robert again. And that kills me inside.

The key slides into the hole and fits perfectly. The lock mechanism is smooth as the key turns with a clunk. The door swings open and an unfamiliar scent floats towards me from inside. It's dust, mixed with something else. Something that I can't quite place.

The cupboard is much larger than it looks from the outside,

stretching back over a metre. It has been used as a wardrobe: there's a hanging rail full of clothes, and a small set of drawers at the bottom. And a stack of shoes next to it.

My body turns cold, the hairs on my arms standing on end. Something isn't right. My body knows it before my mind catches up.

The scent suddenly triggers something, and I know: it's a woman's perfume.

Frowning, I reach up to the rail and slide the coat hangers along, examining each piece of clothing. A woman's clothes. And a woman's shoes.

I don't understand.

I pull open the top drawer of the little dresser, my breathing speeding up. Underwear. Black and lacy. *Lingerie.*

Then in the next drawer down, socks. Socks far too small for Robert's feet. And a pair of purple cotton pyjamas, carefully folded.

Robert's wardrobe is in the bedroom, a few outfits hanging up, but lots of empty space as he didn't store much here in this cottage. He mostly brought a bag with him and didn't leave much when he left. There would be space in that wardrobe for all of this stuff, but instead it's packed away in this cupboard, locked out of sight.

What is this? Who do these clothes belong to? Why are they hidden?

I don't have a clue, but I know it's not good. I don't *want* to know, I realise. I wish I could close the door, lock it and throw away the key.

But what I have found today can't be unseen. And I need answers.

I slide open the final drawer, expecting more clothes, but this one is different. It's filled with the type of stuff kept in the top drawer of a bedside cabinet: a necklace, a notebook and pen, a thermometer, a half-finished pack of ibuprofen... and a photo album with silver cursive lettering on the front.

I drop to my knees, my vision blurring.

### OUR WEDDING

I lift the book from the drawer with shaking fingers. It can't be true. This has to be some horrible mistake.

His mentor, I realise. The man who'd left Robert this cottage. This stuff must have belonged to the mentor and his wife. It's not Robert's wedding album. After all, Robert had never been married before. He would have told me.

That must be it. Robert just didn't clear out some of his mentor's stuff from the cottage. He didn't need this cupboard so he just left it to deal with later and never got around to it.

I pull back the front cover to see the first photo: a bouquet laid on perfectly manicured grass, two shiny wedding rings in their box beside it.

I flip to the next page. It's a woman sitting on a stool, her back to the camera. She's wearing a white wedding gown and her hair is beautifully swept back into an updo, loose blonde tendrils on either side to frame her face. She's looking at herself in the mirror, the camera focused on her reflection as a half-smile graces her lips. She's stunning.

Frustrated, I flip through pictures of someone touching up the bride's make-up, the bride climbing into an adorned wedding car, and then, finally, the picture I've been looking for.

Robert in a navy-blue suit, pinning a thistle to his lapel.

I slump to the floor, the breath leaving my body. A tear tracks down my cheek before I even realise I'm crying.

My fiancé was already married.

## 15

### GILLY

'It's you, isn't it?' the voice says, a tremor behind the words. It's a woman's voice.

Gilly swallows and glances up at Henry's window again. He's still on the phone, his mouth moving and his hands gesticulating. Not listening. She doesn't know how to respond. If she says 'yes', she's violating the anonymity rule for both herself and this caller. She opens and closes her mouth. 'Um...'

'We spoke last week.' There's a tearful laugh on the other end of the line. 'Well, you spoke. I cried.'

A smile creeps across Gilly's face and her whole body floods with relief. She realises now that what she's been dreading is the powerlessness of the silence. Having to listen to someone's anguish and being able to do nothing. And that powerlessness is gone. The caller wants to talk. She releases her held breath in a rush and says, 'Yes, it's me. I was so sorry to hear how sad you sounded.' She's careful not to lead the conversation, to let the caller guide what direction they move in.

'You really helped me when no one else would. I wanted to thank you.'

Gilly closes her eyes briefly. Moments like this are why she volunteers here. 'You're very welcome. You can tell me anything. Safeline is here to help.'

The caller sniffs and when she talks again it's clear she's crying, but she's much more in control than last week and Gilly can understand what she's saying. 'I just...' She clears her throat. 'Something awful has happened and I don't know what to do. So many awful things, really. It's like I'm living in a nightmare.'

Gilly pauses, making sure to leave space in case the caller wants to continue. 'Do you want to talk about it?'

'I don't know. I know I need help but I don't know where to turn or who to tell. It feels like there's no one left. No one on my side.'

'That sounds really difficult,' Gilly says.

'I... I don't even know where to start.' The caller takes a shaky breath and releases it into the phone speaker with a *whoosh*.

Gilly pulls the headset away from her ear as the speaker rattles. When she returns the headset to her ear, the caller is speaking again: 'I thought I was sorted, you know? I had everything I needed; everything I wanted. And then overnight it all disappeared. Even my memories don't seem true any more. And I still don't know if I could have done something differently to stop it all from happening and keep my life the same. Or if it was my fault.' She suppresses a sob. 'Did I do this?'

Gilly shakes her head, not able to say much in response to this. She's not got enough information. She waits, knowing that this caller will tell her more eventually and everything will slot into place.

She hears the caller taking a breath, ready to speak again. 'I wish I knew your name.'

Gilly purses her lips, preparing to rebuff, deflect, divert. Anything to avoid making the same mistakes again. But the caller doesn't wait, continuing without needing Gilly's response. 'Maybe I'll call you Ruby. Or Sadie. Maybe Katherine.'

Gilly forces a light chuckle, just to make a sound more than anything.

'Tell me something, nameless Safeline volunteer. I have my suspicions and I want to know more about you. Nothing that breaks the sacred vows of anonymity or anything, of course. But I want to know this.' The caller pauses, leaving a crackling silence on the line before she continues in a whisper now. 'Have you ever destroyed someone's life? Even if you didn't mean to?'

Gilly's vision narrows to a pinprick, but this time it's not because she's so hyper-focused on the call and in her element, tuning in to the training and doing a great job at offering support. No, not this time. *Have you ever destroyed someone's life?* Her vision blurs and narrows, turning black and white like static on an old TV. A deafening ringing begins in her ears. She can't breathe.

Her tenuous hold on her calm is gone, replaced with a soaring nausea and a precipitous feeling, like she's standing on the edge of a ten-storey building, about to step out into empty air.

Because the answer to the caller's question is *yes*.

How would a caller know to ask a question so pertinent? A question that soars straight to the heart of everything Gilly has spent her adult life running from?

She's going to faint.

She pushes her chair back from the desk and leans forward, her head between her knees. She tries to gulp air but she can't get enough into her lungs.

*Have you ever destroyed someone's life?* The question runs through her brain over and over, echoing alongside the ringing in her ears, everything getting louder and louder until it sounds like she's surrounded by yelling and screaming. She rips the headset from her ears and drops it to the floor, and at the same time she feels a hand on her back, rubbing and coaxing.

'Gilly,' comes the faint voice, almost drowned out by all the noise inside her head. 'Take a deep breath. I've got you.'

## 16

### MAEVE

As always in times of stress and pain, I try to outrun my thoughts and feelings. But this time, I have nowhere to go. Over the next few days, I push my body to its limits hiking and running in the hills, trying to be so exhausted by the time I fall into bed that there's no space for thinking. No energy for sleepwalking or insomnia. No space to remind myself that Robert lied to me.

I'm never going to be able to ask him why.

I climb to the top of the biggest hill for miles and stare out at the landscape – my prison. The wind buffets me hard and for a moment I'm tempted to just let it push me down, fling me into the ether.

I try to get the images out of my head, but it's impossible.

The rest of the photo album was just as damning. There's no way he was just a wedding guest, or some crazy, wild hope that had crossed my mind when I first found the book. No, the book shows everything in stark, painful relief: the look of joy on Robert's face when he first sees his bride-to-be walking towards him down the aisle; the tears gathering in the corners of her perfectly made-up eyes as she reaches him at the altar; the delight on the faces of the congregation. And in the congregation is a betrayal which feels just as stark and raw.

My best friend was at that wedding.

Yep, Sarah's there with blonde highlights and a red fascinator, sitting on the front row to watch her brother marry someone else.

Why did she never tell me? She was my best friend practically since the day we met at university; I knew her before I even met Robert. But she'd never mentioned her brother being married, that I recall. Although, I suppose when I finally met Robert and asked, 'Where have you been hiding him?' she'd shrugged and mentioned he'd been travelling. Travelling with his wife, I suppose.

I've been doubly betrayed – once by Robert and also by my best friend.

And where is she now, this woman? His wife?

There was no date on the wedding album, but Sarah looks only a little younger in those pictures than how she did when I saw her just last week. Her cheeks are fuller, her jaw less angular. But even so, the wedding couldn't have been that long ago. She's even holding her phone in one picture: the same pink case she has now. I noticed when I looked through the wedding album for the fiftieth or sixtieth time last night, poring over every detail as the orange light from the open fire cast a warm glow over the plastic-covered photographs.

And I know that divorces take a while. Years, sometimes.

I met Robert two years ago. Was he married to her, then? Did he sneak out of his marital home to meet me? Was I the other woman?

My stomach heaves and I bend double, my face close to the heather at the top of the hill. Nothing comes out, and I straighten up, staring down at the little village huddled in the miniature valley below. It's just a tiny lane, flanked by cottages,

Robert's included. From up here it looks like a toy village, like a boy's train set might loop around it.

Did she live here with him? Is that how he led the double life? The cupboard didn't have a lot of stuff in it – not enough clothes, shoes and general belongings for a woman's whole life. Did Robert have another house? One where he lived with her?

With a lurch, I wonder: do they have children? Does she know he's dead?

I run back to the cottage, my breath coming in ragged gasps and my knees screaming as I plunge down the hill. I don't care if it hurts. No, I do. I *want* it to hurt. I want to feel anything except the pain in my heart, and if that's pain in my lungs and my knees, then so be it. Bring it on.

How can I continue to love him, knowing he lied? Knowing he wasn't who I believed him to be?

Robert loved me, I do believe that. But I also know that Robert was a man who loved steadfastly. He wouldn't have divorced one woman and married another within two years. It doesn't fit the man I knew.

Yet was he capable of an affair?

I can't imagine it. But here is the evidence, sitting in that horrific wedding album – the wedding another woman got to have and I didn't.

Someone took it from me.

I stop running with a gasp and almost fall with the shock.

Did she do this? Did she kill Robert, knowing he was about to marry me? The vengeful wife who had discovered her husband was about to bigamously marry the other woman? But, oh, of course, of course, I realise as I reach the lane and my footsteps echo off the walls of the empty cottages.

The ultimate revenge. Kill the husband and frame the other woman.

## 17

### MAEVE

I'm in the bedroom, his wife's clothes scattered around me on the bed and on the floor. I'm going crazy. I feel hysterical, like I could burst into peals of laughter at any moment.

My feet are half a size larger than hers. I know this because I've tried on all her shoes, now. She had good quality hiking boots, and some really nice sandals. The sandals are mine now, I've decided. The hiking boots can stay in the cupboard – they'd give me blisters in moments.

A strange, lunatic laughter tickles at my throat, even though I'm not happy. I don't know how I feel. But I do know it wasn't me. I didn't do it.

That's the one gift that this discovery has provided: I'm no longer terrified that I'm a murderer and that I killed Robert in my sleep. I can sleep again at night without fear of what I might be capable of. I might be trained to kill, but I'm not a killer. I didn't slice my fiancé's jugular with a knife.

Her mascara and liquid eyeliner have both dried up, but her blusher is velvety and smooth on the apples of my cheeks. She had good taste in beauty products. The perfume is too floral for me, I decide. But I don't throw it away. I can't. It's not my place.

What I also know is that I can't hide here much longer. In fact, it's a miracle I've been able to hide here for as long as I have. There's a woman out there who's capable of murder, and she knows this cottage exists. It's only a matter of time before she comes here, or sends the police here.

I pull on one of her jackets, a delightful tweed blazer that wouldn't look out of place in an episode of *Downton Abbey* when they all go fox hunting or something equally countrified.

It fits perfectly around my shoulders, and the length in the arms is just right. Perhaps Robert's wife and I were a similar size. Perhaps he had a type, I think with resentment.

But the buttons on the jacket won't fasten around my middle. I tug them together but I can't make them meet. My once-flat stomach is rounding out beneath my layer of abdominal muscle.

The baby is growing. Soon I'll be visibly pregnant.

## 18

### GILLY

By the time she arrives at the Safeline office for her next shift, she's back to normal happy-go-lucky Gilly.

She heads to the kitchen to make tea, dunking the teabag with a spoon until it is the perfect colour and then carefully pouring the milk into her cup.

She savours the momentary calm. It's a new day.

Henry's not in today, and Gilly's grateful that she hasn't needed to have a proper conversation about what happened at the end of her previous shift. But she's ready to talk if she needs to. She has nothing to be ashamed of. It's happened to her before; it'll happen again. Panic attacks can happen to anyone, be triggered by anything.

*Have you ever destroyed someone's life?*

It wasn't a big deal, after all. After a few minutes, her breath had steadied and her vision began to clear. Her lungs loosened so she could finally take a breath, and she noticed the small glass of water on the desk in front of her, which someone must have brought her.

She used to get panic attacks all the time, back in her early twenties and then again in her early thirties. Every so often they still rear their head, plunging her back to her lowest moments as if no time has passed. This time it must have been the tension of the unknown – that caller had really managed to tap into something deep in Gilly's psyche, even without realising it. All the anticipation, the caller's crying, their anguish, and then the waiting over the weekend and all through that shift, meant she was a bundle of nerves by the time the call even began. And then that question: *Have you ever destroyed someone's life?* Just perfectly phrased and poised to send her spiralling back into her past, back years and years to another time she barely thinks about any more. A time she knows wasn't her fault, doesn't deserve the guilt she puts on it.

'Destroyed' is such a harsh, violent word, she's always thought. It makes her flinch every time it's used in the context of putting dogs to sleep, for example. There's something so total and final about it. Destruction. Obliteration.

By the time she was sipping the water, holding the glass in her shaking hands, Vivian was back at her own desk, having transferred Gilly's call through to her phone, and Henry was sitting next to Gilly, a concerned look on his face. She'd managed to brush off the incident, blaming the flu, and got out of the door in time to collect Polly and Jake from school, only a mild tremor in her hands giving away the depths of panic that had wracked her at Safeline.

And now she's back for her next shift, ready to take on the world again.

But as she's returning to her desk, cup of tea in one hand and a bourbon biscuit in the other, she sees that the light on her phone is flashing to signal there's an incoming call. She quickly glances around the room, but every volunteer is busy. Her stomach knots and her mouth fills with saliva. A prickly sweat breaks out on her upper lip.

She's been telling herself it's no big deal, but the way her body is reacting tells her she's dreading her first call. All calls.

She doesn't know who's going to be at the other end of that line, what problem they might have, what horror story they might want to tell. It's fear of the unknown, that's what's going on.

*It's anxiety*, she tells herself. *You're feeling anxious.* Name the feeling. Acknowledge it. Then let it go. She knows all the techniques. She's read all the books, listened to all the podcasts. Breathing, stretches, naming things, journaling, gratitude diaries, scheduled worry time, feeling the fear, trusting her instincts... all of it. None of it works. How can she trust her instincts if her instincts constantly signal danger?

It could be hormones – she's in her mid-forties, after all. Her friends have mentioned this: the first sign of menopause for many of them was a deep anxiety which left many of them unable to undertake their normal day-to-day lives. One friend gave up driving until her doctor found the right dose of HRT. Another took up smoking, claiming it was the only thing that would calm her down. She makes a mental note to contact her GP even though that's always a last resort, and she takes a fortifying breath before crossing the office to her desk and sliding the headset over her ears.

'Hello, you've reached Safeline. How can I help?' She holds her breath.

There's a rustling at the end of the line, and then a happy hum. 'Oh, it's you! I'd recognise your voice anywhere. I've been hoping to catch you.'

It's them. Her senses heighten immediately. There's something familiar, the buzz of the line, the intonation of their voice... her body reacts like there's a wild animal ahead of her. Instinct.

Gilly's heart rate speeds up but she holds it together. The caller sounds OK, almost cheerful. Today's not going to be as challenging as the last few calls. Gilly decides not to confirm or deny. 'How are you today? It's nice to hear from you.'

'I should be asking you – your colleague said your phone stopped working. I was disappointed we couldn't continue our chat. You know, when you've developed a rapport with someone it's hard to start up with someone new.'

Gilly murmurs an agreement. 'You know, I could give you some resources to put you in touch with a therapist, if you'd like to set up something regular. It might be a bit easier than—'

'No, thank you.' Her voice is sharp and firm. 'I don't know,' she continues, her voice softening. 'There's something about you – I know you get it. You were there for me for hours when I was at my lowest, when others would have given up. There's something special in you, and I just really feel like you're the person I need to talk to.'

A smile crosses Gilly's face. This is why she volunteers, she reminds herself. 'Well, thank you. I'm so glad this service has helped you. Is helping you.' She takes a sip of tea and lets the quiet sit for a moment, but the caller doesn't fill it. 'Is there anything you'd like to talk about today?'

Her heart starts to calm, and she focuses on loosening her muscles, rolling her shoulders and wiping her sticky palms on her thighs. Her panic was silly and unnecessary. This is a normal call, just one which began in an unusual way.

She's dying to ask what happened that first day, why the caller was so distraught. But she has to follow the policies and let the caller lead the direction of their conversation. She can't be directive.

The caller releases an almighty sigh. 'I have no idea where to start,' she says with a mirthful chuckle. 'There's not just me to think about any more. My decisions will affect other lives. Lives that didn't ask to be involved. And I'm running out of time.'

Gilly pauses, hoping she'll say more but she doesn't. 'Time for what?'

'I need to—' Another sigh. 'I should have called the police.'

Gilly closes her eyes. She's out of her depth. She's been

dreading a call like this, one which might involve a crime. Safe-line's policies on involving authorities are scant. They're designed to protect the caller in all circumstances, and there are only very, very rare situations where it's possible to contact the police about a caller. If they're suicidal and divulge their loca-tion. If they're holding a weapon with intent to use it... and divulge their location. Otherwise, there's nothing Safeline can do. There's no caller ID, no way to trace where a caller might be located. Gilly just has to listen, no matter what.

A caller could be pointing a gun at someone's head, and there'd be nothing Gilly could do.

It's terrifying. Callum has been warning her about this from the beginning, she thinks with a roiling feeling in her stomach. And she ignored him, even though he's always got her back. Even though he's so often right. *His* instincts work properly.

'Why did you need the police?' She tries to keep the tremor from her voice.

'I wanted to call. I almost did, when I woke up that morn-ing. But I just...' She sniffs, sounding like she's crying. 'I realised they wouldn't believe me. I couldn't call. They never believe us, do they? Women, I mean.'

The caller can't see her, but Gilly nods, feeling her agree-ment deep in her soul.

'And the sun was starting to rise. And he was just lying there, so still, as if nothing had happened when actually every-thing had changed. No going back. I had to get out of there before it was too late. I didn't want anyone to see me. But I should have called the police.' There's admonishment in her voice, as if she's disappointed with herself. 'Let justice be done.'

She knows what this caller is talking about, even if she shouldn't assume. She knows because Gilly's been through this herself: waking up the next morning next to a man she didn't know, with no memory of the night before. Sore and broken, her body understanding that something horrific had happened, even if her brain couldn't tune in to what it was. Not able to face the truth, just desperate to leave before he woke up.

'People won't believe me. I couldn't sit there in a police station, give a statement about what had happened and then have them turn around and tell me I was to blame; that I'd done it.' Her voice cracks and Gilly hears quiet crying. 'I've already lost so much. It's not fair.'

Gilly looks up. Henry's office is in darkness, the door firmly closed. It's his day off, so in reality she can say what she wants. No one is listening, and these calls aren't automatically recorded. Around her, her colleagues are focused on their own worlds, chatting to each other, or immersed in their calls.

She swallows, and then starts talking before she can stop herself. 'It's possible you won't be believed, yes. And if that happens, it'll be the hardest thing you'll ever go through. But the only thing you have is the truth. Lies always get found out. Remember, this wasn't your fault. Nothing you did made it happen.'

'I didn't think...' Her voice fades.

'I'm listening,' Gilly whispers.

'I didn't think there'd be so much blood.'

## 19

## MAEVE

Lentils. Pulses. Potatoes. Canned vegetables. I'm sick of them.

I'm making a vegetarian chilli, stirring the bubbling red sauce with a barely contained fury as my mind flits here and there, hardly allowing my thoughts to rest on a worry or a frustration before finding the next one.

I want a rich, buttery chicken curry or a huge cheeseburger. I want a whole punnet of strawberries and a family-sized bag of Doritos.

But the money I found in Robert's wallet is starting to run low. Every time I make a meal, I mentally calculate the cost of each serving, the nutritional value for a growing baby... those things are more important than my pregnancy cravings. But what I wouldn't give for variety and taste. A takeaway delivered to my door.

I put a lid on the pot and start to measure out rice, careful not to spill even one grain or make too much. I can't waste anything.

The low level of panic in my chest rises a little with every passing day as my baby bump swells. It was still so early in the pregnancy when Robert and I were due to get married. We knew I wouldn't be showing yet, so we'd kept our secret, stealing snatched joyful glances if conversation strayed near the topic of children. I'd have a couple of sips of wine to keep up appearances, but never more. I loved sharing a secret with him like that. Something only we knew.

I place a hand on my little baby bump, a warm glow in my chest as I think of it – her, I've decided – as the only remaining piece of Robert left on this earth. But then, as has happened over and over since opening that cupboard, a mental cloud covers the sun and I remember he's not the man I thought he was. He betrayed me. His actions led me here, to hiding out in this tiny cottage, cooking with canned vegetables and afraid to waste one grain of rice.

It's still a tiny bump – no one would know I was pregnant if they passed me on the street. My old clothes still fit. My gait is still the confident stride of an athlete. But even while my body remains as strong and familiar as ever, over the past few days, the reality of my situation has started to strike me, and with every new realisation I'm more and more terrified.

Within the next few months I'm going to need medical care. It's not just me, now. The welfare of my baby is at stake, too. But to see a midwife you need to give your name. And my name is all over the news.

Even more urgently, I need money to be able to feed myself and nourish the baby as she grows. After that, I'll need nappies and baby clothes.

My situation is unsustainable and terrifying. And he did this to me. To *us*.

With a rush of fury, I shove the pan of rice onto a burner and stomp upstairs, into Robert's art room. I've avoided coming in here, still holding onto the idea that Robert's art is somehow sacrosanct, the last piece of him that no one else has touched or seen.

But now I push the door open with my shoulder and pull a

painting away from the wall, barely seeing it as I punch and kick through its papery layers, scraping at the paint with my nails and snapping the frame under my feet until I'm left exhausted in a heap in the middle of the room, my face on the bare paint-splattered floorboards, sobs wracking my body.

From downstairs, I hear the hiss of my pan of rice boiling over and I howl with frustration. But I haul myself to my feet and trudge down the stairs, unable to waste a whole pan of rice.

Halfway down the stairs, however, I freeze, staring at the front door ahead of me. Silhouetted in the blurry glass of the top of the door is a figure. Someone is standing on the doorstep.

I don't move. Did they see me? I don't know how long they've been standing there. Did they hear me?

The figure moves, reaching a hand up.

And then they knock on the door.

## 20

### MAEVE

The knocking doesn't stop. It gets louder, as if the person on the doorstep is willing to batter the door down if they have to.

My eyes are wide, my breaths shallow. I'm terrified.

Slowly, I sink to a sitting position on the stairs, my legs not strong enough to hold me up. Perhaps it's the postman, or a political canvasser, I try to convince myself. But those knocks aren't the knocks of someone doing their job or trying to deliver a flyer.

*Bang. Bang. Bang.*

There's determination in there. Violence, even. This person isn't going away.

Above my head, the little bell inside the phone tinkles lightly, reverberating with the power of the knocks at the door. It's such a bright, cheerful little noise, like the phone is offering me a lifeline. If only I had anyone I could call, someone who could help get me out of this mess.

No one knew about this cottage except Robert, he'd told me. He'd called it his secret getaway. A place he went to paint in peace. No one is meant to know it exists. No one should know I'm here. So who is here? And why are they knocking?

Whoever it is must know Robert is dead. Even if it's not a family member or a friend, his face will have been all over the news.

Which means only one thing. They're here for me.

## 21

## GILLY

She's exhausted today, her eyes gritty and dry. She pushes her glasses up onto her forehead to rub at her eyes, while the old lady continues talking at her, her voice reedy and thin.

'Well, you know, I remember the coronation. There was only one person on our street with a television – a little black and white box, it was – and they pushed it up to their window and we all crowded around to see Princess Elizabeth get her crown put on. None of us were royalists usually, but we were that day.'

The lady has been talking non-stop for almost an hour, and Gilly is grateful for it. She'd been up and down all night with Polly, who said she had an earache but Gilly suspects it was a ruse to get cuddles on the sofa and watch Netflix for a little while. Gilly doesn't wake Callum for help on nights like that, even if she's exhausted; he's got the high-flying money-making job and Gilly's a volunteer. Her time feels less valuable, and if she's tired during her days, she's tired. It doesn't matter as much.

But time seems to be passing extra slowly today. To an extent it's a relief that the caller doesn't seem to need any input from her except the occasional mumbled 'mmhm'. And Gilly is glad that she can be here to assuage the loneliness of an older person.

And, she has to admit, it's a plus that being tied up on the line means she doesn't have to answer the phone to anyone else. There's no risk of picking up the phone and hearing those sobs, that breathing, or anything else. For a brief moment, she allows herself to relax. She feels the muscles in her shoulders ease and a loosening in her forehead as she releases an ever-present frown.

*I didn't think there'd be so much blood.*

She shudders, thinking back to her previous call with that woman. A rape victim, she's pretty sure. And a brutal assault, if there was blood.

Can she handle it, if she calls back again?

Gilly thinks back to her training, to the afternoon when all the new trainees were taken aside into a private room and quietly questioned about triggers, trauma and other things which might mean Safeline wouldn't want her as a volunteer.

Her own 'trauma' happened so long ago that Gilly hadn't even thought to disclose it. Half her life ago. She hadn't even thought about it in years, until recently.

Once, in her twenties, she'd been defined by it. She'd wanted to go up to people on the street and tell them what happened in the same breath as telling them her own name. But now she's a wife, a mother, a survivor with other parts to her life. Or so she'd thought, before the caller had asked that question about destroying another person's life and plunged her right back to those horrifying days and weeks.

And then the caller had mentioned blood.

'My sister – Noreen, her name was, God rest her soul – she never believed me when I said I could remember watching the television that day. She said I was too young... I was only a toddler, you know. But I've always had an uncommonly good memory, even now when most folks my age are rocking and dribbling in an old people's home somewhere. Not me. Although...'

Gilly can hear a phone ringing somewhere else in the office. She frowns, tuning out the old lady for a moment. Usually calls are picked up quite quickly, but as she looks around she sees that all her fellow volunteers are either on calls or away from their desks.

The ringing stops at an empty desk and then starts elsewhere.

At the desk opposite, Vivian gives her a shrug and continues with her own call. It happens sometimes: a caller will bounce around from phone to phone until finding a line that's available.

'Anyway, I must let you go. I've talked your ear off and I'm sure you have other people who need your help. I just like a chat, you know.'

Gilly pushes a smile into her voice, hoping someone else picks up that call before she hangs up this one. She could do with a break and a cup of tea. 'I've really enjoyed hearing your stories,' she says, and she means it. It's been a relief. 'That's what we're here for, and I'm glad you called.'

Just as she hears the old lady returning her phone handset to the cradle the line buzzes, she sees Vivian press buttons on her own phone and answer that call with their familiar Safeline greeting.

The ringing stops and she lets out a relieved breath, standing up to stretch her legs and maybe get a cup of tea. She wonders what biscuits they have in the kitchen—

'Same to you, asshole,' mutters Vivian, pulling her headset from her head.

Gilly gives her a quizzical look.

'Called me the C-word then hung up,' she says, shaking her head.

'Lovely,' Gilly says with a sigh. 'Cup of tea?'

But before Vivian can answer, the phone on her desk starts

ringing again. Gilly signals to Vivian that she'll bring her one, and heads into the kitchen.

When she returns, she can see that most of her colleagues are off their calls, too, sitting around chatting and filling in call details on their computers. Sometimes it happens like that: everyone's busy at once and then there's a lull. Her personal theory is that it's bored people at home, calling Safeline for something to do in the ad breaks between episodes of *Homes Under the Hammer* or *Bargain Hunt*.

She sits with her cup of tea and starts to complete her log for the old lady (o16 – loneliness), when something strange starts to happen: each of her colleagues gets a call, picks up the phone and then the call ends almost immediately. A hang-up. And then the next desk phone starts to ring, gets answered, and then hung up. Then Vivian's. More silent calls, going through each of their phones one by one. It's like watching a tsunami heading towards her, helpless on the once-idyllic beach.

Then her own phone starts to ring.

'Hello, you've reached Safeline. How can I help?'

'Help,' the familiar voice whispers, and Gilly's skin turns to ice.

She's found her.

## 22

## MAEVE

'I know you're in there. Open the door,' a voice yells through the letter box, sending a chill through the deepest recesses of my soul.

I huddle closer into the wall, the stairs jutting into my back and the banister knocking against my head. As if making myself smaller will protect me somehow.

It's a woman.

Normally that information would bring me relief. After all, isn't there a statistic somewhere that women are more afraid of bumping into a man alone in the woods than a bear?

But just a few weeks ago I woke up in a pool of blood next to the body of my fiancé. And now I think his wife killed him, angry that he was cheating on her. Determined he wouldn't marry someone else. And for all I know, I'm next. A woman should feel safer, but I'd give anything for that voice to belong to a man.

A hand snakes through the letter box slot and I see manicured blood-red fingernails reaching into the entrance hall, groping around... for what? My heart sinks as I remember the old-school methods of leaving keys for holiday renters, before lock boxes were common: you'd hang the key behind the letter box on a string, and the renter could reach in and pull the string to get the key.

This woman's trying to get inside.

But then something even worse happens. The figure disappears from the top window, and a pair of hazel eyes appear through the mail slot.

She can see me.

'You,' she hisses, her voice dripping with hatred.

## 23

### GILLY

'How can I help?' Gilly asks, trying to keep the shake from her voice. She's embarrassed by how much this caller unbalances her. She wants to be neutral, to follow the rules and treat each call like an individual caller, unconnected to the last, but she can't shake the unsettled feeling that this person gives her. There's something so invasive about every interaction they have, and Gilly can't put her finger on why.

Perhaps it's the lack of information. Gilly still doesn't know what this caller wants from these calls, what she believes will help. She doesn't even really know what their problem is, she can only assume.

On the other end of the line, the shaky breaths begin.

Gilly swallows and braces herself, immediately remembering the endurance test that this caller's initial phone calls were when she wouldn't speak, would only cry and scream and sob and breathe into Gilly's ear for hours. She doesn't think she can do that again. Not today. Not when she's so tired, her nerves strung taut ready to snap.

'When we talked last time...' the caller says, her voice a whisper. This time it's different; instead of an oppressive silence, today there's background noise. A banging and rustling, like the caller is calling from a building site.

Gilly releases a silent breath of relief, so glad the caller is talking, that this will be an equal exchange, not a hostage situation.

The caller clears her throat and tries again, her voice clearer as she raises it over the background din. 'When we talked last time, you said that what happened wasn't my fault. That I didn't make any of this happen. Do you remember?'

She closes her eyes and slumps forward, her forehead almost touching the desk. She reaches down and grabs a handful of each thigh in her hands, squeezing and pinching to hurt herself. *Stupid, stupid, stupid.*

This is another reason why this caller unsettles her so much. It's not just the lack of control. She's constantly pushing the rules, testing Gilly, trying to breach the boundaries of anonymity and confidentiality. And Gilly let her guard down.

This caller inadvertently found Gilly's weak spot and exposed it. It's not the caller's fault, Gilly knows. It's her own. She purposefully kept an incident from her past secret during her training and that incident influenced her ability to act in a professional manner. She said too much, made assumptions. And now that's come back to haunt her.

She lowers her voice, glancing up at Vivian, who's looking at her mobile and not paying attention. 'I shouldn't have said that. We're here to talk about you.'

Henry's on holiday, his office window dark. No one knows this is happening. No one is listening. Thank goodness.

Gilly loves Safeline, she realises now. This role gives her a purpose. Here, she's not just a wife and mother, she's a volunteer, a friend, someone making a difference. And this caller is threatening all that, pushing her further and further away from her training, the handbook and the rules she's meant to follow. Henry has already pulled her up for breaking the rules, and she had to abandon a call during a panic attack. Is that two strikes? What happens if there's a third?

She doesn't want to find out. She can't lose Safeline.

She tries to shift the conversation, and adjusts her tone, trying to sound breezy yet firm. 'Would you like to tell me more about what happened?'

She's pushing the limits of the rules again, directing the conversation instead of letting the caller lead. But she needs to get her away from this. Away from prying into Gilly and pushing things further than Gilly wants them to go.

But the caller won't let her get away. The background noise subsides a little and Gilly hears her clearly: 'How did you know it wasn't my fault? Is it because this happened to you?'

The line crackles in her ear and she holds her breath, images flashing in front of her eyes. Images she's been suppressing for decades.

Waking up next to a dark figure in a strange bedroom, disoriented and bleary, more thirsty than she'd ever felt in her life. Little memory of the night before. A deep ache between her legs. Fingertip-shaped bruises on her wrists. A chunk of hair missing from her head. A used condom tied in a knot on the bedside table. Lips bitten and bruised. Dawn creeping up to the window, and a whisper of a feeling: *get out of here. Run.*

'Hello? Are you there?' The caller sounds irritated, and Gilly snaps back to the present, releasing her grip on her thighs, her hands shaking. She swallows down the bile that rises in her throat.

*Enough. Get a grip,* she says to herself. The usual calming techniques won't work on this. Screw the breathing exercises. If she could slap herself in the face, she would. But colleagues would see. She satisfies herself with a brutal headshake, like a dog climbing out of the sea. And she fills her lungs with air, mentally blowing the images away when she exhales.

It was a long time ago. She is healed. She has moved on.

She has processed all of it. Yes, she has. Years of hard work, of introspection, of pain. And now she's a new person. This caller doesn't have to affect her like this. Gilly can choose who impacts her and who doesn't. Who can hurt her and who can't.

Like she's mentally turned to a new page, Gilly sits up straighter. From now on, full professionalism. Following the rules like they're tattooed on her heart. No deviating, no allowing herself to be pushed or prodded away from the line. She won't be manipulated. She won't lose this job.

This is a new caller, and Gilly knows nothing about them or their life. She's never spoken to them before, and she's there to listen. That's it. That's what Safeline is for.

'I'm here,' she says in her soft voice. 'Sorry if we lost connection for a moment. Is there something you'd like to talk about today?'

'Yes, there is.' There's a prickliness to the tone as she raises her voice over some muffled shouting at the other end of the line.

Gilly can tell she's irritated the caller.

'I want to know what happened to you. Why you know so much about what's my fault and what's not,' the caller demands.

Her cheeks grow hot, but Gilly's resolve doesn't waver. 'I'm here to help you, and I'm afraid I can't talk about myself.'

The caller laughs, a cruel mirthless chuckle. 'That's not what you said last time. You were practically telling me your name and address.'

She straightens her shoulders, berating herself again for telling them her volunteering hours. 'Safeline is a safe and confidential helpline. That means we won't ask you any details about yourself other than what you're willing to share. And your call handlers are also anonymous too, providing confidentiality for anything you'd like to—'

'Shut up with your bullshit sales pitch,' the caller practically spits.

Gilly's mouth falls open. Her world narrows to a pinprick as she focuses only on the fierce growling words pouring into her ears.

'You think you know it all. You think everything is black and white. You think you know me but you don't. You pretend you want to help people but if you really wanted to help you'd be real and honest. Instead, you're just a liar like everyone else. You can't hide behind your stupid scripts and policies for much longer. I know the truth about you.'

Gilly stays quiet as the caller continues goading her, getting more and more insulting and abusive the longer Gilly remains quiet. At the caller's end, the building site noises and the shouting seem to have subsided, the line descending into quiet once more, even while the noise in Gilly's mind gets louder and more intrusive.

At some point, Vivian must have noticed Gilly's pale face and frozen demeanour, and she crosses around the desks and puts a reassuring hand on Gilly's shoulder. Gilly doesn't move.

She knows that most people move into fight or flight when they feel threatened. Gilly used to fight. She used to bristle at the slightest danger, ready to protect herself and everyone around her. But since... she doesn't know when, perhaps since having her kids, her reactions have shifted and now it's not fight, and nor is it flight. It's freeze. And she's frozen.

Vivian gives her a gentle shake, just as the voice on the end of the phone utters the most heinous, violent and abusive threats that Gilly has ever heard. They call her names, they wish her dead, they wish her maimed and raped and diseased.

And finally, Gilly is released from the prison of her mind. She utters the words that were drilled into them in Safeline's first training session, to be used only in very specific scenarios:

'Safeline doesn't accept calls of this nature.' And she hangs up the phone.

# 24

## MAEVE

'I can see you, sitting on the stairs,' the woman says through the letter box, her voice clear and cutting.

I close my eyes, as if that will somehow make me disappear. My body is wracked with shivers. I still haven't moved, even as I heard her circling the house, trying the back door and the windows.

'Open the door,' she hisses.

I shake my head and swallow a whimper. I don't want to face this.

The woman doesn't care, her voice getting louder as her frustration mounts. 'If you care about me or my brother at all, you'll open this door. Now.'

She's so determined, as always.

'Sarah,' I croak, my voice shaking. But surely I don't need to be afraid any more. She's my best friend. Or... is she? She's also Robert's sister, after all.

If she's found me, it probably means the police aren't far behind. There's no way she'd come here on her own. She'll hand me in within moments, and I wouldn't blame her. From her perspective I'm a cold-blooded murderer who stabbed her brother to death and then left his body. On our wedding day. She won't have come alone.

I don't move.

The letter box rattles and I hear her muttering to herself from the doorstep, frustrated.

'Just let me in, Maeve. The longer I stand here, the more likely it is that someone sees me, and I know you don't want anyone to know you're here. Let me inside.'

Her voice is so familiar, the same voice that has teased me, comforted me, talked me through the toughest parts of my life up until today. There's a pull from my heart to her, and I long to step forward and open that door.

I look up, a frown on my brow. If she's brought the police with her, why would she be concerned about being seen? There'd be police cars on the lane outside, uniformed officers behind the hedge waiting to storm in and take me down.

Maybe she's just saying that to get me to let my guard down. That must be it. Lull me into a false sense of security and then the moment I open the door I'll be pounced on, thrown to the ground and immobilised until the handcuffs close their cold metal around my wrists. I'll be bundled into the back of a police car, someone's clammy palm on the top of my head as they shove me roughly inside. Treated like the criminal they think I am. The criminal everyone believes me to be.

Someone broke into my house to commit murder. Someone who knows me. I can't trust anyone. Not even Sarah. And definitely not the police.

Could I fight? My body responds to the thought like an instinct, my muscles tightening in readiness. I can immobilise a grown man in moments. I've been trained to fight multiple assailants, armed and unarmed. I can injure. I can kill. I'm strong and I'm fit. But I can't hurt Sarah. I love Sarah. And I can't take on a group of policemen. They might have tasers.

And maybe even guns. They'll be prepared for that. They think I'm a murderer, after all.

No. I can't fight.

Could I run? The cottage has a door out of the kitchen, leading through the backyard and into the little lane that runs behind the cottages. I'm not wearing any shoes. My belongings are scattered around the house, stuff in the bathroom, living room and bedroom. If I leave now and manage to get away (and that's assuming the police aren't around the back, too, waiting to stop me if I try this) then I'll be lost and alone with no coat and shoes in the middle of the Highlands. I wouldn't last the night, even at this time of year.

But the alternative – opening the door, allowing myself to be arrested when I know I've been framed and have no evidence to prove it... it's not an option. I'll go to prison for the rest of my life. It's what Robert's wife wants, and if she managed to get into our home undetected and kill Robert while I stayed asleep, she planned this carefully. She knew what she was going to do and she knew who I was. Those injuries on Robert's body... I shudder just to remember them. So carefully orchestrated to look like they were performed by someone who knows how to butcher and kill. Someone trained. Someone like me.

So I can't predict how much more Robert's wife had planned. What else she has planted on me to make this look even more incriminating than I've already uncovered.

I curse myself for spending these last couple of weeks pacing the cottage, feeling sorry for myself, obsessing over Robert's betrayal of me. I should have been doing more, finding out where this woman could have gone, how she might have given herself away. Instead I've been staring at these walls, fretting about how I can go into hiding with a baby. At this rate I won't have a baby. She'll be taken from me at birth as I live the rest of my life without her, behind bars.

I can't let that happen. I have to run.

I stand up, dart down the stairs.

'No,' Sarah shouts as I turn the corner to the kitchen. 'Don't do this, Maeve. Face me. Look me in the eyes and tell me it wasn't you. Please.'

I freeze. She's still my best friend. That voice and beseeching tone I've heard so many times over the years when she wanted something from me. I can't just walk away.

But I have to.

'Come on, Maeve. I cancelled three meetings for this.'

I almost laugh. Almost, but not quite. From anyone else that wouldn't mean anything, but for Sarah skipping work is massive. One year she even missed her own birthday party to finish a report. So her presence here on a work day says a lot.

But not enough. I shake my head and take another step towards the back door.

'I saw your vows. What you were planning to say to Robert at the wedding,' she shouts, her tone pleading. 'You left your notebook on the coffee table in your living room.'

My mouth goes dry as I realise what that means: she came to our flat the morning of our wedding. Sarah was the one who found his body, who called the police. She saw the blood-soaked bed. Robert's grey, lifeless face.

I close my eyes, letting that sink in. I'm flooded with guilt and self-doubt. If I hadn't run, I could have prevented that.

'Your vows were beautiful. There was so much love.' There's no accusation in Sarah's voice, just understanding and affection. 'You couldn't have written them if you didn't mean it. I know you couldn't.' Her voice catches and I draw in a breath, letting myself hope. She clears her throat, and her next words are almost a whisper: 'I know you couldn't have hurt him, Maeve. You loved him.'

I stop again and turn towards the door. She's still crouching at the letter box, and I can see her eyes. She's crying, mascara gathering around her eyes as the tears fall. She reaches a hand out and wipes them away, smudging her mascara more.

And all I want to do now is reach out and hold her again. I've held her so many times while she cried. Terrible boyfriends, failed exams, bad haircuts – a whole range of causes. Except this time, it's a dead brother. And she doesn't think I did it.

I know her well enough to be able to tell when she's lying. I believe her. She knows I'm innocent.

Before I talk myself out of it, I step towards the door and unlock it.

## 25

## MAEVE

Sarah spills forward and quickly rights herself, rising to her feet and facing me straight on. Her eyes search mine, flicking from side to side as she examines me. She has Robert's eyes, I notice for the first time with a pang.

'You didn't do it. Did you? You loved him. You wouldn't. You couldn't.' Tears are streaming down her face and she doesn't bother reaching up to wipe them away.

I start to cry, too, sobs wracking my body. We fall into each other and I bury my face in her shoulder. It's been so long since I've touched another person – or been touched – that as soon as her arms close around me, I fall apart. I hadn't realised how much tension I'd been holding in every muscle of my body, and suddenly I'm jelly. I lose all control of my emotions, the grief spilling out of my mouth in an animal-like wail. I feel Sarah's grip on me tighten as my legs almost collapse under me.

'I didn't do it, Sarah,' I choke out through my sobs. 'I didn't do it. I didn't do it.'

I say it over and over until she shushes me and pulls back, looking me in the face again.

I blurt out the story of waking up in the bed, covered in

blood, the knife in my sheets. My body shakes with the same terror I felt that morning as I relive every painful, awful moment. Until I get to the description of his injuries. I can't describe that to her. She should never have to picture her brother that way. I can't share the images that haunt me, flashing behind my eyelids as I try to drift away to sleep every night.

'And the self-defence methods I was taught, when I went abroad to study... some lethal methods, to be used only when your life is in danger. I've never used them. But whoever did this, they wanted to make it look like it was me. I didn't kill him, Sarah. But I know it looks like I did.'

She holds my shoulders. She looks me straight in the eyes, her own bloodshot and red, just like mine must be. 'I believe you.'

I usher her inside and glance outside at the deserted street. No one's around, although something niggles in the back of my mind, a little voice asking, 'Do you trust her?' I pause, my eyes roaming over a couple of parked cars, and I glance down the street to the post office, where the sign sits out on the pavement and the door is propped open. Everything looks normal. And behind me inside the cottage is the only person in the entire world who might believe me. The only person who might help. I *need* to trust her, I realise. Otherwise I'm totally, completely alone and I don't think I can handle that.

But I'm not ready yet to tell her about the baby. That's still my secret to keep. Mine and Robert's.

I close the door quickly, rush to the kitchen where I remove the pan of ruined rice from the stove, and then follow Sarah into the living room, where she's standing by the fireplace holding that photograph of me and Robert from that barbecue, a sad smile on her face. It looks genuine.

'He really loved you, you know.'

I slump down onto the sofa, exhausted. Just a few days ago

that might have given me solace, helped ease my grief. But now I've seen the wedding photos.

She looks up, eyes clouded with concern as she notices the shift in my body language at her mention of Robert's love. 'What?' She puts the picture down on the mantelpiece, still staring at me. 'You were about to marry him. You loved each other. What's going on?'

I shake my head, unable to form the words as my mind whirls. I don't even know where to start. On the one hand, Robert was her brother, after all. She must have known all along.

She let me fall for Robert and get engaged to him, all while knowing he was married to someone else. I've seen the photographs in that wedding album: Sarah was there at their wedding. Just like she would have been at mine. Would she have thought about that other wedding day while watching me walk down the aisle to my fate? Would she ever have told me?

And now she's here, in this cottage that Robert led me to believe no one else knew the existence of.

I fold my arms across my chest. Maybe letting her inside was a mistake. Maybe I shouldn't trust her, even if I want to.

But if I can't trust Sarah, I'm so alone.

So on the other hand, Sarah is meant to be my best friend. She's the first person I've spoken to since it happened. This is the first time I've felt safe. I've had no one to talk to, no one to share anything with. I need to talk to her about it. I need to know the truth. But I'm terrified the truth will take away the one person I have left.

'How did you know I was here, Sarah?' I ask, my voice quaking.

She nods. 'It was a lucky guess. After Robert was kill—' She stops herself and swallows, not wanting to talk about that yet. She starts again: 'I hacked his emails and found this address.'

I force myself to push more, terrified of what I'll find, but desperate for information. Desperate for the reassurance that I have one friend in the world. 'Robert said no one knew about this place. That he'd kept it quiet from his family.'

She nods, her face unreadable. 'I knew he had a cottage somewhere up in the Highlands. He didn't keep it secret; he needed somewhere with space to paint and think. He wasn't hiding this place or—'

'Or hiding another wife?' The words emerge from me in a rush before I can stop them.

She freezes, her back to the fireplace. I see little goosebumps rise on the bare skin of her forearms, the blonde hairs standing on end. She wraps her arms around herself as if she's freezing cold.

'Why didn't you tell me, Sarah?'

I don't move from my seat on the sofa but she backs away, her heels butting against the stone hearth. Her eyes flick from side to side as she tries to think. Is she conjuring a lie?

'Sarah,' I whisper. 'You kept this huge secret from me and—'

She lets out a big breath, shaking her head. When she opens her eyes, they twinkle with unshed tears. 'I wanted to tell you. You deserved to know.'

'So why didn't you?' I try to keep my voice steady even though my heart is beating too fast.

'It wasn't my secret to tell. If Robert had wanted to tell you about her, he would have.'

Suddenly I'm not just devastated; I'm angry. I ball my hands into fists and punch my thighs in frustration. 'You don't think I had a right to know who I was marrying? When you were dating that guy and I saw him in Alberto's with someone else, I called—'

'What are you talking about? This is nothing like that. Paul was a cheater and Robert—'

'*Was married to someone else,*' I shout, hot tears rolling down my cheeks once again. I don't care that my voice is loud, that I'm behaving in a way that Sarah has never seen. I've been betrayed in so many different ways, and I've been so alone. I'm so angry with the world and here is someone safe, someone I can rail and wail at without consequence. And so I do.

'Do you know how I found out he had another wife? I found his wedding album here. I saw pictures of him marrying someone else. Of him looking happy with her. Of him, *alive*. It's like I lost him all over again. She got everything I will never have. And now he's dead. And I want to know why. Who is this woman who gets so much when I got nothing? I don't even know her name. Why don't I even know the name of my fiancé's wife?'

Sarah turns away and pulls out a chair, sitting at the wooden dining table in the corner. She's not facing me, but I can see her profile as she battles with emotion. Sadness, frustration, anger.

My heart's pounding like I've run a marathon, and I'm out of breath after my rant. A faint feeling of guilt and something else creeps into my heart. Doubt.

Sarah looks down at the table, using a fingertip to trace the patterns in the scrubbed wood. 'Her name was Elodie,' she whispers.

## 26

## GILLY

For the first time, Gilly calls in sick to the helpline. She can't face the idea of answering the phone to that anger-filled growl one more time. Of having to listen to the streams of abuse. Of being told this is her fault, that she invited this. Although that last one is her own doing: she's so angry with herself for breaking the rules and letting that caller push the boundaries until she clearly believed Gilly owed her something.

The rules are there for a reason, she berates herself now. Henry told her as much.

And even though there are no longer any Safeline drop-in centres, and the caller couldn't know where she lives or where the Safeline offices are located, a feeling of being watched prickles the back of Gilly's spine everywhere she goes.

As she walks from the big Tesco to her car, pushing the trolley piled high with their weekly shop, she glances over her shoulder to check no one's watching her, an ever-present feeling of dread gnawing at her stomach. As she stands on the sidelines at Jake's weekly football practice, she scans the faces of the other parents, looking for anyone unfamiliar. As she drives the kids home from school, fielding school project questions from Jake about her long-abandoned career aspirations, she glances down side streets as if expecting the caller to jump out in front of her car. And every time she hears a phone ring, a cold dread steals its way through her guts.

Late one night, as Gilly and Callum are drifting off to sleep, she hears the sound of sobbing float through their open bedroom window from the summer evening outside. She freezes in fear, thinking the caller has caught her.

She knows it's stupid. She knows the woman can't find her. But still, she's afraid. She freezes, except for shivers that rack her whole body. She tries to tense her muscles, to hide the shakes from Callum even though he's used to hearing her frequent anxieties. Even though a hug from him is like being wrapped in a warm blanket. This time she just can't share.

She hasn't told Callum anything, really. He knows she hasn't been to a Safeline shift in a few days, but he believed her when she told him that she wasn't needed, that they've reduced her hours because of a couple of new trainees getting started and picking up more shifts. She's been waiting until Callum leaves the house for work before calling Henry to tell him she's still not quite herself, but that she'll be back soon.

Callum must have noticed something, though. She sees him looking at her with concern sometimes, when he thinks she's not paying attention.

And when she froze at the sound of the sobbing, he got out of bed and crossed to the window. 'Just a teenage girl on the phone. Must be having an argument or something,' he whispers. Always patient, always reassuring.

It makes sense: they live on a bus route into town and occasionally they get intoxicated teenagers heading home after pub kicking-out-time. This must be one of them, winding her way from the bus to her parents' house after a bust-up with her boyfriend.

'Poor thing,' she mumbles, the relief rendering her incapable of anything further.

Halfway back into bed, Callum pauses. 'I'll go and check she's all right. It's late and she's on her own.'

She gives him a grateful smile and that concerned look flits across his face once more. Ordinarily she'd be getting up with him, pulling on her dressing gown and switching on the kettle in case the girl needs warming up. Not now. Her generosity is on pause, while she overreacts to every tiny threat as if it's that woman storming at her, holding a machete. More so than usual, it's like she can't regulate her response to fear any more. It's all life or death. Every phone call. Every loud noise. Terror.

Given some time away from the call centre, she starts to realise just how much she had deviated from the regulations of Safeline, and just how damaging that had been. Yes, out loud Gilly's only real transgression was telling the caller when she would next be on shift, but in Gilly's mind she'd done the rest. The caller mentioned not being believed, not wanting to call the police, and those feelings were so familiar to Gilly... so valid, that Gilly had wanted to help this woman in the way that she herself had needed all those years ago.

She'd taken scant information and blown it up into a huge narrative that fitted Gilly's own past and experiences. Without the caller saying it, Gilly had assumed she was a rape victim.

*I didn't think there'd be so much blood.*

But now, with some distance, Gilly realises that the caller could have been talking about anything at all. Perhaps instead of being a victim, the caller was actually a perpetrator. That would explain the shock at the blood. The hesitation to call the police. The fear of not being believed.

What if she's a murderer?

It would explain the pure fury directed at Gilly when Gilly wouldn't bend to her will. The wild escalation from ingratiating conversation into hatred, threats and insults. The kind of reaction reserved not for a victim but for a criminal.

Gilly lets it sink in that she perhaps spent hours consoling and comforting someone who had hurt another person. Telling her everything would be OK, that Gilly was there to listen.

She wishes she could go back in time, do it all right. Be totally impartial and above all not make assumptions about anything.

After all, it's also possible that none of it was true at all. She's heard from other volunteers that they secretly believe 60 per cent of the calls they receive to be total bullshit – mad inventions from the callers who just want to live in a fantasy world. Inventing problems and personalities and spinning webs of lies to helpless volunteers, held hostage at the end of the phone line, imprisoned by restrictive rules and unable to verify anything at all.

Maybe that was what this woman did. Perhaps while she cried and sobbed and moaned for hours, the caller was sitting in a perfectly comfortable semi-detached villa in a nice part of Edinburgh, a cup of tea steaming on the coffee table in front of her. Playing games from her perfect life. Toying with volunteers.

There's no way to know.

She prays that whatever problem that caller had is resolved. She hopes they never call the helpline again.

She feels guilty about the last few days she's spent at home, cleaning out the spice cupboard and defrosting the freezer, scrolling mindlessly on her phone, arriving ten minutes early for Polly and Jake's school pickup time. She could have been there, helping people. She can't let one nasty caller stop her.

After a few days, Callum's concerned looks have now turned into questions, and Gilly steels herself to return to Safeline tomorrow, now she's given enough time to realistically recover from the fake stomach bug she invented for Henry. But first, she heads into town for some new underwear for Jake, who helpfully informed her last night that he'd thrown all his boxers away because they were too tight. Every single pair.

Kids. She can't help but laugh as she locks the car and walks through the Kingsgate multistorey car park, which is strangely quiet for a Wednesday morning in July. She feels normal, she realises. The bubbling feeling of dread has started to fade; the break from her volunteer shifts has helped her get things in perspective. It was just a normal caller, someone having a bad day, a bad week. They don't know her. They can't find her. She's safe.

There's a chill breeze whistling around the dimly lit concrete pillars, and her footsteps echo off the walls. The fluorescent strip lights above her head buzz and flicker, momentarily plunging her into darkness before they snap back on once more to illuminate the neat rows of car bonnets packed together in the shadows. No daylight reaches into the depths of the car park.

She picks up her pace, her eyes trained on the lifts. As she punches the button for the lift to take her into the familiar, bustling shopping centre, her phone starts to ring in her bag and she reaches for it, her stomach clenching with anxiety as it always does when someone calls while the kids are at school. *An accident in the playground*, her mind always leaps to. *Or worse.*

Her palms turn slick as she fumbles to get her phone from her bag, steeling herself to see the kids' school number on her caller ID. But it's not the primary school; it's a withheld number.

Probably spam. Nothing to worry about. Most people let calls from withheld numbers go straight to voicemail, and she's always tempted, just to save herself the faff. But still, when she's away from her children she answers every call, just in case the imagined worst-case scenario lurks around the next corner.

Even as she distances herself from the irrational fear response, she realises she'll never quite get used to the intense fear caused by having children, the terror of having a little piece of your heart running around in the world without you, unprotected. The world is a much scarier place when everything important can be taken away from you in a single instant.

*Hello Safeline,* she nearly says, but catches herself in time. 'Hello?' she asks, trying to ignore the slight waver in her voice which never used to be there.

Next to her, the lift arrives and the doors slide open to reveal an empty carriage, graffiti scrawled across the mirror on the rear wall. She looks at her reflection, not stepping inside: she might lose signal and she's still waiting for the caller to speak.

Definitely spam. There's always that pause while the bot assigns a call handler.

She holds out a hand to the door sensor, holding the doors open for an extra beat. She gets ready to hang up the phone and step into the lift. But then—

Breathing. She can hear breathing on the other end.

Her body freezes, her muscles tense.

She thought she was OK. She thought she was ready to return. But now she knows she isn't. She's too afraid. That Safeline caller, by doing nothing except breathing, crying and then shouting, has burrowed their way into her subconscious like a parasite, leaving her utterly defenceless even when she's out of the Safeline offices, living her normal life.

But this isn't Safeline. This is her own mobile, and it's just a spam call, nothing else. There's no way the caller could have her mobile number, could be calling her now while she's out shopping for new underwear for Jake.

Her skin feels hot, then cold.

'Hello?' she says again, trying desperately to keep the shake out of her voice.

More breaths, slow and regular.

She could just hang up. Pretend the line went dead. Henry's not listening. There are no rules she must follow. Her hand twitches towards her phone screen, ready to push the button.

'Is there anyone—'

The caller clears their throat. It's her.

'I'm sorry,' the caller says, her voice clear and regular now.

Gilly's vision sparkles and she realises that in her panic she forgot to breathe. She drops her hand from the lift and the doors slide closed; there's the whir of the lift's mechanism as it descends without her. She turns back to the multistorey car park, casting her eyes around the concrete floor and walls, the deserted cars, the pillars... all the places someone could follow her, could hide.

Her hand shakes, and she presses the phone closer to her face, trying to keep it steady. She opens her mouth but she can't speak.

How did this caller get her mobile number? What is going on? Gilly needs information. She needs to know how much danger she's in. How much danger her family are in. She takes a deep breath and attempts to override her terror, to focus on the moment and gather information.

'I'm sorry I got angry last time. I just hate liars.' She has a faint Scottish accent that Gilly can't place. Somewhere central, she thinks. But it could be anywhere, really. Gilly's never been good with accents.

Gilly doesn't know what to say to that. She hasn't lied to this caller. She just backtracked on how much she could give. She reverted to the rules. A hard lesson learned. She opens her mouth to say something – anything – she doesn't know what. She needs to know how this caller got her number. That's the only important thing right now. But before Gilly can get her thoughts in order or utter a sound, the caller continues:

'I'm ready to talk. And I want to tell you everything.'

## 27

## MAEVE

Elodie. Suddenly I have a name to fit to the face in those photographs. The beautiful blonde with love in her eyes who got everything I wanted and then took it all away.

*Her name was Elodie.*

Doubt intensifies and curdles in my gut. 'Was? But I thought—'

Sarah looks up, her expression sharp. 'Stop talking for a minute and *listen*, OK?' She straightens her shoulders as if trying to reset herself, and goes back to tracing figures on the table, her voice calm once more. 'I know Robert never mentioned her to you.'

I nod, willing her to blurt out everything so I don't have to wonder any more.

'I begged him to tell you. It all happened before you and I became friends, otherwise I'm sure I would have mentioned some of it. And then when it was all over and you and Robert got together, I pushed him and pushed him to tell you everything. After a few months I just assumed he had, until the week of your wedding and it came up again. He confessed you still didn't know.' Her face crumples, her cheeks blotching red as she swallows down tears. 'He was a kind man; you know that.'

I nod, my heart aching at her use of the past tense.

'And sometimes kindness is misdirected. He didn't want to upset you or hurt you. He avoided uncomfortable truths. The last time I talked to him was on the phone, ranting at him about how you had the right to know he'd been married before. I wasn't nice to him. I threatened to tell you myself if he didn't. And then I told him I wasn't coming to your rehearsal dinner because of a stupid meeting.'

She grabs a tissue from her pocket and blows her nose. I remember Robert whispering down the phone to her a few days before our wedding, a dark expression on his face. I'd assumed he was just angry she was missing the rehearsal dinner, normal brother-and-sister frustrations. Not that Robert was keeping something from me.

I reach out and grab Sarah's hand, trying not to squeeze too hard. 'Tell me now. Please.'

She takes a breath as she prepares herself. 'They met in their mid-twenties. They were sweet together, and very happy, but I suspect they would have gone their separate ways eventually, except then Elodie was diagnosed with brain cancer.'

I close my eyes and sink deeper into the sofa.

'It was inoperable, and they predicted she had six months. Maybe nine.' Sarah looks over at me then, tears in her eyes and a little contempt. 'They got married. They managed a year before she died.'

I drop my head into my hands, guilt and shame swirling in my gut. 'I thought—'

'That Robert was a bigamist?'

I don't move.

'You knew him better than that, Maeve. Come on.'

'I didn't know what to believe, honestly. I'd found Robert dead next to me, and had no idea who could have done it. Still don't. But suddenly there was a potential suspect in the spurned wife, and I ran with it. I needed something to cling to. Because otherwise, who could it be?'

We are quiet for a few moments. Even though Sarah is looking down, I know she's got tears in her eyes. I try to slow my breathing as I pluck up the courage to say the thought that's been haunting my sleepless nights. Robert's wife was my prime suspect; now I've found out it's not possible that she killed him, I have nothing. No other suspects, except myself.

'For a few days I even thought it could have been me. In my sleep.' As the words leave my mouth, my heart rate speeds up.

I wrap my arms around myself and close my eyes. I can't have killed my fiancé. I just can't.

She stands and crosses to sit next to me, a comforting hand on my leg. 'This must have been so awful for you.'

I close my eyes and let the wave of renewed grief crash over me. Finding the woman's belongings in that cupboard had given me an excuse to build a dam shutting out all my loss and sadness, and now I have to dismantle that wall and feel it all over again. I've got my Robert back; he wasn't a bigamist or a cheater. He was the good, kind human I knew and loved.

I blink back tears and focus on Sarah. My one true connection in this hellscape of my life right now.

'And awful for you, too,' I start, pausing to clear my throat. 'I've been thinking of you all, you know. Knowing you probably all hated me, but I wished so much I could be with you and your parents, to hug you all and cry.'

She lets out a little giggle. 'Not sure you'd be getting a hug from Mum any time soon.' She covers her mouth, as if the words came out without her permission.

I sigh, but I'm not surprised. Sarah's mum tolerated me well enough when I was only Sarah's best friend, visiting their family home for the occasional weekend or birthday party. But as soon as I started dating Robert, she turned cold and distant. I always felt like she thought I wasn't good enough for him.

'She believes I killed him, then?'

Sarah's cheeks flush, but she doesn't deny it. 'She's heartbroken, of course. For her, I think she just wants a resolution, you know? Someone arrested for the crime.'

I lean against her, exhausted. 'He deserves justice. We all do.'

She nods, but I can tell her mind is elsewhere. She stares into the empty fireplace, her eyes unfocused. 'I'm going to find out who did this, Maeve.'

I stand up, gathering my hoody from where it's hanging on the back of a chair, and the battered Regency romance I've been slowly trying to read for the past two weeks, desperate for distraction. 'I'll pack my stuff. We can drive back down to Glasgow. Or is there a police station near here? I'll turn myself in to the police, let them question me. At least then we can make some progress. They'll arrest me at first, but I'm sure they'll... I'll go to prison if I have to. We'll get to the truth eventually.'

Sarah holds out a hand. 'Stop.'

I pause on my way to the kitchen, my arms full of belongings.

'I hate to say this, but you can't do that.'

'I can't do what?'

She swallows and rubs her mouth with the back of her hand. 'Your picture is all over the news. The papers are writing about this case like it's a done deal. They're calling you "The Bloody Bride".'

*Of course.* My mouth turns dry as I recall Ella's face on the TV, denouncing me to the media and demanding justice for Robert. I step into the kitchen and down a glass of tap water and return to the living room, shaky and fizzing with the shock of having to face this reality.

Sarah's still on the sofa, staring at her hands linked together in her lap, her long red hair falling over her face. 'The police took away all of Robert's paperwork, both of your laptops and phones. Analysis of equipment like that can take months, which is probably why you've been OK for the last few weeks, but it was easy for me to find this address when I started looking. It won't be long until they learn about this cottage, or someone recognises you and turns you in.'

'What are you saying?' My voice croaks, coming out at barely a whisper.

'I'll help you get away. Start a new life somewhere with a new identity while I try to find out the truth. I've got legal connections, I've got investigative skills. I won't let Robert's killer get away. And I'll always be there for you when you need me, but you can't be here and you can't be... *you.*'

I feel bereft and exhausted all at once. I've already run. I've been wearing a baseball cap and paying for everything in cash for weeks. But my hair is growing longer, poking out of the hat. The money is running so short that I have no idea what I'll be eating next week. And the baby inside me is growing; I can't hide this pregnancy for much longer. Sarah's right: this current situation cannot continue. But more running? I can't bear it.

I want stability. Honesty. Openness. Somewhere I can raise my child without peering around every corner expecting to be thrown to the ground by armed officers.

I shake my head, panic welling in my throat. I thought this was temporary. I was always going back. Back to my house, my life, my friends, my job. But now she's telling me I can't have any of it. And I can't handle that thought.

I grip my fists around the paperback, twisting it in my hands. 'I can't do it. Not any more. I'm so alone, Sarah. I just want justice for Robert. I want to walk into a police station and tell them everything I know. I want them to find the absolute monster who killed my fiancé. I want them to pay for what they did with their freedom. I can't be the one to pay by sneaking and lying and hiding. It's not right.'

She nods, but I can see the resignation in her whole body.

'I understand. I really do. I feel for you. It's a horrible situation. A literal nightmare and you can't wake up. But you can't turn yourself in.' She looks up, her hazel eyes steely and determined. I can tell by the set of her jaw that she's about to pull her trump card. 'You know better than anyone, Maeve. Justice doesn't always get it right. You didn't get justice last time, did you?'

# 28

## GILLY

The caller's words echo in the air, and Gilly's guts churn. She's trapped on the line, like a worm on the end of a hook.

A car creeps by, its tyres rumbling on the car park's concrete floor. Gilly can't see the driver's face, can't move in order to signal for help. And what could another person do, anyway? It's only a phone call, after all. It's not like this caller is holding a knife at her throat, even though that's how it feels to Gilly.

The caller doesn't wait to hear Gilly's reply. 'I like this anonymity thing,' the voice continues.

Gilly leans against the cold concrete wall next to the lift, her legs shaking so hard she's not sure how she's still upright. *But this isn't anonymity any more*, she wants to scream. *You have my phone number. What else do you know about me?*

The caller continues, her voice unnaturally cheerful, drunk on the power she holds over Gilly. 'I could be anyone. I could be famous... a criminal on the run, even; my face all over the news, and you would have no idea. Or the other way around; *you* could be the criminal.' She laughs softly. 'That's the whole point of your little helpline, right? No one knows anyone's true identity.'

*But you must know mine. How?*

Again, the caller doesn't wait, taking a breath and plunging right back into her softly spoken words. 'I think you'll like this story. You seemed to know what I was going to say, when we last talked. Like you understood me. Like you'd been through it, too. So I'm going to tell you everything I know and you can tell me if it sounds familiar.' She giggles; a small, chilling sound.

Gilly swallows the saliva building in her throat. Even though the caller has apologised, has expressed their intention to talk openly, there's something threatening in her tone. A challenge. Goading.

*Hang up*, she tells herself. This isn't Safeline any more; she doesn't have to follow the rules. She can just press the red button and move on with her life.

She moves the phone slightly away from her face, her thumb wavering over the red button.

As if the caller knows – *as if she can see Gilly*, she thinks with a stab of terror, glancing around once more – there's an intake of air at the other end of the line. 'I wouldn't hang up, if I were you.'

Gilly freezes, her eyes flying open to scan the deserted car park. Nothing. No movement.

'Why not?' she chances, unable to conceal the tremor in her voice.

'Why not?' the caller laughs. 'Three words. Jake. Polly. Callum.'

Gilly's blood turns to ice.

'They're why not. And if you want to keep them safe, you'll stay on the line. Pretend I'm still one of your Safeline callers.'

Gilly's vision blurs. If she abandons this conversation right now, she'll never know how much this caller knows. Does she, for instance, know where Gilly lives? Where her children go to school? If she's got Gilly's mobile number and knows her kids' names, she could have more information. And hanging up right now might be even more dangerous than staying on the line.

She closes her eyes and breathes mindfully through her nose, trying to regulate her breathing, for once grateful for the coping tools her anxiety has forced her to develop.

If she was at Safeline right now she'd have learned from her mistakes: she'd treat this call independently of any other previous calls. She wouldn't assume it's the same person as previous calls, and she certainly wouldn't try to guess what the caller's talking about. She would take this caller's words only at face value. No judgement. No directing. She'd be here to listen.

She'd be writing a note to Vivian, asking her to make tea – their little system, when one of them thinks they're on a call for a long haul. She feels a pang of longing for the simplicity of the call centre, the protection of the anonymity that she once took for granted.

She rubs at her face with her free hand, drawing her palm across her eyes and dragging down until she brushes her mouth with her fingers, trying to centre herself. Trying to work out what to do to protect herself and her family.

'I'm listening if you're ready to share,' she says finally, trying to keep her voice steady.

Her mouth is dry and her legs still quake underneath her weight, but Gilly pushes herself off the wall she'd been leaning against and walks on shaky legs back to the car, trying not to let her footsteps echo off the bare concrete walls. She unlocks the car and slides inside, pulling the door quietly closed behind her as she leans back into the driver's seat. She catches sight of her reflection in the visor mirror: her eyes look haunted, bloodshot and sunken. Her face is a ghostly pale, the phone clutched to the side of her head with a white-knuckled hand.

She could flag someone down, put the call on mute and ask them to call the police. She turns in her seat, scanning nearby cars for any movement, but there's no one around. And it's not like the police could trace this call immediately. Things like that take hours to set up, and by then this caller will be long gone.

She's wrenched from her desperate planning as the caller continues in a raspy whisper. 'Let's talk in hypotheticals. Say... you were at a party a while ago. Years ago, maybe. A student party. You know the kind: lots of drink, probably some drugs although you don't tend to touch them, do you? Just alcohol for you. What's your drink again?'

Gilly almost drops the phone from her sweaty grasp, managing to fumble it just in time. What is this caller doing? Is she testing out some experimental second-person storytelling technique, using 'you' instead of 'I'? But Gilly knows that's not the case, not really. She opens her mouth and closes it again without uttering a sound.

She stares at the windscreen in front of her, eyes unmoving, her whole body frozen except for terrified tremors. She's a captive, kept prisoner on this call by how much the caller knows about Gilly and her family. And this caller knows it. She's been working up to this moment for weeks, testing Safeline's policies, calling over and over again to make sure she understands the rules. Pushing the boundaries like a tiger in a cage, and slowly learning more and more about Gilly in the process. And now, somehow, she's got Gilly's personal number and the names of her family.

The caller's voice pierces her consciousness once more, not waiting for Gilly to answer. Not even pretending she's going to. This isn't a two-way conversation. 'Ah yes, I remember. You liked Malibu and Coke, didn't you? And sometimes wine. Rosé and white. Never red. You said it stains your teeth.'

Gilly says nothing. Yes, she doesn't drink red. Not often, anyway. And she did used to drink Malibu, back when she was a student. Before everything. Now, just the smell of it makes her feel ill.

'You get messy drunk. So drunk that your friends can't get

you to leave with them. You want to stay and party some more. You're dancing, stumbling, laughing. You get so drunk that they leave you behind. Silly girls. They have no idea what they're doing. What impact that decision could make.' The caller pauses, her breath coming in short bursts, like she's running.

Who is this? Is it someone Gilly knew, once? Someone who knew her favourite drinks, her avoidance of recreational drugs.

Or is this the caller's own story, told in a strange and invasive way? Perhaps this is the caller's way of distancing herself from her own rape, telling it like it happened to someone else.

Gilly's story isn't unique, after all. Sadly. Lots of people have stories of getting too drunk at a party. Of their friends ditching them when they couldn't get them to cooperate.

'At some point, you fall asleep at the party. Maybe someone looks after you. A man. Barely. Well, a boy really. He takes off your shoes and tights. Lies you on your side, covers you in a blanket. Maybe he's drunk, too, so he lies down next to you. Maybe he wants to make sure you don't choke on your own vomit.

'When you wake up in the morning, hung-over and in bed next to a man, you grab your stuff and you leave. You don't wake up the man who helped you. You don't speak to anyone. You don't thank him for taking care of you.'

Gilly doesn't move. Doesn't make a sound.

'You probably go back to your flat, have a shower, share stories with your flatmates about the fun party last night, laugh about your drunken stubbornness. Maybe you vow not to drink so much next time. Maybe your hangover is bad enough that you joke you won't drink again. Maybe you even mean it, for a short while.'

She can't listen to much more of this. Bile rises in the back of her throat and she lurches forward as her stomach heaves, her head bumping against the cold leather of the steering wheel.

She manages to swallow down the burning acid in her throat. Her forehead is clammy and cold.

'You don't call the police that day.'

Her hands are numb, as if all the blood has rushed from her extremities to protect her internal organs from the threat her body perceives. And it is a threat. This person is threatening her in the most invasive, terrifying way anyone could ever threaten another human being without holding a knife to their throat.

*I know everything about you*, this person seems to be saying with their every sentence. *And I'm going to use it against you.*

'Why didn't you call the police that same day, if you were so sure a crime had been committed against you? No, for some reason, you wait until the day after that to walk into the local police station and tell them that the nice boy who looked after you when your own friends wouldn't... you tell the police that he raped you. That he drugged you. That he held you down and took advantage of you when you weren't able to say yes or no.'

Gilly can barely breathe. There's no air in this car, and no daylight. It's like being buried alive.

How does she know all this? How has this caller found her? Safeline is meant to be anonymous. Volunteers are encouraged to only tell their next of kin that they're involved with the helpline, just so that someone knows where they're going and where to find them in an emergency. The only person in Gilly's life who knows she volunteers at Safeline is Callum.

Lovely Callum, who adores her. Who only cares that she's safe, that she's happy. There's no way he told someone about her shifts at Safeline. Why would he?

'What you did to him was a crime. Yet he was punished.'

She can't think. Her thoughts are jumbled with panic, echoing through her skull even as the caller keeps talking, rambling on and on.

She doesn't care about following Safeline rules. This is her own phone, her own time. Her own safety on the line, and that of her family. She needs this to end. She's going to hang up on this caller and never return to the Safeline office. Her days of volunteering there are over. There are too many terrifying people in this world, and the most terrifying one of them all is on the phone to her right now, hissing into her ear.

And all Gilly has to do is hang up and it'll be over.

Her thumb moves forward to the phone screen about to stab the button and sever the call.

But the voice slices down the line once more, before she can hang up. 'And even though you didn't call the police straight away... even though you'd already showered by the time you walked into the police station, and even though the rape kit found no DNA evidence on you when you went into the police station that next day, the police arrested that boy, didn't they? And then there was a trial.'

Gilly's hand freezes. She can't hang up. The only thing she wants in the entire world is for this call to be over. She wills her hand to move, to push the button and end the call. She knows what the caller is going to say next and she can't bear to hear it.

'You lied, didn't you? That's why you didn't call the police that first day after the party. Because there was no rape. And, of course, we can't guess why you lied. Maybe your friends talked you into it; maybe you were embarrassed at spending the night with a stranger. Maybe you really thought he had done it. It didn't matter because the jury knew you were lying, didn't they?'

Finally, Gilly wrenches herself out of her stupor. She can't listen to any more of this. 'Stop it,' she whispers, her voice trembling. Her whole body trembling. 'You don't know who I am. You don't know anything about me.'

'You're wrong,' the caller shouts down the phone, so loud that Gilly's whole body jolts at the sound. 'I know everything about you. I know that even though you lied, you walked away from court that day and got to continue your life as if nothing had happened. *He didn't.* Even though the jury didn't believe you, he still had to live with the accusation, with the trial by court of public opinion. People spat at him in the street. Someone graffitied the word *rapist* on his mother's front door. No one would give him a job. All because you lied.'

'None of this is true. I—'

'You don't speak, now. Safeline is a listening service, as you've told me many times. So shut your mouth and listen.'

The caller's voice is so harsh, so violent that Gilly clamps her mouth shut so hard that her teeth jangle.

'You got to live your life twice over while Simon got nothing. He killed himself because of you, did you know? He hung himself by the neck in his childhood bedroom.'

Gilly pushes open her car door and leans out, her stomach heaving as she empties its contents onto the concrete floor of the car park. The voice ignores her retching and continues pouring poison into her ears through the mobile phone she doesn't have the strength to move away from her ear.

'His suicide note said he was innocent. That he couldn't take that everyone believed you. Did you know that? You destroyed a man's life with no consequences. Until now. And now those consequences are coming for you. All your lies are about to be uncovered.'

From the corner of her tear-filled eyes, Gilly sees a woman rushing across the car park towards her, feels a hand on her back and a tissue thrust into her hand. She can't move. The voice is still talking.

'I found you. I know who you really are, *Maeve.*'

PART TWO

## TEN YEARS BEFORE

'Maeve doesn't exist any more,' Sarah says to me as she moves from room to room in Robert's cottage, grabbing my scattered belongings and throwing them into a plastic bag. 'You're not a self-defence instructor. You don't live in Glasgow. You can't see your parents or your friends. Not even me. You're done. A ghost.'

Sarah is saving my life. I know it.

I don't know what I would have done if she hadn't turned up at the cottage yesterday, making me face the truth. I'm in a terrible situation, and I was paralysed, unable to move forward or make any decisions. An understandable paralysis, to be sure: my fiancé is dead, and I am in the frame for his murder. But still, I had no plan. I'm running out of money. And I'm pregnant with Robert's baby.

'You have to tell me everything about the murder. All the details, everything you can remember. And then you must let go of the life you once knew.'

My eyes fill with tears. My parents. Aside from a quick chat at the rehearsal dinner, I haven't seen them since a couple of days before my wedding. We pottered around the garden while

Mum showed me her new raised beds and Dad trimmed the hedge with his newly sharpened clippers. How have they been coping with the news that their daughter is a suspected murderer?

I open my mouth to ask, but I catch myself before the question emerges. It's too painful. Deep down, I know I can't bear to hear her answer.

'You can't stay here. It's been long enough, and, as I said, if I can find you then the police won't be far behind.'

I trail after her, my guts churning. I've been feeling sick every day, and I don't know if it's anxiety and fear, or morning sickness. Maybe a bit of both. I have no idea where I can go. But I underestimate Sarah.

She carefully removes my piercings from my ears and slides them into the coin pocket of her purse. 'I'll keep these safe. You can have them back when we've exonerated you.'

She drives alone into the nearest town and comes back with a box of Lindt truffles, sharp scissors and hair dye. My red bobbed waves are gone, replaced with a white-blonde pixie cut which highlights the hollows in my cheeks. Gaunt with fear and stress.

When I look in the mirror, I see a stranger staring back at me.

'Good,' Sarah says when I tell her. 'That's what we want. Now, a name. You can't be Maeve any more. You need to pick a new one. When you were a kid, what did you wish your name was?'

Despite everything, I watch in the mirror as a smile flits across my lips. A flash of colour appears on the apples of my cheeks. 'Sparky, for a bit. Then Meadow.'

She bursts out laughing and pats me on the shoulder. 'Probably not either of those, eh?'

I shrug, not able to compute the decision she's asking me to make. Does it matter what name I choose? Surely it won't be long before they find Robert's real murderer and I can be Maeve again, go back to my normal life. This can't go on forever.

Suddenly freed by the inconsequential nature of this decision, I skim my memory of childhood. Not for the names I wanted back then – already written-off for good reason, and definitely too memorable for someone trying to fade into the background – but for who I wanted to become.

An image pops into my mind, someone I haven't thought about in years. A cool next-door neighbour I had when I was a kid. She was a few years older, could skateboard, and she used her brother's punchbag in the garage. She'd hammer at it for hours, and sometimes he'd come in and help her refine her punches and kicks. I decided I wanted to learn to fight just like her.

I pause for a moment, wondering why I'd never made the connection before. I'd thought my pursuit of a career in self-defence was solely motivated by the rape in my early twenties, the need to be able to defend myself and to never feel powerless again. But maybe it's been burgeoning much longer than that.

'Gilly,' I say in a quiet voice, and Sarah claps her hands in glee.

'Perfect,' she says. 'Not memorable at all. Gillian, if we manage to get you passports and papers, etc? I can unearth some contacts through work; dark web stuff that won't get traced back to me.'

I nod, and raise one shoulder in a half-shrug to show how little this matters. 'Surely we won't need to go that far? Once they arrest someone...'

Sarah's face falls. 'Like I said before, Mae— Gilly.' She gives me a pointed look. 'You told me what happened at the trial. The justice system never helped you before. Why would it now? It can find guilty people to be innocent, and innocent people guilty. A wrong verdict ruins lives.' She pauses, and we both remember the trial I had to sit through, the terrible verdict and its tragic aftermath. Sarah and I had met and become friends just after the verdict, while I was still clawing myself out of the darkness. She has always been livid for me that I had to sit through that trial and face my attacker on the stand, get grilled by the defence and prosecution, delve into my sex life and drinking habits, and all to be told that no crime had been proven.

For some reason, though, Simon's suicide was more traumatic to me than any of the trial and aftermath. Every time I think about him, there's an underlying nausea and responsibility there. *He died because of me.*

Shaking off the moment, Sarah bustles over to the cupboard in the corner of the bedroom and opens the door, peering inside. 'And in this case a wrong verdict would be your life ruined. You'd be in prison for the murder of your fiancé. Then there'd be years of appeals. Hundreds of thousands in legal fees. So as much as I want to say "life will be back to normal soon", I don't think we should plan for that. We plan for me to uncover as much as I can about who really did this, until we have incontestable evidence that it wasn't you. Until then we need to plan for you to be Gilly, for your hair to be different, your hobbies and job to be different...' Her voice fades away as she surveys the insides of the cupboard.

She turns back to me, her face ashen. 'Is there anything of yours in here?'

I shake my head, flicking my eyes over Sarah's shoulder to skim the rows of clothes belonging to Robert's dead wife.

She runs her hands along the soft cotton of a summer dress, before pulling her hand away as if burned. 'I'm sorry I never told you about her. I assumed Robert would eventually... and it didn't feel like my place.' Her eyes skim my face, searching for my forgiveness.

Of course I forgive her. Sarah's fiercely loyal, and kind to a fault. There's no way she would have kept anything like that from me without good reason. And when she found out Robert was keeping that secret, she confronted him straight away. Had he lived, she'd have hounded him until he caved and told me everything. She's relentless about the things that matter to her and I love that about her. I feel so lucky to have her on my side.

I sit down on a paint-splattered chair. I'm overtaken by a sudden wave of exhaustion, at everything that's happened to me over the past few weeks. Everything I've learned about my fiancé, about the world, and now about my future. The life I'd once imagined has been wrenched away.

I'm not a happily married woman on her honeymoon with her new husband, a baby on the way. I'm not Maeve. I'm Gilly. In seven or eight months I'll be a single mum with a new identity purchased on the dark web.

Sarah runs her hand along the row of Elodie's clothes. 'I'll clear everything out of here, put Robert's paintings into storage and turn his studio into a second bedroom,' she mutters, almost to herself. 'I'll need to get new carpets.'

I baulk. 'His studio? Why?'

Even though I know he has no use for it now, I'm crushed by the idea of destroying his beloved art room and turning it back into something as ordinary as a bedroom. If Robert had died under different circumstances and I'd had the chance to be a traditional mourning widow instead of a suspected murderer on the run, I'd have kept his studio exactly as it was for as long as I could. A small memorial to my calm, quiet, gentle and artistic love. A shrine.

Sarah turns to me, her jaw set in a determined expression. 'You're going to need money. You can't work until we find a way to get you stuff like a National Insurance number. I've got some savings; I can help you for a while until we work out something more solid to keep you going.'

My shoulders slump in relief, but my stomach twists. As much as I'd been going along with Sarah's plan, it didn't feel real. It felt like we were children making sky-high schemes which would never come to fruition because they were too far-fetched. But Sarah really means this, and this is the first piece of the plan which feels tangible and real. I'm going to need money. An income. And a fake identity.

'I'll pay you back. Every penny,' I say, and I mean it, because I believe in Sarah and I know once she's decided she'll help me, I'm in good hands.

Sarah's a determined person. She always has been. She decides something about herself, or her life, or the world around her, and she works to make it happen until it's done. Partway through her degree, she decided English Literature wasn't going to get her where she wanted to be (rich, I think was her main goal), so she switched majors and worked her arse off to catch up and graduate with a Law degree instead, and now she's a data technology lawyer with a huge client list. She knows a lot about blockchain, AI, and the dark web, and she works very long hours.

Today I'm lucky enough to be the target of her determina-tion. I'm grateful. I couldn't do this on my own. But at the same time, I'm terrified. I know that Sarah gets what she sets her mind to, which means that if Sarah has decided I'm changing my identity, then that's what's happening.

No more Maeve.

I'm Gilly now.

## 30

## NINE YEARS BEFORE

'Gilly?'

I'm in a Starbucks in Kingsgate shopping centre, all glass walls, warm lighting and various shades of beige and brown. Very little natural light makes its way deep into this cave, which suits me.

'Gilly?'

Maeve would never have come into a Starbucks. Maeve liked artisan roasters and independent cafés on the back streets of Glasgow. But Maeve is gone, and Gilly has to blend in. In Dunfermline, a Scottish city between Edinburgh and Glasgow small enough that no one will look for me, and big enough that no one will find me if they did.

'Gilly! Flat white and a croissant!' the barista yells, exasperation behind his tone.

I snap out of my reverie and raise a sheepish hand. 'Here. Sorry. Miles away.' I try an apologetic smile but the barista has already turned away with slightly rolled eyes, onto the next customer. It's taking me a while to get used to my new name, my new life.

My new baby.

Jake coos at me from the pram, his eyes starting to take on the hazel shade of his father's eyes. I'm lucky, I know it. At four months old he's a calm, happy baby. As long as he can see me, he's happy to entertain himself. He smiles a lot. Laughs occasionally. He can sit up, and he's about to start crawling.

If I've got nothing else, I've got him. I have love. Even if it's not Robert. Even if I'm not me.

I slot my coffee into the cup holder on the pram handle and slide the croissant's paper bag into the basket underneath Jake's seat. As I leave the coffee shop, I catch a glimpse of myself in a mirror by the door and I almost freeze in shock.

It happens less and less frequently, but it's sometimes a jolt when I see my reflection unexpectedly. I'm softer now. I don't teach self-defence any more – I barely even have time to exercise – and I'm only a few months post-partum, so my once-muscular physique is bigger and less compact, my face rounder and piercing-free. My hair is bottle-blonde in whatever box dye I can find at the local Superdrug when I need it, and it's cropped in a short pixie cut, totally different to the wavy red bobbed hair of Maeve. I look like a stranger.

One day I'll look in the mirror and it'll feel normal. The reflection I see will look like me, Gilly. But I'm not there yet.

I am different, both outside and in. Where Maeve seemed to be surrounded by an emotional exoskeleton, Gilly is more permeable. Perhaps it's having a child, or perhaps it's the loss of the love of my life, but I feel exposed and vulnerable all the time. Everything is scary. I never feel safe. And with that comes the constant hum of anxiety, which occasionally raises itself to a roar. Somehow, I have to learn to live with that.

I smile at Jake in his pram as I push him around the shops, popping into Next to look at the baby clothes, although I won't buy anything unless there's a sale. Jake's growing fast, and apart

from a few mums in the baby groups I attend, I know no one.
It's hard to make friends when I can't be my whole self, and I'm
using a new name. I don't have social media, and I don't let
anyone take my picture. I'm an island and I can't let anyone in.

So there are no hand-me-downs from friends with older
children. No presents from relatives. My parents don't even
know he exists. Everything he has is from me, and I have to be
careful with money.

We have Sarah, of course, who puts money in my bank
account as regularly as she can: as Robert died without a will,
his estate went to his mum. At her age she had no use for a
remote cottage, so she signed ownership over to Sarah, who
secretly sends me the proceeds from renting it out. And, I
suspect, some extra here and there. Although we never see her,
and I can't contact her to thank her. Our only communication is
one-way, in the eighteen-character limit references on the bank
transfers.

*Miss you*
*Thinking of you*
*ur parents are ok*
*Hope baby is well*
*All good here*

I always wish I could reach through the computer screen
and grab her and hug her and cry into her shoulder for everything I've lost. I wish I could thank her.

I wish I had my family.

As if the universe wants to rub salt in my wound, I pause to
glance through the window into the toy shop and see a family
roaming the aisles: a mum and a dad wrangling three kids as
they jostle each other and laugh together, picking up toys and
putting them back in the wrong places. Joy and chaos.

I look down at Jake, who's starting to fall asleep in his pram.

It's just me and Jake against the world. It's nice being in our little bubble, but sometimes I find myself distraught and guilty, knowing that we're so alone and he's so isolated because of me. He'll never have siblings. He'll never have a dad. His life will be small and quiet and I'll never be able to tell him it's because the world thinks I'm a murderer.

## 31

## EIGHT YEARS BEFORE

I rush into the dentist's examination room, Jake in my arms, and see the dentist's brown eyes twinkling at me over the top of his surgical mask. I look away; not inviting attention. I'm used to this, now. I've decided it was Jake and me against the world, the two of us alone for ever. And that means not making eye contact with twinkly-eyed dentists.

The smell of disinfectant tickles the back of my throat and I slide into the chair, Jake on my knee.

The dentist leans over me to move the pink mouthwash out of Jake's reach, and as he does, his forearm brushes against mine. And I almost fall apart. That is the first time a man has touched my skin in almost two years.

The hair stands up on my skin and I shudder.

'Everything OK?' the dentist asks, turning to his assistant and moving his arm away. 'Could you turn up the radiator, please, Marianne? I think it's a bit chilly in here.'

I open my mouth to protest, but the dentist doesn't notice, turning his attention immediately to Jake. The patient. 'Now, little man. Have you been to the dentist before?'

'He hasn't,' I answer for Jake, who's a year old, starting to say a couple of words. He started walking early, and wants to toddle everywhere by himself; he'll scream if I try to confine him in the pram when he can get there on his own legs. But he's not old enough to answer questions yet. He's too busy reaching up for the twinkling lights, batting the little sink and trying to pick up the plastic cup of pink liquid. I hold his arms by his sides and kiss him on his fuzzy curls.

'Well, Jake. This is going to be an easy one for you today. I'm going to look in your mouth and count your teeth, and then I'm going to ask Mummy some questions about brushing, and then you can be on your way. It won't hurt and it won't be scary.'

Jake coos and laughs at the dentist, enraptured by his deep voice and kind tone.

The dentist pulls down his mask to reveal a beautiful smile, and a dash of stubble along his jaw. 'You just need to open your mouth and say "ahhh".' He demonstrates, and then looks up at me and gives me a wink. My stomach flips and I can feel my cheeks heating up, but I can't help but smile back.

Our eyes meet, and there's a *zing*. A zing I haven't felt in years.

The transition from newborn to baby to toddler brought new challenges for me, of course, but also the clouds of the baby months have begun to clear and with it a new realisation of the reality of my situation. I can't live in our bubble any more. It can't be just me and Jake against the world. It isn't fair on either of us. I need something else. A job, maybe. Childcare, definitely. A life.

'And does Mummy need a check-up, too?' the dentist asks, eyes twinkling at me again.

I flinch. I've been lucky since leaving Robert's cottage. Sarah came through with the paperwork to make Gillian Bookman official so I could get a midwife and medical records that I needed for a safe birth, and I could technically register with a GP and a dentist if I needed to, but I prefer to stay as under the radar as much as possible, unless I really need something.

I stammer, unable to form a sentence immediately under the power of this man's stare. 'Um. Er.' I shake my head, trying to clear my thoughts. I have to look away from his eyes, which gaze at me like I'm pinned to his chair. Only when our eye contact is broken can I form a coherent sentence. 'Oh, I'm not registered as a patient here. Just Jake.'

'Okey doke,' he says, turning his attention back to Jake. For a moment I'm disappointed, like the sun has gone behind a cloud. I like this man, I realise.

I've not looked at a man with interest since Robert died. Until today. And I'm not sure whether it's because I'm ready for a connection – I've grieved, I've processed, and I've waded through the weeds of the newborn era and come out the other side – or because this man is special. I think he might be. And there's a connection here.

The dentist must feel it too, because after we're done and I've made Jake's next appointment, he bursts out of his examination room, his surgical mask around his neck, and catches me as Jake and I are about to head out of the door.

His cheeks are flushed and he looks nervous. 'I don't normally do this,' he says in a voice low enough that no one in the adjoining waiting room can hear. 'But would you like to go for a drink next week?'

I open my mouth and close it again, ready to step into my normal routine of deflecting any meaningful friendship or connection with another human being, when something else takes over. Before my mind can run through all the arguments against letting someone into my life, my mouth opens and words spill out as if someone else is speaking for me:

'That would be really nice. Thank you.'

## 32

### LAST SEVEN YEARS

Callum is the exact right person for me at this stage in my life, and our first date turns quickly into seeing each other a couple of nights a week, Callum appearing on my doorstep with a bottle of wine and a bunch of flowers after Jake's gone to bed.

A successful dentist with his own practice, Callum had been single for so long that he'd filled his life to the brim. Friends, hobbies, a strict routine that never deviated. He'd thought there was no space in his life for a partner – he'd almost purposefully designed it that way, keeping busy to stave off the loneliness – and then Jake toddled into his dental surgery for his first check-up and everything changed.

After a few months, we see each other so often and we're so comfortable that he invites me to give up my poky studio flat and move into his house, a four-bedroom semi-detached villa with a garage. It feels like a palace.

Callum is gentle and kind, and often wrapped up in his own little world. He spends his weekends hillwalking and wild camping, and at first I try to tag along with Jake, but it soon becomes clear that this is a part of Callum's life which can't easily accommodate the two new additions into his world.

Toddlers and camping are a tricky mix, so after a couple of disastrous outings involving too many midge bites and running out of dry clothes after falling in streams, Jake and I stay at home pursuing play dates and playgrounds while Callum explores the wilds. He returns tired and happy and sweeps us both into his arms, his hair smelling like the Highlands: wind, grass and fresh soil. Sometimes when I'm doing his laundry I get a faint scent of the air and hills around Robert's cottage and I'm catapulted back in time to that awful few weeks hiding out in the middle of nowhere, pregnant, grieving and alone.

People who meet later in life often move quicker – we know what we want and what we don't, I guess – and within six months Callum and I are married in a tiny ceremony with only three guests: Callum's best friend and brother as witnesses, and Jake. Callum doesn't mind how small it is; he thinks it's romantic, and he understands that I don't want a big wedding this time. I tell him part of the truth: that I was engaged to Jake's dad, who died before he was born.

Callum adopts Jake without hesitation. They even look alike, Callum with his brown-caramel eyes and Jake with his hazel. No one would guess they weren't related. He's an amazing dad, patient, kind and loving. Callum and I decide not to tell Jake about his real dad, not until he's older.

We don't actively try to have a baby, but we agree we're open to it if it happens. A part of me doubts pregnancy will happen again for me: I've been through so much in my life up to now that I assume my body won't do that any more. That I'm somehow in 'self-protection' mode as I approach the peri-menopause. But not long later Polly is born healthy and perfect, and I know in my heart that my family is now complete. I've got everything I once dreamed of, and which I thought I'd never have again. I'm content.

Callum earns enough from his dentist practice that I don't have to work, which although it makes me feel uncomfortable to be financially reliant on him, it's more important that I continue to live under the radar as much as possible. I don't want HMRC poking around in my taxes, or an employer doing a background check.

So I keep our home beautiful, cook tasty meals, entertain our children, and develop a social circle of other mothers with children Jake and Polly's age – friendships which maintain a surface-level connection but which will never delve into the past, into deeper issues, lost loves, unpleasant experiences.

Sometimes when I'm walking down the street or doing the weekly grocery shop, there's a moment when I almost think I see someone from my old life. From Maeve's past. An old client from my self-defence classes, or a friend of my parents'. There's always a brief second of joy and relief – the feeling that I could just step forward and hold out my arms to greet them and be Maeve again – before it disappears, replaced by fear of discovery and the desire to run and hide myself away. But I'm Gilly now. Even if it was someone I once knew – and it never is – they wouldn't see Maeve.

I've successfully transformed myself into the type of person that no one would look at twice if they passed me on the street. Maeve is gone, her life reduced to nothing but memories, as if she's the fake one and only Gilly is real. Even my own parents wouldn't recognise me. I'm a ghost.

But by the time Jake and Polly are both at school full-time, I'm bored out of my mind.

And one day, while I'm reading the back pages of a local newspaper as I wait in the foyer of our community centre to collect the kids from Cubs and Beavers, their shouts echoing off the parquet floor in the next room, I stumble across a little obituary:

**Shirley Ross (1945–2025)**

Born in Dunfermline but resident in Glasgow for most of her adult life, Shirley Ross passed away last week at the age of 79. She was happily married to husband Neville (1940–2023) for 40 years, and is survived by their beloved daughter. Shirley was a homemaker and volunteer, in later life becoming an active campaigner for overturning wrongful convictions and miscarriages of justice. A remembrance service will be held in Crow Road Church, Glasgow, next Friday at 1 p.m. In lieu of flowers, please send donations to Project Innocence UK.

I sit silently, staring into space as I listen to the chirping voices of the kids on the other side of the wall, playing games and running about as their activity comes to an end.

My mother died.

My father was already dead.

And I didn't know.

For a moment, I feel a flash of annoyance that Sarah didn't tell me. But then how could she, when our only method of communication was the eighteen-character-limited reference that accompanies a bank transfer? She must have known I'd find out some other way. Perhaps she even submitted my parents' obituaries, hoping I'd see them. After all, it's not like their daughter was around to write one. I choke down my guilt, trying not to draw attention from the other waiting parents in the community centre. But the thing that makes my throat feel clogged with cement is that last line: *donations to Project Innocence UK*.

My mother had always supported local charities that aligned with what affected her, the stage of life she was in. War veterans' support, because her dad had fought in WWII and come back 'a little funny', she'd always said. Child poverty relief, when I was little and we'd just begun to claw our way up the social ladder into the lower middle classes and had a tiny bit of spare cash. Then cancer research, when my parents and their friends hit middle age and started feeling their mortality. The last time I saw them, Mum was full steam ahead on an elderly befriending charity: linking isolated older people with volunteers in person and on the phone, to alleviate loneliness. I'd thought it was sweet. I'd wondered if Mum was lonely, even though she and Dad were so close.

But she'd been resistant to my questioning, trying instead to get me to sign up to be a phone befriender and call an old person every week to have a chat.

I'd brushed her off. Maeve was too busy. Too busy teaching self-defence, drinking in pubs, working out, planning a wedding, about to start the rest of my life.

So after the elderly befriending service, it seems like Mum's attentions had turned to miscarriages of justice. My eyes filled with tears. Even after all this time, my parents believed in me. They knew I was innocent.

They were waiting for me to come back so they could help fight the accusation alongside me.

My vision blurry with tears, I flick past the obituaries, barely reading any of the text on the page. Just trying to hold it together until my kids come out of the community centre and I can drive them home and sit them in front of the TV. Maybe I can cry a bit in the kitchen while I cook their dinner.

But then my eyes fall on an ad for a local charity looking for volunteers:

Do you want to make a difference in someone's life? Can you spare a few hours every week to offer a listening ear?

Join Safeline's volunteer programme to become part of a like-minded community; a generation of listeners changing lives and forging connections with those in need. Enrich your daily life today by joining our volunteer training programme.

I turn the page, and when Jake and Polly come barrelling

out, their uniforms crinkled and their neckerchiefs askew, I shove the newspaper into my handbag for later. I don't have much from my previous life; a small box secreted behind one of the eaves in the attic is all Maeve has on this earth, that I know of. Especially now that my parents are gone. This newspaper belongs in that box, a little piece of my parents held close to me.

I'm an orphan now. And I can't tell a soul.

I can't attend the remembrance service. If the police are still looking for Maeve this many years later, that'll be the place they look. I can't even donate to Project Innocence UK on behalf of Mum and Dad, even if it's anonymous – there'll be ways of tracing payment details.

While I silently grieve over the next few days, my mind keeps coming back to the Safeline ad. I can't donate or attend the remembrance service, but I can honour my parents in another way.

A charity to support, just like Mum always had. Making a difference. Changing lives.

And, more selfishly, the promise of a purpose. A community.

Even though I have a family now, people who love me and would notice if I disappear, a part of me still feels like that lost soul wandering from room to room in Robert's cottage. An island in the isolated wilds of the Highlands, in hiding. Robert was gone; my parents had each other back then. I wasn't special to anyone. I had made no impact on the world. If that person – Maeve – had disappeared for ever, who would notice?

And I've had my answer, now: when I left the cottage and returned to the world, I saw the news stories:

*Bloody bride still on the loose!*

*Where's Maeve? Police baffled by disappearing killer bride.*

*Robert's murderer sighted in Switzerland?*

And I saw the media attempts with my friends and family, camera crews shoving their lenses in the faces of people I loved, journalists shouting questions at them. 'When did you last see Maeve?' 'How does it feel to be related to a killer?' Mostly my loved ones seemed to try and ignore this intrusion, muttering a 'No comment', or shielding their eyes from the flashes. But sometimes they'd give little titbits – like I saw from Ella that day on the wall of televisions in Currys – and that'd give the newspapers some fodder to dine out on for at least three days.

But within a few weeks the searches stopped, the news stories dried up. There were brief mentions on the anniversary: one year since, then five. And now my parents are dead... it is as if Maeve had never existed.

As the children grow older and forge their own friendships, their own hobbies and eventually go out into the world to establish careers and their own families, where would that leave me? Callum has his job, his hobbies... what do I have?

It's not healthy, being so wrapped up in your family that you have nothing else to focus on.

And so, just a week after I learn I'm an orphan, I fill in the Safeline online application form and become a volunteer.

## 33

### NOW

'I found you. I know who you really are, *Maeve.*'

I wrench the phone from my ear, mashing the hang-up button over and over, my vision blurred with tears. Even though the call has ended, I feel no relief. I have no idea if I'm crying or if the tears are from the vomiting out of the car door.

Maeve. No one has called me that name in years.

'Are you OK?' The passer-by woman is still there, trying to check up on me as she hovers by the side of my car.

I throw my phone across the car and shove the car keys into the ignition, ringing in my ears. I can't hear what the woman is saying, whether it's curious or comforting or what. It doesn't matter.

I need to get out of this cave of a car park, into the daylight and then away. I don't know where. But if this person knows so much about me and my volunteering, they'll know where I live. They'll know about my children. About Callum.

I'm so paralysed with fear, but there's no time to succumb. Not when my family are in danger.

I look up briefly to see the woman still standing by my open car door, a crumpled tissue in her hand and a concerned look on her face.

It's rude, but I don't want to talk to her. I motion for her to move back and slam my door as soon as she's out of the way. My tyres squeal on the tarmac as I accelerate out of the car park and out. There's no time to waste.


I barely see the trees streaking past as I drive, and it's lucky the roads are quiet. It's not school pickup time yet, so I only come across a few other cars as I head to Jake and Polly's school. I have no idea what I'm planning to do, I realise.

I won't collect them from school right now, make them realise something's wrong. I can't draw attention to myself among the school staff by summoning them out of class early. I'll wait outside in the car until it's time. I just need to be near them. To make sure they're safe.

I pull up at a red light and the caller's words echo through my brain. *You got to live your life twice over while Simon got nothing.*

At first that didn't make sense to me. Live my life twice over? What was she talking about?

But as the light turns green and I pull away from the junction as fast as I can accelerate, it slots into place: unlike anyone else in the world, this caller knows the full trajectory of my life. She knows I was once Maeve. She knows about my rape in university, the trial, the 'not proven' verdict, the accused's suicide. I lived life twice over: once as Maeve and once as Gilly.

But I didn't get to just continue with my life, unscathed. I didn't 'destroy a man's life with no consequences', like she spat at me just minutes ago. I was left with PTSD so complex and unmoving that therapy wouldn't touch it. I stopped drinking. No more parties. No more boyfriends. Not even male friends. I gave up on my plans to join Sarah in a career in law – I'd seen how unjust the law could be – and I packed a bag. I needed to get away. As far away as possible.

I keep an eye on the speedometer, keeping as close to the speed limit as I can without going over. I can't be pulled over for speeding. I can't face that delay. That risk of scrutiny if my licence is run through a computer system.

That caller must also know my pursuit of protection in the aftermath of the rape: my hastily reconfigured trip around the world after graduation where instead of partying on beaches in Thailand I only felt safe if I was attending self-defence classes, the fiercer the better. I didn't want belts, gradings or formality. I wanted to be able to kill, if I needed to.

I was lucky: within my first days in Singapore (safest country in South East Asia. I'd googled it), I met a man from the Philippines who'd grown up in an organised crime family and managed to get out and become a martial arts master. He taught me everything I know, a combination of the most-deadly fighting styles on earth. Quick and dirty grappling, weapons, and fight-to-kill. He helped me find my physical and emotional breaking points and then push through them to the other side. I became a killing machine even though I've never had to use my skills on another person aside from in class. By the time I completed my training, I could take down a man double my body weight and over a foot taller than me, and force him to surrender.

When I came home, I had enough knowledge to devise my own self-defence class. I didn't teach everything I knew – much of it was too dangerous to demonstrate – but I taught the core skills to three classes a week, and made lots of friends in my students, who often went on to learn more formal disciplines once they'd mastered the basics with me.

If that caller knows about the rape and the trial, they'll also know about my fighting background. I don't even know if I still could, now I'm a soft housewife who hasn't grappled in years.

Surely they wouldn't try to attack me? But they might target my family. And I'm terrified.

Who is she? The thought runs through my head over and over like ticker tape at the bottom of a news bulletin. What does she want? How does she know so much about my life?

*I found you. I know who you really are, Maeve.*

She must be someone from university. Someone who knew me. Someone who knew him, Simon Adam-Todd, and believed his claim of innocence. It wouldn't matter to her that my memory came back to me in chunks over the next few days after that party. That yes, I didn't remember much that first morning, but after whatever date-rape drug he'd given me wore off, I started to remember things.

His breath against my ear.

*I love when they're too fucked up to fight back.*

A voice mumbling into my neck.

*It won't hurt if you stay still.*

His hands clutching at my hips, holding me in place.

Pain.

My friends believed me. The police officer who took my statement believed me. My lawyer believed me. But the jury didn't. And whoever this woman is, she didn't believe me either. She believed Simon. And it sounds like he was part of her life, and now that she's found me, she wants revenge.

I try to remember the faces in the courtroom as I gave my evidence in the trial. There was Simon's mother, pursed lips and folded arms. She shook her head while I spoke, as if she couldn't believe how much bullshit I was spinning. Next to her, his older brother, who glared at me like he'd not hesitate to stove my skull in with whatever heavy object he could find in the moment if we happened to walk past each other in the street. I think his dad was there too, some days, sitting alone in the back in a polo shirt. A girl our age who fiddled with her ring, barely looking up from her lap. His sister, perhaps. Or a girlfriend. And maybe a few friends, for some parts of the trial. They'd mumble and hiss under their breath whenever my name was mentioned by a witness.

I can't remember these faces enough, and certainly can't link them with the voice of the person terrorising me now.

I'm surprised I can remember that much, considering how traumatic I found the whole thing. I lost fifteen pounds of weight in just a few weeks, and I ground my teeth so hard in my sleep that I had to get an emergency dental appointment for a mouthguard before all my teeth turned to dust.

I didn't want to be there. I didn't want to be a rape victim.

I didn't want to be part of a trial which might condemn a man my own age to months or even years in prison. I didn't want anyone to suffer, or his life to be ruined. I didn't ask for this. I didn't ask for any of it. But I knew I'd been raped. I knew I hadn't made it up. And I knew that if I didn't involve the police and suffer through a trial like this, that Simon would do this again to some other girl. Or maybe even more. And I knew he'd probably done it before, too.

The trial turned on the problem of corroboration. No one else had been in the room with Simon and me that night while I was drugged and unconscious. No one witnessed the rape. The drug he'd given me – scopolamine, or 'devil's breath', one police officer had theorised, based on my description of how I'd felt – had disappeared from my system by the time I reported it. The world's scariest drug, news articles said. Because in large doses it turns people into zombies, helpless to the whims of criminals and robbers. It takes away their free will and leaves them only able to follow instructions of their controller.

And although he'd definitely done that to other girls, none of them would come forward and agree to testify. When the final girl – another potential victim who came forward to police during the investigation – retracted her statement on the stand, the only remaining evidence to link him with my rape was the physical evidence: my hair in his bed and evidence of sexual intercourse.

It wasn't enough. The prosecution couldn't prove it beyond reasonable doubt.

His family cheered as the foreman read out the verdict, and I felt nothing but anguish.

Not proven, by a majority. But not unanimous.

A verdict only available in Scotland, and which acquits the accused in just the same legal way as a ruling of not guilty.

As Simon's family and friends patted each other on the back and high-fived, I slipped out of my seat in the back of the public gallery and got on the bus back to my flat, grateful that no one was paying me attention. That I'd insisted my friends not come with me to hear the verdict. I wanted to be invisible, to disappear.

As a survival mechanism in that moment, I allowed myself a little hope: that going through the accusation and the trial had scared my rapist enough that even though he wouldn't be punished for his crime he wouldn't rape anyone else.

I didn't even want further justice. The trial had been such a punishment for me, just being a witness for a couple of days, that I couldn't imagine the torture of being the accused, sitting in the dock day after day for two weeks, staring at the faces of the jury who would decide your fate. Unable to speak. Advised not to take the stand, told that to defend yourself might incriminate you further.

And then he was free. Sure, people still gossiped about it. People from uni messaged me to offer their condolences, and some stopped me in the street to tell me they believed me, that they'd never be friends with Simon. That even though he wasn't guilty in the eyes of the law, they believed he did it.

And then I guess there were some vigilantes. Politically

motivated people who campaigned against Scotland's use of the not proven verdict, believing that it is used disproportionately in rape cases: giving the jury an easy way out in the thorny issues of proving what happens behind closed doors. People who wanted justice that the law couldn't give. The people who graffitied *rapist* on his mother's front door. Who slashed his tyres and poured chemicals through his letter box.

I guess it was too much.

I didn't think he would kill himself. I would never wish anyone dead. But he did kill himself, and there's clearly someone out there who believes he died because of me, and that I need to pay for that.

I'm almost at Jake and Polly's school, but my next thought nearly sends me careering off the road. All my muscles tense, my arms lock and my feet push down on the pedals, hard. The car jolts to a screeching stop, and the car behind me swerves and leans on their horn, filling my head with a long, drawn out honk. But the panicked ringing in my ears drowns it out.

The realisation chills me to the bone.

If the caller has found me, Gilly, they'll also know about me – Maeve – waking up next to Robert's blood-spattered body with a knife covered in my fingerprints. About me going on the run, changing my identity. Becoming Gilly.

The calls were just the start.

I've designed my own downfall. The perfect revenge is just sitting there, ripe for the taking.

That caller has found me and she's not going to let me go. I'm too valuable a find. She's going to get me imprisoned for Robert's murder.

## 34

I somehow manage to start the engine again, waving apologetically to the car behind me, who doesn't release the horn for almost a minute as we crawl through Dunfermline town centre traffic at the twenty-miles-per-hour speed limit. In that way typical of British drivers in small towns, the driver now makes sure to leave only a few feet of space between my back bumper and their front headlights all the way through town, ensuring I'm fully aware of how angry they are and how inconvenienced I have made them with my sudden stop.

Normally I'd feel concerned, or guilty, or maybe even a bit frustrated. But today I'm numb to everything except the enormous mess unfolding in my brain as I realise the significance of what just happened.

The caller knows my real identity. She knows my whole life.

Everything I've been building for the past decade could come crashing down around me with just one call to the police, and I bet this woman – the caller – knows that. I suspect that's why she was calling, really, revelling in how much she knew about me, how much power she really had.

Each phone call where she was breathing down the line, pretending to cry, whispering cryptic phrases – she always knew what her end goal was. Ruin my life. Take away everything I have. She was just playing the long game. Toying with me, like a cat tortures a mouse.

I pull up outside the school half an hour early for pickup, where ordinarily cars jostle for space and everyone's inching past each other at five miles an hour, watching out for kids darting into the road without looking. Right now, the street is quiet and the playground deserted, all the children still safely in class and no parents arrived yet.

I watch a discarded Monster Munch packet skip down the pavement, buffeted by the wind until it gets caught between a lamp post and the wall. An old man ambles by with his dog, a rickety Westie who stops to sniff every three feet.

I don't switch on the radio. I don't scroll on my phone. I just sit and think. Churn. Worry.

The caller's awareness of my true identity has brought everything back, and this is the one part of the puzzle I haven't yet had time to pore over.

As the years have passed, I've revisited Robert's death more times than I can count. The bloodied knife in my bed. The specificity of his wounds. I've never been able to work out what the killer wanted. I've run through it in my head over and over: who would have wanted him dead and why they killed only him, not me. The only conclusion I've been able to reach is that the killer successfully framed me for his murder. That was the intention, and it worked. The only reason I'm not in prison right now is because I ran.

Even if the Safeline caller had nothing to do with Robert's death and only has connections to Simon, now that the caller knows my true identity they could easily throw me in the path of Robert's killer. And if they've killed once, it's likely they're willing to kill again, whether that's me or someone I love.

So now I'm in danger. And so is my family.

The sky turns black and rain starts at the same time as a teacher pushes open the dark-blue painted double doors at the front of the school. Unlike the usual pathetic drizzle of Scottish weather, today's rain comes down in huge drops, hard and fast. One of those sudden summer showers that smells like wet dust. The playground is slick with water within moments, raindrops slapping the windscreen and bouncing off the ground.

Kids pull their raincoats over their heads like capes, not enough time to thread their arms through their sleeves as they run from the school to the gates. Parents rush along the pavement, scooping their children into cars or under umbrellas. I turn on the engine, defogging the windscreen and hitting the wipers to clear the glass.

I see Jake and Polly emerge together, Jake's already dark hair darkening further as the rain drenches him. He's wearing his blue raincoat, but his hands are busy as he helps Polly into her own purple coat. They jog across the playground and I wave to them as they get closer to the school gate, but I look down to check the car doors are unlocked and when I look back up, they've gone, subsumed into the crowd of parents and children milling on the pavement around my car.

They don't emerge from the crowd.

My children have disappeared.

My breath catches in my throat and I scrabble to roll down my window to get a better view. I'm only twenty feet away from the school gates – parked as close as is legally possible to get outside of the zigzag lines they paint on the road outside schools. And our car is distinctive: a bright red Toyota RAV4 that Callum insisted would be useful for icy roads and hill-walking excursions. Surely they just got held up, chatting to a friend? But in this rain, certainly not.

I unclip my seat belt with shaking hands and shove open my car door, nearly smashing it into a passing car. Another parent, driving off with their kid. They toot their horn and swerve around me as I stumble into the rain and rush around the car onto the pavement, into the crowd of milling parents and kids.

I stand on my tiptoes, squinting through the rain, scanning everyone's faces and the bright colours of all the kids' raincoats.

Suddenly, I spot them: a blue raincoat and a purple one, hoods now pulled over their heads. They're on the pavement by the gates, huddled together in front of a tall figure in a dark coat, hood pulled up and tightened around their face so their features are indistinguishable. Another parent?

They could be asking about a play date with a friend, or having a last-minute chat with a teacher, but my gut tells me that's not the case.

The hooded figure doesn't have a child with them. Instead, they reach out a hand to each of my children, as if inviting them to be lead away.

No.

'Jake! Polly!' I yell, my voice shrill and panicked. Several parents' heads snap up to stare at me, making a scene. I don't care.

I'm drenched already, my short hair dripping into my eyes. I wipe it out of the way with my forearm and stride through the crowd towards the children. Knocking into people as I go.

A kid barges into my legs on his scooter and I nearly trip over him, grabbing the fence to right myself and when I look up, Jake and Polly are standing in front of me, bemused smiles on their faces. The hooded figure is gone, melting into the crowd and indistinguishable from all of the other hooded parents now leading their children away from school, back to warm homes, dry clothes, dinner, bath and bed.

'Hi, Mummy,' Jake chirps, and I sink to my knees on the pavement and gather them both into my arms, their raincoats slick against my bare arms. 'Where's your coat? You're all wet.'

I can't answer him. I bundle them into their booster seats in the back and climb into the car, turning on all the blowers to max to demist the windows as all three of us steam up the car from the combined heat of our damp bodies. I'm relieved that I can't see through the windows, that I have an excuse not to pull away and join the traffic, when my whole body can't stop shivering in shock and fear.

'Who was that?' I ask, and Jake shrugs.

Polly's staring at the window, tracing raindrops down the pane with her fingertip. Always in a daze. Her sandy blonde hair's already forming damp ringlets around the ears.

'Who were you talking to?' I ask again, my tone harsh.

I watch them in the rear-view mirror as their heads snap up, their faces serious at my unusually snappy voice.

'Don't know,' says Polly. 'She said she was your friend, Mummy. She said she'd come to pick us up because it was raining.'

Jake nods. 'She said you knew she was coming.' He lisps his vowels, still unfamiliar with the large adult teeth in his childlike mouth.

My breath catches in my throat and I'm grateful I'm not yet driving. I'd have run the car off the road again. I bombard them with questions: what did she look like, what were her exact words? I interrogate them on their knowledge of our family rules about pickups: that it'll only ever be Daddy or me collecting them, and never to go with anyone else.

But part of me doesn't see much point in pursuing this line of lecturing, because my old, familiar instinct has kicked in. I've done it twice. I can do it again.

My children will never be in this kind of danger again.

It's time to run.

## 35

As the garage door descends behind us, the daylight disappears and we're plunged into orange artificial light. The kids are out of the car and into the house through the side door before I even have chance to unfasten my seat belt and pick up my phone. My movements are slow, muddied by exhaustion. The adrenaline high of the last couple of hours has worn off, replaced by depletion and fatigue.

In the kitchen I switch on the kettle for a coffee and the oven for a quick dinner. Usually I feed the kids something easy and then make something more lavish and sophisticated for Callum and me to savour once Jake and Polly are in bed – the privilege of being a stay-at-home mum – but today I pour enough chicken nuggets and chips onto baking trays for all four of us and pull a can of baked beans from the cupboard. And then I head into the living room.

The kids are already glued to the TV – some show about deadly animals in the jungle. I open my mouth to talk at the same time as a crocodile almost grabs the cameraman. Jake and Polly watch the near-death action, mouths open.

I wait for a break in the action and then grab the remote, pausing the TV to a chorus of protests.

'I'll put it back on in a minute. I just want to quickly talk to you both.'

'Can we have a snack?' Polly asks, swivelling around on the sofa so her long skinny legs go up the wall. She watches me, head hanging upside down off the edge of the sofa, her hair trailing on the carpet. 'Crisps?'

I shake my head. 'I need to talk to you.'

She whines and slumps down onto the carpet in a tangle of limbs. 'I'm starving. I'll even have an apple. Anything.'

I swear under my breath and stride to the kitchen, coming back with two bananas. I hand them to Jake and Polly and wait for a second while they peel the bananas and take a big bite each. Kids finally quiet, I start to talk.

'We're going to surprise Dad,' I say, trying to sound jovial and excited even though I'm making this up as I go along. 'When he gets home from work, we're going to be all ready to go on a special trip, just for him.'

'For his birthday?' asks Jake.

I smile. He's such a sweet boy, and he knows it's Callum's birthday next, in about six weeks. 'Yes, an early birthday surprise. So once you've finished this episode, I want you to go up to your rooms and find clothes you want to take on holiday. Your hiking shoes and waterproofs, some books to read and games to play. Don't forget underwear and pyjamas. And a couple of toys.'

I'll check their bags and add anything they've forgotten, but it feels important to let them get started, to pick their own outfits.

'But we have another week of school,' Jake says, a worried expression on his face.

'They'll understand,' I say. 'Holidays can be educational. Sometimes more so than school.'

'I haven't said bye to my friends. And there's sports day next week. And a disco,' says Polly, now lying on the floor, half-eaten banana in her hand. She doesn't sound upset, as such. Just confused.

I choose not to dwell, but also try not to dismiss either. 'There's sports day and a disco every year. And we'll see your friends for play dates when we get back from holiday.'

Polly takes another bite of banana, seemingly satisfied with my answer. I'm lucky she's a fairly independent, resilient kid. 'Where are we going?'

I purse my lips. I want them to think this is fun. Not that Mummy is on the run.

'Somewhere nice. It's a surprise.'

And that's going to have to do. Because I, too, have no idea.

I stand up and clap my hands, emulating an excitement I just don't feel and hoping they'll run with this so I don't have to drag them. I brush off more questions with a very parental 'wait and see', un-pause their TV show, and head upstairs, where I quietly pull down the loft hatch and slide down the telescopic ladder. They had at least ten minutes left on their show, so they're unlikely to come upstairs and ask what I'm up to in the attic. I'll be up and down before they see me.

Up in the loft, I grab a couple of empty suitcases and place them by the hatch, ready to take downstairs. One for the kids, and one for Callum and me. They're the large ones we've used for long trips in the past: big enough to hold two weeks of clothes at least. Big enough to hold enough clothes for each of us when we don't know when we're coming back. If we're coming back. And I'll use the unpredictable nature of Scottish weather as an excuse to encourage them to pack as much as possible.

Pack light, we're always telling them. Only this time I'll be telling them the opposite.

Confident I've created a little barrier with the suitcases around the hatch, blocking me from view if either child climbs the ladder out of curiosity, I step over the random boxes and objects we've thrown up into our attic over the years: an IKEA high chair, a couple of boxes of Christmas decorations, a rocking horse, some old picture frames stacked against the wall, a broken TV... Finally, I get to the far end of the loft, where the light barely filters from the tiny window in the eaves. It's filthy over here, my feet making prints in the dust of the plywood floor. I'm completely out of sight from the hatch now, and I can't hear any sound from the house below.

Callum boarded out the loft years ago, before I moved in. He did a great job, and instead of the usual joists-and-insulation death traps that many British lofts provide, with boxes balanced precariously and one wrong move and you'll plunge through the ceiling of the room below, this attic is practically a normal room. Except at the edge here right at the back, where Callum clearly ran out of plywood towards the end and began using offcuts to finish the job.

I found it a few months after I moved in, and was thankful for the discovery.

I crouch down and lift up a smaller piece of plywood, revealing a soft pillow of yellow insulation. I hold my breath against the plumes of dust, and lift up the insulation to reveal an old green box, one that once contained wellington boots. I set it down on the floor and lift off the lid.

Everything inside is just as I left it: a small velvet box with two never-worn wedding rings; a set of house keys, and an old address book full of names, numbers and houses belonging to people I no longer know. Who no longer know me. Except one.

I get out my mobile and key in a number, and then press the green button to dial.

## 36

Like the kids, Callum is wary but amused when he returns home from work to find two packed suitcases lined up by the door. The kids are running wild around the house, finding snacks and entertainment for their 'hand luggage' – the backpacks they'll have with them in the car to keep them busy on the journey.

I've checked the oil and the screenwash on the car, and we've got three-quarters of a tank of fuel.

Over chicken nuggets and oven chips, I tell Callum a semblance of the plan. 'And I called Diane, she said she'd call a locum in to cover your appointments next week. That it's quiet because the kids are still in school anyway.'

He spoons baked beans into his mouth and chews thoughtfully. 'But why not just wait until term ends?'

I stand up and start busying myself with the kids' plates, scraping the leftovers into the food waste bin. 'Lots of reasons. Holiday prices are cheaper in term time, the weather is meant to be great this week, Jake only has two years left of primary school – there's not many more opportunities to take him out of school without consequences.' I pause, waiting for more arguments and confusion from Callum. They don't come.

I turn around, shoulders tense and breath coming in short gasps. I cough to cover it up. I wish he was as easy to trick as the kids are, but he's not clueless. He knows me too well. Well, as much as he can know Gilly.

Callum's staring at me, a concerned look on his face. He notices things. He pays attention. When we first met, I didn't tell him about Robert straight away. He knew I was a little fragile, and of course he knew I had a young son. But it was a few months into the relationship before I confessed that my fiancé had died.

'I'd guessed it was something like that,' he'd said when I eventually told him, omitting the murder, the blood and the change of identity. He'd reached out and pulled me to his chest. 'No man in his right mind would leave you willingly. And your eyes were so sad. So I knew.'

And I'd sunk into him, confident and safe in the knowledge that Callum was an intuitive man, someone who didn't ask a lot of questions but who soaked in the world around him and understood it well enough. Someone I could trust with my life and trust not to poke around too much, too. An ideal match for Gilly.

And now, I know, this wonderful trait in my wonderful husband has come back to bite me. He knows this isn't just a holiday. He knows there's something wrong. But he's not going to ask too many questions, not yet. He's in his information-gathering stage right now.

He's watching every move I make.

And he's probably not the only one. So we need to get going, fast.

## 37

I insist on taking the first driving shift, for many reasons: this is meant to be a surprise trip for Callum, so he has no idea where we're going. But also because I actually also don't totally know where we're going, and I'm going to need to decide as we drive.

It's just turned six o'clock by the time we get on the road, and I'm thankful for the long Scottish evenings with the late-setting sun. We've got a big tent and sleeping bags in the car, so if inspiration doesn't strike from a familiar piece of scenery or an exciting signpost on the drive north, we can pitch our tents next to a picturesque river somewhere and resume the journey in the morning.

I flick my eyes up to the rear-view mirror as often is safe, scanning the other cars in adjacent lanes, checking no one is following. A black SUV. A white BMW. A grey Transit.

'Maybe we'll try some wild camping,' I mention in an off-hand way, when Polly asks for the fiftieth time where we're going as we pull out of our estate. I'm laying the groundwork for anything. Maybe we'll end up camping, or in a B&B, or maybe I'll keep driving through the night as my family sleep in the car beside me, putting miles and miles between me and my faceless pursuer.

A cream Mini Cooper. A black Audi. Another black SUV. Or the same one?

'Wild camping!' shrieks Jake, bouncing up and down in his seat. They've done a bit of camping with Cubs and Beavers, and both kids love it. Callum's taken them once or twice, but they've always been a bit young.

'Too much of a handful,' he'd say when he returned with two incredibly overtired children, dark circles under his own eyes. I never offered to accompany them, firmly sticking with my own position as a lover-of-a-proper-bed and someone who likes a functional, flushing toilet.

Now, Callum gives me a suspicious side-eye from the passenger seat, and then glances back at his phone where I can see he's skimming through the dental appointments for next week.

A blue Hyundai.

'Camping?' he whispers with a smile. 'Who are you and what have you done with my wife?'

Black SUV.

I try to shrug and smirk and chuckle all at once, but it probably looks like I'm having some kind of brief breakdown. 'First time for everything,' I splutter, and turn up the radio to deter further questioning.

But I know he's going to ask more. There's no way his homebody wife who's never loved the outdoors and (as far as he knows) avoids hiking and camping like the plague has suddenly had a massive character transplant. And as much as Callum isn't a particularly curious or nosy person, he's not going to let this go easily.

Suddenly the black SUV is right behind us, the evening sun glinting off the windscreen and obscuring the driver. I shift lanes, and the SUV follows. I change again. It stays in its lane, and I let myself breathe.

But then without warning, it accelerates rapidly, under-taking me on the inside and then pulling aggressively into my lane, only inches from the front of our car. I slam on the brakes and swerve into the next lane, narrowly missing another driver who honks their horn at me angrily. Sweat breaks out on my upper lip.

'Whoa. What's their problem?' Callum asks, shifting in his seat. 'Are you OK?'

I can't answer, fear crowding my brain. Has that car followed us all the way from home? Are they trying to run us off the road? I pull into the furthest slow lane, and watch with dread as the SUV slams on their brakes and starts to move across the motorway towards us, changing lanes rapidly.

At the last minute and while the SUV is still ahead, I take a sharp exit without indicating and pull off the motorway and into a service station.

I stay by the car while everyone uses the bathroom, checking for a black SUV. It was just an aggressive road-rage driver, I tell myself. You're being paranoid. But still... can I risk it? Would I bet my husband and children's lives on it?

No.

Even if the black SUV was a complete stranger, I'm the dangerous one. To keep my family safe, I need to get them some place secure. Then get myself away.

After ten minutes I give up my vigil and follow them into the station, where I buy the kids McFlurries, a very rare treat which is probably a bit of bribery on my part. While I queue to collect them and the kids bicker at the toy-in-a-plastic-ball machine, Callum sidles over to me.

'Everything OK?' he asks, nudging me with his arm. He doesn't move, his warm bulk next to me, propping me up. I wish

I could tell him everything. I should. And I will. But I can't right now. I can barely hold everything together as it is.

But, I realise, we've done it. We've escaped unscathed.

I've driven us out of the town, away from our home, and as far as I can tell no one has successfully followed us. We're safe. For now.

My shoulders slump and I let out a huge breath of relief as I let that sink in. I wrap my arms around Callum's waist, pulling him to me.

'I'm OK. Everyone important is here. And I love you.'

He kisses my forehead. 'I love you too. And I'm here, when you're ready to talk.'

I look into his brown eyes and try to signal everything to him, everything I can't say: that whatever I'm doing right now is in our family's best interests; that my priority is him and our children. Nothing else matters. Not even my own life. That I'm so sorry to have dragged him into this; that our children might be in danger and if they are it's probably all my fault.

That's the biggest question flicking through my mind as we head back into the car and I shrug off Callum's offer to drive. How did that caller find me? How did they know I volunteered at Safeline?

I pull out of the services and onto the quiet motorway, the Friday night traffic easing as we head into the evening and the sun begins to slip lower in the sky. The black SUV doesn't make another appearance, but I scan my mirrors incessantly, while Callum places a calming hand on my knee.

We're still headed north, and in my mind I'm heading for a bothy I visited years ago, in one of those endless summers between school and my first term of university. Before any life-changing damage happened. When I was soft-hearted and trusting Maeve, who nothing bad had ever happened to. No rape. No murder. No grief. No death.

I'd gone up there with a group of school friends, in someone's third-or-fourth-hand Nissan Micra. The car was weighed down with Tennent's, Tunnock's, and Walkers multipacks – in that way that eighteen-year-olds somehow can subsist on nothing but sugar and salt and yet wake up every morning feeling totally fine and not pre-diabetic and dehydrated.

We'd swum in the freezing cold sea every day and drank beer around the campfire every night before falling into our sleeping bags in fits of giggles as the sun finally set at nearly midnight, and the next morning we'd wake up ready to do it all over again. Until we ran out of midge repellent and started craving food with actual nutrients, and had headed back down to our families in Glasgow to show our faces before heading off to halls and a new grown up phase of our lives.

I told Callum all about this bothy when we first met and he has camped up there on his own some weekends. I haven't camped since my sexual assault, terrified of the lack of protection offered by the thin material of a tent, or the perpetually unlocked door of a bothy. I used to love it. But as far as my family believe, I'm not outdoorsy at all. The lie was easier to tell that way.

In the rear-view mirror, I can see Jake in the back seat, his face lit blue with the light of his tablet. Polly has fallen asleep, her tablet resting on her lap, still grasped in her loose fingers. A very different generation. I wonder what their lives will be like when they're eighteen. Whether they'll still consider camping and no electricity a fun holiday with their friends.

We try to monitor and restrict their internet use, but on travel days all the rules go out of the window in favour of keeping them entertained and happy. We use parental controls, special apps that monitor what they do, and they know they're not allowed social media until they're a lot older. But I can't block everything. I can't watch everything.

It just takes one moment of inattention, a small lack of awareness and the defences are down, like the last time Jake's friend Tim came for a play date and disabled the tablet's parental controls.

'What are you doing on your tablet, Jakey?' I ask, trying to sound nonchalant. I've spooked myself now. But in a way it's really nice to be worrying about something else as opposed to the threat I've been driving away from all evening. It's a relief to have realised that we're free, for a while.

'Just reading something,' he mumbles, his tone distracted as he taps away.

'What is it? Your project?' Callum tugs on his seat belt and turns around to look at Jake.

I feel a pang of guilt. For the past month, Jake has been working on a project for the end of term, with his friend Tim. Tim of parental-controls-removal fame, although I'll try not to let that cloud my opinion of him forever. I guess Jake won't be able to hand in his project next week if we're on holiday.

It was some kind of research project about parental careers, and for the past few weeks he's been following me around the house with his tablet in hand, asking me questions about my life. Questions that luckily don't probe too deep into anything I've been trying to hide. I guessed that each kid in his class was gathering information about what jobs their parents did and what they studied and what experience they got to get there.

'What's your year of birth?' he'd ask while I was loading the dishwasher.

'What subjects did you study for Highers?' he asked, when I was driving him and Polly to school.

The questions always came while I was doing something that required part of my attention. I'd suggested a couple of times that he ask Callum about his dental career, but I think my availability was an attractive factor, whereas by the time Callum was home we'd all want to slump in front of a movie with some popcorn, homework forgotten. And I'd have loved to sit down with Jake and really dig into whatever he wanted to know all at once, but the questions seemed bitty and occasional, and when I did have a free ten minutes and said, 'Did you need to do anything for your project?' Jake would go all coy and mumble something about the next batch of questions not being ready.

'Yeah, it was the project,' says Jake, sounding a little irritated. I wonder if he's trying to hide his disappointment so he doesn't spoil Callum's birthday trip. He's at this wonderful age where the selfishness of early childhood is fading and he's learning to think of others. It's amazing to watch, and I'm full of pride.

'How's it going?' I ask, trying to sound nonchalant. 'Will Tim be able to finish it without you?'

'Huh?' Jake says, confusion in his voice. 'Finish what? What does Tim have to do with anything?'

My hands go clammy on the steering wheel. Something's not right here. 'Your school project. I thought you and Tim were doing a careers questionnaire. For a presentation.'

Jake laughs. 'Mum, you're woo-woo.' I see him in the rear-view mirror, twirling a finger around one ear. *Crazy.* I hate when he does that and usually I'd tell him off for that but I need to get to the bottom of this misunderstanding. 'It's finished now anyway.'

'Wait, so what have all these questions been about? Your school project, right?'

'No, it's like a meme thing. This friend I have on Snap—' His voice falters as he knows he's just incriminated himself. He's not allowed social media until he's older. He knows that. '—chat,' he finishes, trying to sound nonchalant and style it out.

Something's not right here. I glance at Callum but he's not really listening, back to scrolling on his phone. And, of course, he's not on high alert like I am. Everything is normal and fine in his world, bar a skittish wife. I try again to sound casual, making a note to come back to the Snapchat thing later, to find out what other platforms he's been using without our permission. 'What, like "tell me what jobs your parents have" or something?'

Jake laughs. 'No, silly. It's a game they call The Project. They get twenty questions and then they try to guess who you are, what your name is, et cetera. But this guy said that was boring and we should do it on hard mode.'

My mouth goes dry. 'What's hard mode?' I whisper.

'It's stupid.' Jake rolls his eyes and I watch through the rear-view mirror as he turns to look out of the window at the darkening sky and rolling hills as we drive through the Scottish countryside. 'Just a stupid internet thing. I didn't want to play at first. It's done now, anyway.'

'Jake,' I say, unable to keep the fear from my voice.

He sighs and catches my eye in the rear-view mirror, his face still lit blue from the tablet he's holding in his hands. 'He said "I'm going to ask questions about your mum and then at the end I'll tell you who your mum is." And he's supposed to be able to comb through stuff online and then give me your identity. Your full name, and stuff. Like a guessing game to show how good you are at finding things online. It's done now anyway. The project's finished.'

I stare at him in the mirror as a high-pitched squeal of panic fills my ears. 'Why is it done?'

'It was stupid.' He's biting his lip, knowing he's in trouble even though I've been so careful with my tone. But he thinks he's in trouble for using Snapchat, not that I'm terrified about who this person is and what they've found.

'Jake, why is the project done?'

He raises a shoulder in a dismissive shrug. 'He said he worked out who you were. But he's an idiot. He got your name wrong and everything. Told me you're called Maeve.'

My vision darkens and I hear the blare of a horn as I wrench the steering wheel to the left, off the road.

## 38

The car careers onto the hard shoulder and I shove both feet down onto the pedals, wrenching the car to an emergency stop for the second time today.

Vehicles whizz by my right shoulder, inches from my car door. In the back, Polly wakes up and starts to cry.

'What the heck, Mum?' Jake whines. 'You made me drop my tablet.'

Callum unclips his seat belt and turns in his seat. 'Are you OK? What's going on, Gilly?' He looks concerned and also a little pissed off. 'Did we hit something?'

I can't breathe. I can't comfort any of them. Polly's wails reverberate through the inside of the car.

I place a hand on my chest and manage to choke out: 'Cramp. Just cramp.'

Like a true medical professional, Callum drops the irritated look and immediately checks me over, feeling my clammy skin and taking my pulse. He then comforts the children, hands them a snack and finds their (mercifully unbroken) tablets where they slid under the front seats with the sudden stop.

I stare into space, my breath coming in short gasps. *He told me you were called Maeve.*

So that's how the Safeline caller found me. Through my son, on Snapchat. He must have posted a photograph of our family and someone recognised me. Whoever that was spent weeks – months, even; I can't remember when Jake's little questionnaire thing started – feeding Jake questions to ask me. Questions that would confirm my identity and my location, and expose my past.

I think back on the questions Jake's been asking me, his tablet in his hand over the past few weeks.

I remember the day when he asked me about my job. I was in the middle of doing about fifteen different things: dinner was in the oven and Polly needed ingredients for a cooking class at school the next day, so we were in the kitchen with a list, pulling things from the cupboards and making a separate list of things I needed to buy from the shop tomorrow and drop back off at school. She was stamping her feet and insisting that we dropped everything and went to the shop straight away, that she needed the ingredients at the start of the school day even though her cooking class wasn't until eleven.

While all of that was going on, Jake was hovering nearby, his face buried in his tablet. Homework, he'd said. And he needed my help.

'Mum, what's your job?' he'd asked, and already I felt a little on the back foot. I've never been comfortable as a stay-at-home mum. I'm not the right personality type for it. I get bored, frustrated, caged. Well, Maeve would. Gilly has moulded herself into this place and stuffs down those caged feelings, until I get asked a question like that and things bubble up to the surface, like a poked bruise.

'I look after you and Polly, and Daddy, and our house.'

Then he'd be quiet for a minute as he typed in his answer,

and then he'd come back with another. 'But what do you do with your days while me and Polly are at school?'

At that point, Polly had discovered that we only had self-raising flour and not plain flour, and she began to wail.

'Don't you get bored? And lonely?'

Polly slumped down on the kitchen floor, dropping the bag of self-raising and covering both herself and the lino with flour.

'For God's sake,' I whispered under my breath, as I held out a hand to her and helped her step over the mess, brushing her down to get rid of the worst and stop her spreading it around the house from her clothes. I ushered her out of the room and tried to do the same with Jake, but he was regarding me with a steely, determined gaze, his finger poised over the screen.

It was homework. It was important. I couldn't send my kid back to school the next day with nothing to show for his questions, especially not when he was actively trying to do his work.

I grabbed a dustpan and brush from the cupboard and got down on my hands and knees to sweep up Polly's mess. 'Volunteering,' I threw over my shoulder. 'OK? I volunteer on a helpline for people who need someone to talk to.'

I can't remember if I said Safeline. I was so distracted, so unthinking. Maybe I did.

Maybe I led them right to my own doorstep and gave them the key.


Even though I insist I'm OK, Callum refuses to let me continue driving. My mind is racing so hard that I don't even push back or mention this stupid surprise. I just check my wing mirror and open the door to move around the car and into the passenger seat.

He finds me a chocolate bar and then rests one hand on the wheel, the other on the ignition. 'How's the cramp?'

Even though it's the last thing I want, I unwrap the chocolate bar and lift it to my mouth. I probably do need the sugar. 'Better. Thank you,' I mumble, taking a bite.

'You've been driving for ages. You probably just needed a break.'

I nod blankly and begin to chew.

He glances over at me, love and concern in his eyes. 'Now, I'm afraid you're going to have to spoil the surprise. Where are we going?'

Even though I begin to sweat, I take another bite of the chocolate to buy some time, then I grab my phone off the dashboard holder and check the map on the satnav. My fingers tremble as I slide them across the screen.

It's time to make a decision, and my options have narrowed as we travelled north. We've been driving for almost three hours and we just passed Inverness. Wild camping doesn't feel like an option any more. In my current state, I can't handle the idea of setting up the tent in the dark, finding all the stuff we'd need for a comfortable night, and then lying awake, terrified as I listen for footsteps outside our tent. Even if I wanted to, after Jake's revelation I wouldn't be able to gather my thoughts well enough to navigate us to the bothy I visited all those years ago. And that'd mean at least two hours more of driving too, and a hike in the dark with two exhausted kids up past their bedtime.

No. There's only one place we can go. And thanks to my earlier phone call, she's expecting us.

## 39

As we pull up outside the dark cottage, a feeling of dread settles in my stomach. I haven't been back here since I left with Sarah years ago, with her support and love to get me on the next step of my journey away from being Maeve and into being Gilly. Stepping out of the car and into the fresh Highlands air feels like a dream. Or a nightmare.

Jake and Callum unpack the car as I pick up half-asleep Polly in my arms and carry her to the front door, my muscles weak with fear.

The street is deserted, as it always was back when I stayed here. The night is quiet, not even the sound of traffic from the main road a couple of miles away punctuating the silence. Above our heads, stars twinkle. Hundreds of them. I'd forgotten how amazing the night sky can be, this far from towns and cities.

I fumble around with the keys I retrieved earlier from the box in the attic. Robert's keys. I take a moment to realise that *Jake* has been here before, as a foetus inside me. I want to turn back towards the car, to wrap my arms around him and tell him that this place is somewhere that just the two of us shared, before Polly existed and before I knew Callum.

But I can't. To my family, this cottage is just somewhere I rented online from an anonymous holiday rental site. Not somewhere I legally would own, if I lived under my true identity. Not somewhere I earn money from, when other people rent it on those holiday sites. And luckily, when I called Sarah tonight from my hiding place in the attic, she'd said there'd been a last-minute cancellation and that we'd be welcome to stay at the cottage from tonight. We've got six nights before the cleaners arrive to make the place ready for the next booking.

The keys turn easily in the lock and I push open the door with my hip. I remember the damp, musty feel from my first night here all those years ago. But as soon as I'd aired it out, I remember I could smell my fiancé, his laundry detergent and the soap on his skin.

Now, I'm immediately struck again by a particular scent in the air that's specific to this cottage. Part of it is the fresh Highlands air – the wind and the moors, mingled with woodsmoke. And part of it is the house itself, a comforting, cotton smell. Like Robert.

My eyes fill with tears but there's no time to languish. Robert's gone and I'm here, with my new husband. I've had years to process this. Years to grieve. But tonight it feels like a fresh wound once more, any healing undone.

I step inside and flick the hallway light on.

Everything looks just as cosy and welcoming as it used to. In addition to the masculine touches that Robert left behind – the rattan straw doormat and the wrought-iron light fittings – there are also more feminine touches that I know must have come from Sarah: William Morris coasters, an oil diffuser on the mantelpiece, a vase of fresh flowers on the coffee table in the centre of the room. Sarah has taken great care of this place.

My arms aching under Polly's weight, I leave the living

room and climb the stairs. I push open the door to what used to be Robert's studio and my legs buckle under me. My breath catches in my throat and my muscles seize.

Robert's paintings used to stand stacked facing the bare walls. Now those walls are covered in mounted canvases, Robert's brushstrokes on display on almost every available space. I had wondered what Sarah had done with his art, and now I know: they're all over this house. I perhaps hadn't noticed them as I passed by in the living room, but in this much smaller room they're unmistakable.

Gone are the bare, paint-splattered floorboards, covered now in a new, springy dark-blue carpet. There are now two twin beds, made up in crisp white cotton bedclothes.

I stumble over to one of the beds and lay Polly down, tucking her under the quilt. Her eyelids flutter and she turns onto her side almost immediately.

I stand, straightening my back and easing out my tired muscles. After hours sitting tense in the car, I ache all over. My eyes scan the walls, taking in my late fiancé's artwork. They're all abstract, with bold colours and large shapes. Each one is clearly a place: a waterfall, a landscape, a building. Sometimes you can make out figures on a horizon, or a person seated on a bench. They're beautiful.

I wasn't able to take any of them with me, and it's been years since I've thought about them. I missed them, I realise, drinking in the colours and shapes like they're Robert himself.

I hear Callum's footsteps climbing the stairs, Jake's pitter-patter behind him.

I shake myself, disengaging from the paintings and bringing my consciousness back to the present. 'I'm in here,' I whisper, careful not to call too loudly and wake Polly.

They hover in the doorway, Callum scanning his eyes over Robert's paintings. 'Wow,' he says, admiration in his voice.

I can't respond. I can't say anything. My two lives just collided and I don't know how to compute.

I leave Callum getting Jake settled into bed, and I gather our bags from the door and bring them up to the second bedroom, the double. The room where I spent weeks crying myself to sleep, gazing out of the window across the hills, a prisoner inside a beautiful cage. It looks pretty much the same: the walls have perhaps had a fresh coat of paint, but the bed is in the same position and the curtains are the same thick blackout material to shut out the bright Scottish nights and early morning sunrises.

But one thing has changed, and I freeze, my eyes trained on the wall above the bed. I don't know what to do.

I hear Callum chatting with Jake, his voice a low rumble through the open door. He always sits and chats with the kids before they fall asleep, sometimes telling them stories, sometimes just asking about their days. Today I can hear brief snatches of their chat: he's asking what Jake wants to do tomorrow, how he wants to spend his holiday.

But I can't tune in to that, the buzzing of panic in my ears reaching new heights as I stumble around the master bedroom, trying to work out what to do before disaster strikes and Callum finds out the truth.

Hung on the wall above the bed is a painting of me.

## 40

I've just managed to shove the wardrobe closed when I hear the scrape of the kids' door on carpet as Callum wishes them goodnight and backs out of the room.

'Well, this place is nice,' he says as he enters our bedroom and glances around. It might be my imagination, but I think his eyes linger on the bare patch on the wall above the bed, where the painting hung just moments before.

I try to quell my panicked breathing and nod, glancing around the room as if I've never been here before. I don't know if Callum would have recognised me in the painting, but I couldn't risk it. It was me before: a defined jawline where I'm now soft; red wavy hair which is now short and blonde; glistening, sparkling eyes with a smile in them which now look tired and slightly haunted.

I had no idea that painting existed. I've certainly never seen it before and don't remember Robert mentioning he'd created one. I didn't pose for it. But the artist was definitely him: I recognised his bold brushstrokes and bright colours; the oils creating an almost 3D effect on the canvas; something slightly abstract about the style even when depicting a person instead of a landscape or a building which were his usual fare.

When I hid out here all those years ago I'm sure I looked through all the paintings he had stacked against the walls. I would have noticed that one. I would have remembered it. Possibly even kept it. Sarah must have found it while she was clearing out the room to make the cottage ready for guests. It's kind that she kept it. Lovely that she hung it on the wall. I wonder how many holiday guests have stared at that painting and wondered about the woman in the picture.

Not Callum, though. I can't let him see it. I can't let *him* wonder.

'How did you find this place?' he asks now, climbing onto the bed and patting the empty spot beside him.

I get onto the bed beside him and snuggle into his side, resting my ear on his chest to hear the slow, steady beat of his heart. Alive. Warm. Mine. For the first time in many, many hours, I can feel the tension begin to leave my muscles.

As much as my time here in the cottage was fraught and unhappy, I did feel safe here while I hid in the wake of Robert's death. It's always been a place which represented sanctuary to me, and I'm grateful for it today. For a moment, I feel safe. Until I remember what we're running from.

I close my eyes, focus my thoughts on Callum's question. 'They had a last-minute opening, and I knew it didn't come along very often so I jumped at it,' I say, feeling guilty about my lie but happy that some of what I've said is true: there *was* a last-minute opening, after all.

'And that explains the rush, I guess?' he mumbles into my hair.

I stiffen. He knows something's not right. He's too clever for me to fool. Still, I resist telling the truth. I nod, and utter a vague assent, but he doesn't reply, waiting for me to say more. 'Sarah owns it.'

His body stills as he takes in the information. 'I didn't realise you were still in touch.'

I shrug. 'Sometimes. Birthdays and such.'

'She was your best friend, right? Before you met your fiancé, even?'

'She was.'

He puts a hand on my thigh, and I can feel his warmth through my jeans. 'Why don't you see her any more?'

I pull my sleeves over my hands, inwardly flinching that I can't tell him the truth, why I can't see anyone from my former life. But I tell him a half-truth. The thing that would be true if Robert had died in other circumstances and I'd still married Callum. 'I think I felt it would be uncomfortable to introduce her to my new husband.'

'I'm not your new husband any more.'

I laugh. 'Not in the slightest.' In fact, it's hard to think about sometimes but I've been married to Callum for three times longer than I ever even knew Robert. I flinch from the guilt that Robert still holds such a big piece of my heart that can never belong to Callum.

'And Sarah was supportive of you marrying your "new husband"?' he asks, an amused twinkle in his eyes.

I tilt my head in submission. 'Maybe it's time you met my best friend.'

'If she lives nearby maybe we can see her while we're here,' he says, standing up and stretching so his shirt rides up to reveal a strip of toned stomach peppered with dark hairs. 'Anyway, I don't know about you, but I want a glass of wine and to sit on that very comfortable-looking sofa downstairs. Maybe we can light the fire.'

Before following Callum downstairs, I sneak back into the kids' room and creep inside, carefully trying each floorboard with my weight before I commit.

The kids are already fast asleep in their twin beds, their bodies curled up under the covers. I can hear their snuffling, regular breathing. For a moment I wish I could just climb into bed beside them, inhale their scent and fall asleep myself.

I approach Jake's bed, the one on the left near the window. Sure enough, his tablet is on charge on his bedside table, bulky in its kid-proof case. I grab it quietly and turn to leave the room, but I pause by the door, my hand on the knob.

The cupboard. I need to see inside.

Where once the cupboard was locked with no key, now it slips open without any trouble, and the once-squeaky hinges are now well-oiled and smooth.

With relief and a strange twinge of sadness, I see that the rows of Robert's dead wife's clothes are gone, replaced with stacks of clean white towels, spare blankets and pillows. I wonder what Sarah did with Elodie's things. I wonder what she felt as she pulled them from their hangers and piled them into boxes. Did she keep them? I wonder. Or did she give them to a charity shop? Or discard them with the rubbish?

I grab a couple of towels so I have a reason for being in here if Callum asks, and I lay them on our bed, with the tablet secreted underneath, before heading downstairs.

He's put a match to the fire that was already laid in the grate, and the flames are licking at the logs and starting to reach higher, the heat already emanating into the room. He's filled two wine glasses with red wine and set them on the coffee table, and he's sitting on the sofa waiting for me, an expectant and curious look on his face.

'Hey,' I whisper, still in stealth mode after creeping into the kids' room.

He leans forward and hands me a glass of wine, reaching out with his own to indicate that he wants to toast.

I settle back into the comfortable overstuffed sofa – a new one since I lived here – and for a moment there's no sound except for the crackling of logs in the grate. But there's a tension in the air and I can feel Callum's focus on me even as he looks elsewhere, his gaze flitting around the room.

I place my wine on the coffee table and turn to him.

'Are you OK?' he asks, and I'm filled with a wave of gratitude for him, for the person he is. Instead of asking 'what's going on?' or 'why are you being so strange?' his first thought is for my welfare, and only once he's checked in with me would he ask for more information. Me first, him second. I've never questioned why I married him, but this is surely evidence that I chose right when I fell in love with Callum.

I can't lie to him. I've withheld enough information from Callum throughout our marriage, and I can't add to it now. Plus sometimes it's better to share the burden. Some of it, anyway. And I owe him more of the truth than this. I sit up and face him on the sofa, my cheeks heating up. 'There's something I need to tell you.'

He nods, a resigned expression on his face. 'I thought there would be. You've been acting strange all evening.'

I close my eyes and inhale. I let the breath out slowly and then I confess. 'This was Robert's cottage. Before he died.'

Even though we're not touching, I can feel Callum's body stiffen. The atmosphere in the room changes. He's never been jealous of Robert, always allowed a place for my late fiancé in my life, but he's also never been faced with the reality of him, either.

And I would understand if he did feel a bit of a threat from Robert: it's very difficult to compete with someone dead who can do no wrong. And very easy for the surviving partner to put that person on a pedestal from which they can never fall. We talked about that briefly in the beginning.

'I'm sure he was a lovely man,' Callum had said, squeezing

my hand. 'You're allowed to miss him. As long as you love me, too.'

Now, Callum pauses, letting my confession sink in. 'His name was Robert,' he whispers, after a minute.

I don't move, realisation dawning of what I've just done.

'You never told me his name.'

It must be the shock of being here, so close to the life I used to have, that made it spill out, made me forget what elements of my past I was supposed to be hiding and what I could be open about. 'I didn't realise.'

He shakes his head and I realise he doesn't believe me. He's right not to. 'What was his last name?'

'I...' I stutter and pause to gather myself. I want to be truthful. But there's a limit. 'I can't tell you that.'

He nods, not in understanding, but in resignation. His mouth is set in a fine line, his jaw tense. He's angry with me, I know. Rightfully.

'I'm sorry. I wish I could explain more.'

He places a hand on my knee and squeezes lightly. 'OK,' he says, confusion in every syllable. He shakes it off and tries another angle. 'It must be hard for you to be back here. Why did you choose it if it's so hard for you? And for my birthday? That feels like a strange choice.'

I close my eyes, holding back tears of guilt. Callum's birthday trip should not be haunted by the ghost of my dead fiancé. My *murdered* fiancé. I didn't think any of this through and none of it is possible to explain away.

'We don't have to stay. It was just... a stop on a longer journey.'

'You said it's booked for us for seven nights.'

'It's available for seven nights but we don't have to use it for the whole time. That's just how long it is until the next guests arrive.'

He turns to me and grabs both of my hands. 'Something's going on with you, Gilly.'

He tries to meet my gaze but I can't look into his eyes. He's not normally confrontational, he lets things lie where others would challenge. But clearly bundling my entire family into the car on a Friday night and forcing him to reassign his appointments for next week has made him hit his limit.

'You're not able to tell me what it is,' he says, and it's not a question. 'Perhaps you will be soon?' He pauses but doesn't wait for me to respond. He knows I can't.

He lets go of my hands in resignation and turns to stare at the fire. 'I know you have secrets, Gilly. I'm not stupid.'

I close my eyes and swallow the lump rising in my throat. 'I know you're not stupid. I would never—'

He leans forward on the sofa, his back to me as he stares into the fire. 'Is it a trust thing? Have I ever given you a reason not to trust me?'

I shake my head so hard it's like my brain rattles. 'Never. You've been nothing but trustworthy and kind. For our whole marriage.'

He turns to me again, his forehead wrinkled with suppressed emotion. 'I deserve your trust, Gilly. And I don't know what else I can do to earn it. And I've waited our whole marriage for you to open up to me. I've never understood why you have no friends, why you don't see any family. Why you choose to isolate yourself from social situations even when people are trying to get close to you. You're not a loner type, yet you've forced yourself into that mould. I can tell you're lonely and that you need more. I know you can't let yourself be happy. And I don't understand why.'

My eyes fill with tears. I thought I was pretending well. I thought I'd tricked him. But I didn't give Callum enough credit and I underestimated him. He's a better husband than I deserve. 'I've not been fair to you,' I whisper, still unable to look at him. My vision swims with tears in my eyes as I stare at the fire flickering in the grate.

He groans in frustration. He knows I'm not going to tell him anything. 'Just tell me you're OK. Are you OK?'

My breath shudders in my chest and I shake my head. 'Maybe I just seem off because this place was Robert's. It's strange to be back.'

He turns to me, then, and holds his hands out, palm up. A plea. 'Don't bullshit me, Gilly.' His tone is firm. He sets his mouth in a thin line and a muscle flickers in his jaw.

It takes a lot to make Callum angry but I know I've done it this time. I open my mouth to speak but then close it again. There's nothing I can say. I can't tell him the truth and I don't want to lie.

He stands up from the sofa and heads to the door that leads upstairs. 'I'm going to go to bed. It's been a long day.'

'Wait,' I beg, gesturing pathetically at the half-drunk wine glasses on the table. I'm cold without his presence on the sofa next to me, and as if it senses Callum's movements, the fire flickers in the grate, threatening to go out. I don't want him to leave me. Something tells me that this is more than just him going to bed early. This could be the beginning of him pulling away. And the horrible part is, I get it. Of course he wouldn't want to be married to a half-person; someone with secrets and a past they won't share, someone who refuses all connections and doesn't let anyone get close. What is there here, for him?

For a moment, I imagine Callum with a different wife. Someone gregarious and carefree. A woman who hosts dinner parties and play dates; who goes out 'with the girls' and comes home late to kiss him awake with gin-tinged lips and a giggle in her throat. Someone with nothing to hide. He'd be so happy with that woman. The woman I was, once.

He shakes his head and his hand tightens on the doorknob, pulling it open so the draught flickers the fire in the grate, threatening to snuff it out. 'The kids have been asking to go camping for years. I know you hate it.' His voice is cold and resigned, and I realise how much my holding back has meant I held back from him, from our marriage, too. He rubs his hand along his stubbly jaw. 'Maybe I'll take them up to the bothy tomorrow, give you some alone time. Chance to clear your head and decide if you can tell me the truth.'

I don't argue. This is the best possible outcome for their safety, after all. If they leave me here and go off-grid, they'll be safe. I'll be protecting them by staying away.

I start to cry in earnest now, tears coursing down my cheeks and my shoulders shaking with repressed sobs. I hear the door click and Callum's footsteps as he ascends the stairs to bed, leaving me alone in the living room.

He's never been this angry with me. He's never walked away while I cried. He's never left – and that's what this is, this camping trip. I know that if he returns from this camping trip and I'm not ready to tell him something – anything – then our marriage is over.

## 41

I wake up standing at the living room window, my body shivering with the cold, a kitchen knife in my hand. I don't know how long I've been standing there or what else I've done. What I do know is I've been sleepwalking. Again.

At some point I must have got out of bed in my sleep, walked downstairs and removed a knife from the block in the kitchen. When once I would have feared what that meant, what I'd done, now I know what it really means about me. Even in my sleep, I'm trying to protect my family. Always vigilant. Never resting.

Despite the deep sleep which usually accompanies my sleepwalking episodes, I didn't sleep much last night, lying stiffly next to Callum's huddled form in the double bed that's smaller than the one we have at home. For some reason it felt like I needed to stay awake, to keep vigil over Callum and my family. Someone is after me, and the last time that happened I woke up next to my dead fiancé. So I stayed awake until the sky began to lighten, keeping watch. Listening. Thinking. Finally, I must have drifted off to sleep as the sun rose, only waking with a start when the chill of the morning air became too much for my pyjama-clad body standing by the window. Even while I was asleep, I was on guard.

Now, all my middle-of-the-night fears come rushing back: would he leave me? If he returns from the camping trip and I still don't tell him everything, is he done with our marriage? And do I want to test that?

I'm fighting against a ticking time bomb, and the explosion will be my marriage if I don't find out who that voice was at the end of the Safeline call. And, I suspect, who killed Robert and framed me all those years ago. I really think that the two are linked, somehow. And I need information, something to give to the police, to exonerate Maeve and come clean once and for all. Something to give to Callum so he'll still want me in his life.

With a lurch I realise that not only do I risk losing my husband, but as soon as he knows anything concrete about my past I also risk losing my children as well. Even if he doesn't go to the police straight away to divulge my secret identity, Callum is risk-averse and cautious. He's never even had a speeding ticket. The idea that his wife might be a wanted criminal, someone on the run from the police suspected of murdering her fiancé... he wouldn't stay in the same room as me for a moment. And he'd take the kids with him, as far away from me as they could get.

I'd never see any of them again. And then eventually I'd be in prison. He'd definitely turn me in. No question.

Unless I can find out who killed Robert, and fast.

But before I have a chance to delve further into my theories and fears, or worry about what else I might have done on my nocturnal wanderings – whether I've freaked out my kids or left the door wide open for intruders – I see something that makes my blood run cold.

There's a car parked outside the cottage. A black SUV glints in the early dawn light, everything tinted blue and gilded with dew. It's quite new, with tinted windows so I can't see inside.

I must have been watching it in my sleep, my eyes sticky and sore from staring.

Now awake, I continue to stare at it for what feels like hours, a metallic taste of panic in my mouth and a ringing in my ears.

If I had any doubts about Callum and the kids going camping without me, they're gone now. They're not safe here.

Is it the SUV from the motorway? I don't remember that car being there when we pulled up late last night. The street was empty, I'm sure of it. Now it's parked across the street, outside an empty-looking cottage with a weed-strewn path and dirt-smeared glass. The house looks unoccupied, but the car is clean and newly parked. Is the owner inside the cottage, or in the car, lurking behind the tinted windscreen?

Were we followed here?

I sit and watch the car, scanning the windows of the house across the street, checking for signs of life. After a while with no movement, no indication that anyone's lurking and watching, I shake off my paranoia and ease out my stiff limbs, returning the knife to the block and then burying myself in Jake's tablet, interrogating all his messaging services, trying to find anything from whoever this person is who was gathering information about me from my son.

I find Snapchat nestling in a folder called 'School' which Jake probably thought I wouldn't look in. I flick through his inbox, skimming a list of chats with his friends: Tim, Chloe, Daniel... all names I know, until I come across someone called TheMagician. Their profile picture is an illustration of an upside-down top hat.

I click into the chat, but there's nothing there. All the messages have disappeared. Of course. I close my eyes in frustration.

I know this is the person who's been contacting Jake. The one who instigated 'the project', interrogating my son over a series of weeks, pretending to be playing some identity-uncovering detective game when actually they knew who I was the whole time. They just needed to know where I was. That must be how they found out I volunteered at Safeline.

Although I've never directly told the children that I'm a volunteer at Safeline, I'm sure they'll have overheard the occasional conversation between Callum and me. We didn't think it was necessary to keep it secret from the kids, and in fact Callum felt it was useful for them to see that I gave my time to a good cause. That even though I didn't work, I still lived a useful, productive life which didn't always revolve around the kids. So they knew I went out to talk to people on the phone, people who needed help. I don't know if Jake knew Safeline's name, but he probably knew enough to give a determined stalker some information. Enough to deduce key elements of my life.

But the stalker has been much more careful to conceal their own details. I tap on TheMagician's profile picture and it brings up an almost blank profile page with a UK phone number underneath. I fiddle around in my phone settings, withholding my own mobile number for outgoing calls, and then I copy the number into my own contacts and press save. As a final measure, I edit the number to add '141' in front to be doubly sure I can't be traced. Then I hold my breath and press 'call'.

A computerised voice pours down the line into my ear. *'The number you dialled has not been recognised. Please hang up and try again.'*

I swear under my breath and am about to try again just as I hear Callum and the kids stirring upstairs.

By the time they come down I'm standing by the living room window and staring at the car as I drink. Jake's tablet is on the coffee table in the middle of the room, everything shut down and switched off. All evidence of my snooping carefully concealed.

Jake and Polly barrel down the stairs, shouting with excitement about their camping trip, which Callum must have told them about when they woke him up.

They jump up and down. 'Mummy! Camping! We're going to sleep in a tent!' Polly shrieks.

'I'm going to take my new catapult and we can set up some targets, right, Dad?' asks Jake, miming pulling the elastic and closing one eye to aim.

My thoughts on this trip are a sickening combination of dread and gratitude. I'm hurt and sad that Callum wants to get away from me – and terrified he'll come back resolved to end our marriage – but actually it's ideal. As much as I want to hold them close, they'll all be safer as far away from me as possible. And it gives me time to think. To work out my next move.

Callum follows them into the room, his hair mussed and his face puffy from sleep. I want to run over to him and wrap my arms around him, but his face is still set; anger, tension and hurt lurk in the corner of his mouth and the creases between his eyebrows. *I'm so sorry*, I think. He deserves so much better than this.

He doesn't greet me with his usual 'Good morning' and a kiss on the cheek.

I reach out to him before he can walk past me into the kitchen.

He freezes as my hand touches his sleeve.

'Take your phone for emergencies but leave the kids' tablets behind, OK?' I say, and he frowns, looking at me in confusion. 'I wouldn't want them to get wet or damaged,' I explain, omitting the real reason: I can't risk that my kids might tell the stalker our whereabouts. I can't trust anyone, even my own children.

## 42

After I wash and dress, I help the kids finish packing their backpacks for camping and gather together a couple of days' worth of food for them into a cool bag. Callum mills around the house, shoving things in packs and refusing to meet my eye.

'Will you be OK without the car?' he asks, as he sits on the stairs to lace up his hiking boots, leaving little chunks of dried mud on the hallway carpet.

I nod, surprised at the question. But then I realise he doesn't know how long I lived here with no transport. He doesn't know how normal it will be for me to be alone in this house with no way to leave and no one to talk to. He knows me as the wife and mother living in the suburbs, always surrounded by people and noise, always with someone to care for and something to do.

'I'll be fine,' I say, reaching out to smooth his hair. He flinches away and my hand drops back to my side. I follow him out to the car. 'I'll enjoy the quiet. Maybe read a book.'

I hate lying to Callum. But I know that what I'll really do as soon as the car pulls away is call Sarah and beg for her help. I need to know who's doing this. We need to solve Robert's murder before the murderer finds me.

I load the kids' backpacks and sleeping bags into the boot of the car, alongside Callum's hiking bag, tent strapped to the bottom. It's going to be heavy.

'Remember that the kids aren't seasoned hikers like you,' I say, glancing over my shoulder at the empty house across the road. Did I imagine it, or did I see a net curtain twitch? I blink to clear my vision, but there's nothing there in the dark windows. No light. No shape of a person staring at us. Nothing. The house is empty. I'm imagining things.

He shakes his head and shuts the boot, barely waiting for me to step back. 'It's a robust hike to the bothy, but the kids should manage,' he says, and turns to usher them into the car.

I hug Polly, planting a kiss in her tangled hair. She scrambles into the car and I pull Jake close. 'Did you leave your tablet?' I ask, feigning nonchalance. 'I don't want it to get damaged—'

'Yes, Mum,' he says with a roll of his eyes. 'It's on charge in the living room. Don't look at my stuff.'

I smile at his privacy request, which sounds like the demand of a much older child – a teenager with secrets and things to hide from his parents, not a nine-year-old whose biggest controversy is trading insults on Roblox. I wish I could respect the request. But this is for our family's safety. It's not like I'd read his diary or something. I'd never do that. This is different.

Jake climbs into the passenger seat and Polly begins complaining. 'Mum! Why does Jake get to sit in the front? It should be my turn.' I can hear the tears and hysteria about to follow, like the low rumble of a kettle on a hob building up the heat to whistle.

I close my eyes and take a breath, glancing up again at the house across the street, and the car parked outside. The way they don't match. There's nothing inherently suspicious here, but I fear there's something I'm missing. Something to pay attention to.

Finally, Callum emerges from the cottage, dangling the car keys with a half-smile on his face. Resignation combined with love. 'Couldn't find them. They were in your handbag.'

'Sorry. I was in a total daze when we arrived last night. Wasn't thinking.'

He pecks me on the cheek as Polly's whining escalates further.

'I'd better get on that,' he says, glancing over at the kids standing by the car, tussling. 'You go inside. Might take a couple of minutes for us to get going.'

I wave at the kids and blow them kisses, before I close the cottage door behind me and take a breath of relief. They're safe if they're away from me. They're off the grid, out of danger. But I have no time to lose.

I turn back to the living room, intending to grab Jake's tablet and click once again on Snapchat, to see what else I can find out about TheMagician and run through the other apps. But the coffee table is empty where it was once plugged in to charge, an untethered charging cable snaking down to the plug socket nearby.

Jake must have taken it despite his promises. TheMagician has access to him.

A movement outside the window catches my eye and I glance up.

Our car's still there, the kids both in the back seat now, Jake's head bent over his little screen. But Callum's not there.

My breath catches in my throat and my fingers grip the window sill, nails digging into the white paint.

Where is he? He wouldn't have left them. Not without a fight.

But I would have said that about Robert, too. He would have fought. He wouldn't have just let himself get attacked and killed. He was too alive, too strong. Until he wasn't given a chance.

Where's Callum?

I'm freaking myself out, and I need to stop.

I lean into the window, pressing my face closer to the glass and peering down the street in both directions. And there: a few metres down the street, tucked behind a post box, I see Callum, his back turned towards us. I feel a rush of relief. No one has taken him or murdered him. He hasn't abandoned our children.

I start towards the door, about to march over to Jake and confront him for his dishonesty, when a movement in the street forces me to pause and look again. Callum is chatting with someone, a figure obscured by the post box. Callum moves his arms as he speaks. His body language is relaxed; this isn't a threatening conversation and he's not on his guard. He's a friendly person, and he probably asked for local recommendations or something.

But then Callum reaches out and shakes hands with the figure, putting his free hand over their two clasped hands in a gesture of friendship and intimacy. The kind of handshake you only give to someone you know. Someone you're grateful to. Someone you owe.

He steps away and turns back to the car, an arm raised in thanks to the stranger. And I see the same silhouette that I saw through the rain outside the playground yesterday, talking to my children: a tall figure with a dark raincoat, the hood pulled up around the face.

I can't move. I can't breathe.

I just watch helplessly and frozen as Callum walks back to the car containing my children, starts the engine and drives away.

He knows that person.

I can't trust him. And he's taken the children.

## 43

I brought the danger with me. Callum can't be trusted.

Tears of panic and sadness prick my eyes as I pull back from the window, but I'm not fast enough. I make eye contact with the hooded figure further down the road and they see me at the window.

I freeze.

Time seems to stand still as we stare at each other, two wild animals circling, about to attack. Their eyes are sharp, piercing. Dark holes in a pale, unhealthy-looking face. Full of hatred and intent.

The figure raises their top lip in a snarl, revealing small, pointed canines.

I hiss in air through my teeth like I've just stepped into a lion's den.

I back away, but I can still see the figure across the road, striding forwards purposefully, hands in pockets, their gaze trained on the cottage. On me.

They're coming for me. Callum led them here. I suppress a pang of sadness. Betrayal.

I grab my phone from my pocket and with shaking fingers I

open up the keypad and dial 999. But I freeze before I touch the green button.

I can't call the police. I've managed to go this long without involving myself with the authorities, and I know that the moment they run my name through their system I'm risking them realising that Gilly isn't a real person, that she's a fake identity with papers bought from goodness-knows-where, probably the dark web. Papers Sarah arranged for me.

*Sarah.*

I flip away from the keypad and open up a new text message to the contact I saved in my phone while in the loft yesterday afternoon, and I type out a text as quickly as I can: SOS.

Outside, the figure is still advancing towards the house at an unrushed pace, head down like a predator eyeing their prey.

I look around the living room, panicked. I don't know what to do.

My hands shake as I scrabble around for something. Anything. An idea. A saviour.

No weapons. Nothing to defend myself with.

But, I realise, I don't need a weapon. I might be Gilly, soft housewife and mother of two, but I'm also Maeve: trained fighter. Strong and brave. Fearless because she once had nothing to lose. Or so she thought. Yes, I haven't kept up with my training but the technique is all still there.

I swallow my previous panic and square my shoulders, feeling my muscles come to life, bracing to fight, to protect, to defend.

I wanted answers. I still do. I want to know who's been talking to my little boy, probing him for information about my life, my whereabouts. I want to know who held me hostage on the phone at Safeline hour after hour, shift after shift. I want to know how they know I'm Maeve. How they knew about my rape. And about Robert.

My skin prickles. It's possible that on the other side of the cottage's front door is Robert's murderer. The person who framed me. The reason Gilly exists at all.

My fear evaporates, replaced with rage.

I wrench open the front door. The street is empty.

Where are they?

I stand still, scanning the windows of the other houses on the street until a movement catches my eye in the car across the street. The one I'm sure followed us here. The one I've been eyeing all night, knowing there was something off about it.

Leaving the front door swinging on its hinges, I start to run.

# 44

The engine starts up as I launch myself at the car, my hands scrabbling at the driver's door handle.

She's not fast enough.

It's a woman, her face stricken as I pull the door open and rip the keys from the ignition, shoving them into my pocket. The engine dies.

She screams long and loud, clearly trying to attract attention from nearby houses. Within a second, my hand covers her mouth and muffles the sound, thrusting her skull back against the car seat headrest with a thunk.

'Shut up,' I hiss at her, shocking myself with the force and aggression in my voice.

She puts up a fight, grabbing at my hands, scratching with her nails, trying to wrench herself out of my grip. But she's strapped into the seat belt, pinned by the steering wheel and I can see from her dilated pupils that she's panicking. She's more afraid of me than I am of her. And, good.

I feel her face move under my hand and I pull away before she can sink her teeth into my palm. She doesn't scream again.

I pin her shoulders to the seat with both hands and kneel on her leg to keep her in position. Then I chance a glance up and down the street. Still deserted. Thank goodness for Airbnbs and second homes, emptying our holiday destinations of nosy residents.

'Who are you?' I ask, leaning down to growl into her face. I'm bigger than her, even though I'm not as strong as I used to be. Already my fighting training is coming back, and I'm assessing her physicality, if there are any weapons nearby, how I can use our size difference to my advantage. She's wiry. Probably strong but she doesn't have heft behind her. 'How do you know my husband?'

She ignores my question and just shakes her head. 'What do you want from me?' she asks, her voice trembling.

Her voice sounds familiar, and I feel a bang of anxiety. The voice on the phone. It was her. I know it.

'Take the car, if you want it. Just don't hurt me.' Her eyes dart around, taking in my hands on her shoulders, the deserted street. This helpless act is fake. She's calculating her next move.

Now that I hear her voice in person I know that I've heard it before, and not just at Safeline. I scan her face. A pointed chin, ice-blue eyes, a pinched mouth... where do I know this face? I try to imagine her without the fine lines around her eyes, maybe with different hair. The familiarity niggles at the edge of my consciousness but I can't place her. Not yet. Not while I'm wrestling at her car, trying to maintain a hold on her. But there's a niggle, a faint memory, a shadow... something lurking in my past.

I push her back into the seat again, knocking her head against the headrest again. She blinks, startled by the blow.

'I know you know stuff about me. I'm sure you understand what I'm capable of. If you don't want to get hurt, you'll answer. I said, "Who are you?"'

She shakes her head and I cuff her around the face. Not hard enough to injure, just to surprise.

'You followed us here. You called me at Safeline. You contacted my son. I saw you talking to my husband. What do you want?' I ask again, through gritted teeth.

She pulls away from me and I loosen my grip slightly. Her scared expression disappears, replaced with a derisive sneer as she realises I have so little information, and how desperately I want it. 'I want what you took from me. I want you to know how much it hurts.'

## 45

Stunned, her words echo through my brain. *I want what you took from me. I want you to know how much it hurts.*

What does she mean? What did I take? I can't answer those questions if I don't know who she is.

She sees I'm distracted – a mistake I'd never have made back when I was training and instructing regularly – and she takes advantage, shoving me roughly away and knocking the breath out of me.

She must have removed the seat belt without me noticing. She scrambles across the car to exit through the other door.

She starts to run, her footsteps echoing along the deserted village street.

She's fast, but I've always been a good sprinter, and I shoot after her as soon as I've caught my breath. Even though I gave up my self-defence and have done very little cardio for the last few years, I'm grateful for my regular yoga sessions keeping me nimble and flexible. Even though my body is softer and heavier, my muscles remember. My breath heaves in my lungs and my legs burn, but I gain on her until I can hear her breath too, wheezing in her lungs as she sprints.

She weaves around parked cars, trying to confuse me, but I keep up, catching up to her by the moment.

As she reaches the end of the village, she turns to check where I am and that's when I get the advantage: she stumbles over the post office's chalk sign which sits out on the pavement, and sends it flying. She crashes to the ground on top of the sign, and I don't waste a moment, launching myself on top of her to pin her to the ground. I quickly grab her arms and raise them above her head, pushing her face to the floor with my chest so she can't move. I'm on my knees on top of her, her thin wrists in my hands. A move designed to immobilise your opponent and keep them there.

'What do you want?' I hiss in her ear, as I scan our surroundings. There's no movement inside the post office, and the windows are dark. It's closed. The old postmaster isn't rushing towards the door, phone in his hand. There's no one to see us. No one to call the police.

The woman doesn't answer, she just groans as my weight on her back pushes the air from her lungs.

I push her face harder into the pavement and tighten my hands around her wrists. 'You've been contacting my son. Why? How did you find us?'

She laughs and turns her head away, pulling half-heartedly against my grip. I think that again she's going to refuse to answer, but then she turns her head to the side and looks back at me, her eyes burning into mine. 'Let's just say,' she hisses, 'I never knew you could bake.'

I pause, trying to work out what she means.

'I wonder if your kids' school would even let you through the gates if they knew who you *really* are. And instead they're letting you sell cupcakes and slices of Victoria sponge.'

And then my breath catches in my throat. The school fundraiser, a few months ago. I volunteered to run a cake stall, and I was in the middle of selling the last fairy cake when I heard a camera shutter *click*. I thought nothing of it at the time, but clearly the picture got posted somewhere. I thought I'd been so careful. The school is great at obscuring kids' faces when they post photos online, but clearly they don't extend that to the parents. And suddenly, this woman had everything she needed: she knew where I lived and where my kids went to school.

Once she knew our location, all she needed next was a lucky break on social media: a public Snap or a 'search nearby' and she'd eventually find one of us if she was determined enough.

She grits her teeth and I feel a shift in her weight underneath me. Suddenly, her left thigh hooks over my lower leg and her hands slide quickly along the ground, one hand up and one down, pitching my weight forward and losing my balance.

I'm filled with dread. I remember this move, and I've taught it in class, years ago. How to escape when you're pinned face-down on the ground. Before I can respond, she uses her hooked leg to flip me onto my back and quickly she's on her feet, above me.

Shame and fear wash over me. Ten years ago I wouldn't have fallen for this. I'd have known exactly how to protect against such an attack. But time is unforgiving, and although I still know most of the defence moves I studied on my travels in the years after university – many ingrained on my unconscious like a tattoo – there are some that didn't stick.

She aims a kick at my ribs and I feel something crack. I curl into a ball and scuttle away, my back against the stone wall of the post office, my knees up to my chest to protect my organs from further attack.

But the attack doesn't come.

She stands and stares at me, a look of triumph on her face as all she'd wanted all along was to best me in a fight. Her hood has come down, and her brown hair is escaping from its scraped-back ponytail. Her cheeks are mottled red with exertion, her chest heaving with every breath. There's a sheen of sweat on her upper lip.

She spits on the pavement, her saliva tinged pink with blood. She must have bitten her lip as she fell. 'That always was your blind spot,' she sneers.

And suddenly, I know who she is.

## 46

'Ella,' I breathe, and she kicks out, sending a spray of dirt and gravel into my face.

On instinct, I cover my face with my hands even though I know that makes me even more defenceless. *You've lost your touch*, a voice chides in my head.

But I hear her footsteps running away, towards her car.

She's going to get away. I'll be left with no answers.

Ella Priestley. I'd thought she was my friend.

I scramble to my feet, a tentative hand on my side, holding everything together where she kicked me. I wince at the pain in my ribs but adrenaline courses through my system and I push on, ready to chase her.

She started as a pupil in my – Maeve's – self-defence class, back when I was still dating Robert, before he and I moved in together. Ella was an A&E nurse, she told me during her first class. She loved nursing but had recently had a string of unpleasant encounters with drunk or unstable patients which had left her feeling like she needed more self-defence awareness so she could protect herself. She didn't need attacks, she explained. Just defences.

I gave her both.

Ella became a friend, and continued attending my classes long after she'd mastered all the moves she wanted to learn. I started seeing her socially, even inviting her to my house, and once even half-successfully matchmaking her with Pablo, one of Robert's friends, at a barbecue. She became friends with Robert, too, in a way: spreading the word about his upcoming exhibitions and attending gallery openings to drink the free Prosecco and coo over the paintings.

Of course, we'd lost touch after Robert's death when I left everything behind. But I thought of her from time to time, hoping she was doing well, but knowing I could never contact her to find out. And, of course, I had seen her on the television while I was in hiding, a glint of victory in her eyes as she implied my guilt and demanded justice for Robert.

So why is she here? Why was she contacting my son? What does she want?

I sprint after her, keeping my hand fixed firmly to my side. I can't let her get away.

She hears me chasing and glances back over her shoulder, stumbling over the kerb. I gain on her a little as she scrabbles with the car door. Her hands are shaking. She's afraid of me.

And suddenly, a new surge of adrenaline hits and I'm sprinting faster than I knew I could. She's afraid of me because she knows what I'm capable of. Unlike anyone else in my life, Ella Priestley knows that I can kill with my bare hands. She knows that I'm fast, that I can immobilise a man over six feet tall and twice my body weight.

I'm not just Gilly. I'm Maeve too. And Ella is right to be afraid.

My feet pound the pavement and I catch up with her just as she wrenches open her car door. I grab her before she can slip inside, and I pin her to the back door, my movements fluid and practised. I know how much pressure is needed to break bones, to dislocate kneecaps. I know how to escape a chokehold. I can throw my weight behind a punch hard enough to kill. I remember the lessons I was taught in Singapore all those years ago, and that I passed on in my classes. To pupils like Ella. Where Ella may have forgotten, these moves are written in my bones, engraved in my very being.

I'm eerily calm, as if I'm watching us from above, everything taking place as if in slow motion through my heightened senses.

I assess her demeanour, and can see immediately that she's agitated and scared of me. Sweat beads on her upper lip, she's twitching, and her eyes flit everywhere. She's not able to make deliberate or informed decisions about her movements. I'm already at an advantage.

She struggles against my grip, but I predicted she would and I'm already ready, my body weight primed and my grip on her secure.

I could wound her or even knock her out, but I want answers. I want her conscious, breath in her lungs so she can confess her intentions. I can't wind her. I can't hit her too hard.

Instead, I ease her to the ground and pin her, careful not to leave myself vulnerable to a counter attack this time. Everything's come back to me now.

And with it, comes more memories of Ella.

She was meant to be at my wedding. Robert and I had invited her, and I assume she was one of the guests waiting in the venue that day, the day I woke up covered in Robert's blood.

She'd attended our rehearsal dinner, persuaded me to make a speech. She gave me a card and a present. I remember opening them with Robert by my side later that night, both of us excited that it felt like the first real 'weddingy' thing we were doing together before the actual day.

Suddenly, I have a memory of the 'congratulations' card on the mantelpiece in our flat, written in green ink. I remember

Robert opening the envelope and chuckling to himself at Ella's oddly worded message:

'Till death do you part,' Robert read out loud, holding the card in his hands. 'Almost sounds like a threat,' he had said, laughing even harder when we opened the present and found the set of finely sharpened Sabatier kitchen knives. At the time it was an amusing juxtaposition, something we could laugh off and put down to our slightly dark interpretation of the world.

'Do you think she's trying to tell us something?' Robert joked.

I'd laughed too. Now, standing in the middle of the deserted street facing Ella, laughter feels a lifetime away, now I know how right he was.

My previous calm shatters and I'm catapulted into a world of confusion and pain.

Ella had handed me a glass of champagne and orange juice that night, before I made my speech. The one glass I'd allowed myself, knowing about the tiny baby burgeoning inside me, mine and Robert's secret. I'd drunk the whole thing, assuming the alcohol was diluted by the juice. Soon after, I went home and slipped into the deepest sleep of my life, one so deep that not even my fiancé's murder could wake me. She drugged me, disguising the taste with orange juice, and then Robert's murderer used one of those Sabatier knives, I remember now, my blood running cold. Ella's wedding gift was the murder weapon.

That green-tinged 'till death do you part' was no hopeful wish for a long and happy life together. It was a threat and a promise.

## 47

Ella moves quickly, taking advantage of my distraction. I feel a blinding blow to the side of my head and a ringing in my ears as Ella uses a move I taught her: a slam designed to injure the eardrum and disorient an attacker.

Then she's on top of me, her hands tightening around my neck.

As I feel her fingertips press into my jugular, cutting off my airway, I close my eyes and almost resign myself to my fate at Ella's hands. If I can no longer defend myself, do I deserve to survive?

My lungs heave, trying and failing to drag air into my aching core.

My vision begins to darken around the edges.

'Why?' I croak with the last breath of air in my lungs. And this is the thought that galvanises me once more, dragging me back into the present. Because I still need answers; answers I've waited years to hear. Those weeks in this cottage alone, grieving Robert and terrified that the police were moments away, about to knock on the door and take me into custody as a murderer. And then the years since, letting go of Maeve and starting again as Gilly, still not knowing why this happened to me. My children have never known the real me. My husband doesn't even know my name. My parents died without ever knowing what happened to me, and if I was OK. They can't have gone through that for nothing. I need to know why.

I hear my coach's voice in my head, shouting at me like he used to in his self-defence academy in Singapore. *Focus on your opponent. Ignore everything else. Just because she's on top of you in this moment, doesn't mean she's won the fight. Every move she makes is an opportunity. Take it.*

She's still on top of me, her hands wrapped around my throat and her thighs pinning my arms to my sides. I buck my body, trying to dislodge her grip, and in the process I manage to free my hands.

My movements unbalance her and she releases my neck to steady herself. I gasp air into my struggling lungs. My vision clears and I buck again, shoving her forward above my head. I shoot my hands out to the sides before she can grab them, and wrap my arms around her hips and tuck my head into her stomach to protect my skull. I'm curled up underneath her, like a little woodlouse under a log. Hard shell. Tough exterior.

When she tries to shift her weight back, I climb her body until I can get my arm over hers. She doesn't know what I'm doing, and suddenly I can plant my feet and flip us over, and I'm on top of her, her arms pinned to the ground once again.

'Why?' I scream in her face, my voice echoing off the walls around us. A fleck of my spittle lands on her cheek and she flinches, turning her face away. 'You killed Robert. You framed me. You hounded my son. Why?'

A look passes over her face, almost amusement. She's enjoying this, I realise. Like me, she's waited for years for this confrontation. I suspect she's been searching for me since my wedding day.

I remember her words earlier. 'What did I take from you?'

Her expression changes, the amusement disappearing to be replaced with derision and hatred. She detests me. I know that if I released her hands right now, she'd try to kill me. I can see it in her eyes. I tighten my grip, grinding her wrists into the floor and feeling her bones creak under my weight.

'My future,' she spits. 'My whole life. So I took yours.'

I stare into her ice-blue eyes, the hatred in there piercing me. But I still have no idea why Ella should hate me so much. We were friends. She was my student. Nothing more. I did nothing to her. Why would she kill my fiancé? Frame me for his murder? Hunt me down a decade later? 'I don't understand,' I say.

Her whole body tenses and I feel the anger and hatred emanating from her in waves. My instincts tell me this person is dangerous, to let go and run, run as far away as I can. But I can see her determination. Now that she's found me she's never letting me go. Or my family. We're not safe and I need to know why, so I tighten my grip and wait for her answer.

She breathes in and out once, twice, taking her time before giving me my answer.

'Because,' she says, her voice trembling with emotion. 'You destroyed an innocent man's life. And then when justice came knocking you slithered away into the shadows. I won't let you get away with it again.'

## 48

*An innocent man's life.* Realisation hits me. I can barely suppress the scoff of derision that rises in my throat like bile.

I remember him sitting in the dock, staring straight ahead at the jury, no expression on his face. Appearing to the jury like a promising young man with his whole life ahead of him. Side parting, comb marks in his sharp new haircut still fresh from that morning. Brand new slim-cut grey suit, white shirt, black tie.

My whole body recoiled when I saw him. The only time he moved was when I took the stand, and then his blank expression shifted. Like a curtain lifting for just a moment, suddenly a sneer parted his lips. And then, as quickly as it appeared, it was gone again and replaced once more with his blank, neutral face. Before anyone else could see.

Simon Adam-Todd. That's who this is about. My rapist. The man who assaulted me and got away with it. Who walked free from the courtroom that day and never served time for the crime he committed against me. And for some reason Ella feels that I am responsible for what happened to him next. For his suicide.

I shake my head, dumb with incredulity. 'He ruined my life,' I breathe, my voice dripping in disbelief.

Her eyes are wild and filled with hatred. 'Your life looked perfectly fine to me. Handsome fiancé, running your own business, nice little flat. The only person whose life was ruined was his. You killed him.' She rears back and despite my restraint, she manages to spit in my face.

I recoil as the glob of saliva spatters on my cheek and drips down my face. My hands are on her, holding her down; I can't wipe it away, and I shudder at the slimy feel.

'He killed himself,' I say with a tremor in my voice, before I can stop myself. I mentally kick myself for rising to the bait, for showing I let her words affect me. Anger bubbles up in my throat and my next words are gravelly with rage: 'That man raped me. No matter what the jury decided, I know the truth. Who are you to determine what really happened? I was there. It happened to me. It was my body. My life. Everything that happened to him – *everything* – was a consequence of his own decisions and actions. Not mine.'

I've had years to think about this. And I have. I know that Simon was guilty and that I did the right thing in reporting him and pressing charges, no matter the consequences. Perhaps he'd have gone on to rape more women, if the police hadn't come knocking on his door a few days after that party. Maybe it wasn't a one-off. Maybe my actions protected other women.

I'm sure he believed he was innocent. And I'm sure that the court's 'not proven' verdict reinforced that belief of innocence for him. And I'm also sure that many of his friends and family believed him to be innocent, too. And held me accountable for what happened next.

I stare into Ella's face, trying to parse what she wants, what her connection is with that time in my life. I don't remember knowing her while I was at university. I don't recognise her from that time. Only from later, when she wandered into one of my self-defence classes and declared herself in need of support against attackers. Against men like Simon.

And then the thought hits me which chills my blood to ice. Yes, if I hadn't gone to the police, Simon would still be alive. And so would Robert.

That day I went to the police to make my report, I could never have had any idea of the butterfly effect I was putting in place. That my decision that day was the wing beat that would cause the tsunami leading to the brutal murder of a man who at that point I hadn't even met yet.

*When justice came knocking you slithered away into the shadows*, Ella said.

She was talking about when I changed my identity to avoid being framed, I realise with a jolt. A flash of anger sears through my chest and I squeeze her wrists tight until her expression crumples with pain.

I lean into her face until I can feel her breath on my saliva-dampened cheek. 'Justice?' I hiss into her ear. 'You think killing Robert was justice?'

Without thinking, I move my head towards my shoulder, trying to wipe her spit from my cheek.

'It should have been,' she snarls, and takes advantage once more of my moment of inattention, shoving me off her and scrambling to her feet. She tries to run, but I catch up to her quickly, landing a blow to the head which knocks her back to the ground.

It wasn't enough. Killing Robert wasn't enough for Ella, for whatever reason I don't know. But it doesn't matter.

I stand over her, knowing I could kill her if I wanted to. But I'm not a killer. I feel responsible enough for the deaths of Robert and Simon, without adding a deliberate death to my roster.

*It should have been.* Justice. She's still hunting her version of justice.

And my blood turns cold.

She's not here for me, I realise. She wants my family. She's going to kill my family. That's what she sees as justice.

I don't care about Ella, revenge, clearing my name... or anything, except my husband and children; I need to get to them.

I aim a swift kick at her ribs, in the same place she kicked my own just a few minutes ago, feeling her ribs crack under my foot. And then I run.

Her car's still on the street, door ajar and keys in my pocket. I slide into the driver's seat and start the engine, just as I see her in the rear-view mirror, sprinting down the street from the post office.

The wheels spit gravel in her face as I pull away, whisking out of the village and into the hills, watching the village get smaller and smaller in my mirror as I drive, until eventually the road winds around a hill into a glen and I can't see it any more.

My heart finally slowing slightly now I'm miles away from Ella, I stop at a petrol station in the middle of nowhere and fill the tank, keeping my head down and not engaging too much when the lady behind the counter tries to make conversation as I tap my card on the card reader to pay for my petrol, water, and a cheese sandwich. I answer her questions in quiet monosyllables, trying to be as forgettable as possible: yes, I'm on holiday. Yes, I'm pleased that the weather is holding up. No, I haven't yet been bitten by midges. Yes, I'll take some repellent, thank you.

I'm good at being forgettable. I've had years of practice.

There are a few other customers at the petrol station: a couple of bikers standing next to their motorbikes in their leathers, chatting while they sip their coffees; a supercar driver with a yellow Lamborghini, presumably up north to take advantage of the winding roads, and a hiker with a massive backpack, shoving a Snickers in his mouth as if that's the only sustenance he's had in days. I make eye contact with no one, using the bathroom and returning to my stolen car as quickly as I can.

I wonder if Ella has reported her car missing yet. I wonder if anyone's looking for me.

I need to get to my family before I'm found. Before anything stops me. I need to warn Callum.

*Callum.*

My stomach sinks as I get back into the driver's seat. Callum was talking to Ella in the street before he left with the kids. I haven't had time to process what that might mean, but guiding the car through the winding lanes of the Highlands with nothing for company but the static of the radio trying to find the signal means I've had time to ruminate on it now.

Callum knows Ella. That handshake I saw was one of friendship, of understanding. An exchange, or an agreement. That wasn't just someone Callum had met in the street and briefly chatted with.

My heart aches with hurt as I run through the possibilities while I drive.

He has betrayed me in some way, that much must be true. Has he been part of Ella's plan from the start? She's clearly willing to play the long game, attending my classes for months and forging a friendship so she could take my fiancé away at the most painful moment; calling Safeline over a period of weeks just to toy with me like a cat plays with a mouse before killing it. Ella wasn't in a rush to get the justice she sought. Maybe Callum's the same. Was our whole marriage a lie? Was he... working for her?

Or did he meet her recently and she's managed to infiltrate his life? He would have mentioned a new friend, unless there was a reason to keep her existence secret. Perhaps it was an affair.

My muscles clench, my body reacting to this thought on instinct. But my mind is clear on this one. Not an affair. Not Callum. He wouldn't. He couldn't. He's steadfast, straightforward. He wouldn't sneak around, wouldn't betray me like that.

*But he knows Ella*, another voice pipes up in my mind. He *has* betrayed you. The only question is to what extent.

How much does he know? I wonder if he's always known about my past, about Maeve, about Robert.

But then if he did know my truth from the start of our relationship, that would mean Ella had, too. And if my whereabouts and identity were both known for years, why wouldn't one or both of them just hand me into the police? So no, I don't think he's always known about my past. But at some point recently – perhaps around the time Ella's calls to Safeline began – she must have also infiltrated my family through Callum, as well as Jake. Perhaps she contacted Callum through work, sidling into his life under the guise of friendship. Or maybe she masqueraded as an old friend of mine, manipulating him into believing I knew her somehow.

The only way for me to find out is to get to Callum and ask him. And if I can't get any answers, at least I'll be with the children. Jake and Polly are my only priority now. Getting them to safety, keeping them by my side no matter what. I'll take them away from their dad if I have to.

My fingers grip the steering wheel until my knuckles turn white, as I turn off the main road and down the series of single-track lanes leading to the place where I'll leave the car and set off on the hike to their campsite.

What if they're not at the bothy? What if he's taken them and disappeared from my life, just like I did years ago? Maybe that's what the handshake was about: Ella had somehow convinced him to leave with the kids, to disappear.

Maybe they're at an airport as we speak, queueing to get on a plane and leave the country.

Tears prick my eyes. I've lost everything before. I can't do it again. I can't live through that again. Losing a love is one thing, but losing my kids is a hell I couldn't live with.

## 50

My hike from the car to the bothy is the longest of my life, stumbling along stony tracks and boggy trails. My ribs still ache where Ella kicked me, and when I raise a hand and press into my side, a sharp pain travels around my abdomen. I turn every corner hoping to hear the laughter and shouts of my children but there's nothing but the wide expanse of hills, the call of sheep and the whipping of wind in my ears.

At some point I take a wrong turn, following what must have been a sheep's track instead of the footpath and then having to double back and retrace my steps when I realise my mistake. Tears of frustration prick my eyes when I realise that's cost me over an hour of time I sorely needed to reach my children.

I'm grateful that the weather is mild, when Scotland's days can turn as fast as a finger click, going from warm sunshine to driving rain and fog in an instant. The ground is damp and soft under my walking boots, the long grass leaving my trousers damp as I push through it, my boots sinking into mud if I don't pay attention to my footsteps.

As I walk I try to choke down some of the cheese sandwich

I bought at the petrol station, but it turns to paste in my mouth and even glugs of water don't help. I throw it into a gorse bush for the birds and stride on, my thoughts festering with fear of what I'll find when I get there.

The sun hovers at eye level, searing my retinas as I spot the slate roof of the bothy tucked into the bottom of a glen, with a river winding its way through the valley behind, and the sea in the distance. It's a tiny little cottage, with two small windows on either side of a door in the middle of the stone walls. A building originally built as a basic shelter for a single farm labourer to sleep while he tended his livestock out to graze for the season. Not big enough for a modern person to live, so now repurposed for campers looking for shelter and somewhere to rest their giant packs while they explore.

The windows are dark and it looks uninhabited, I notice as I descend the steep hill towards the bothy. I hadn't considered that my family just... wouldn't be there.

I swallow tears of frustration and fear, my breath catching in my throat as my steps turn into a run, the knee-high grass lashing at my legs.

Where are they?

The reality sinks into my soul. Callum's betrayal goes deeper than I'd anticipated.

He's taken the children. This whole journey was for nothing.

## 51

They have to be here. They must be. I repeat the words under my breath, my fists clenched by my sides as I scramble to my goal.

I cross the river, its waters rushing past quickly as I hop across the stepping stones and then scramble up the bank to approach the bothy from behind. Where there are two windows and a door at the front, the back wall of the bothy is solid stone, no windows. It must be dark and dingy inside, with so little natural light. No electricity. No running water.

The door is unlocked and I push it open, holding my breath. The room is empty.

My knees give out and I sink to the bare wooden floorboards in despair.

Where are they?

The air smells of damp and the ashes in the fireplace, which is empty and cold. But it's surprisingly clean and comfortable. There's a large scrubbed wooden table by the window, and at the other end there's a raised wooden platform which must be where campers can lay their sleeping bags. It's basic, but it's dry and probably better than sleeping in a tent, when the Scottish weather is at its most wild. I understand why Callum brought them here. *If* Callum brought them here.

I don't know what to do now.

I had been so sure I'd find them here. So sure that my next step would be to talk to Callum, to come clean about everything. To ask him why he betrayed me. To beg for his help, and his forgiveness for not telling him the whole truth.

I'm miles from the car, and when I look out of the window at the horizon, I can see that the sun will set within the next hour or so. I won't get back to it before darkness.

I drink the remaining water I bought at the petrol station and I refill the bottle from the stream. The water is clear, cold and clean, and I gulp it down, filling my empty stomach so it sloshes as I move. It chills me from the inside. I regret throwing that cheese sandwich into the bushes now. I'm furious with myself for not planning this better.

It's summer, yes, but people die in the wilderness of Scotland at all times of year. It's a harsh place for the unprepared and inexperienced, and I am both. I am stupid. And hungry. And tired. And alone.

I curl up in a ball on the bare wooden platform, my arms wrapped around my knees. And I finally let the tears flow. I cry for Robert's loss, for Callum's betrayal, for fear for my children. The death of my parents, never knowing if I lived or died, but knowing I was innocent of the accusation thrown at me by the newspapers. But mostly I cry for Maeve; for that hopeful, ambitious girl who went to sleep next to her love the night before her wedding with hope for her future in her heart, with nothing but love and ambition. Who had it all wrenched away when she awoke the next morning.


The self-pity party doesn't last. I don't have time. My stomach aches with hunger, and I pull myself up from my huddled ball on the cold wood and head to the little kitchenette area: there's no sink or oven, but there's a wooden work surface and some cupboards underneath for plates and pans to use on the top of the wood stove tucked inside the fireplace.

I open a couple of cupboards and then I get lucky: there's a bag of dry pasta and a glass jar of tomato sauce. I almost cry with relief.

I light the stove with a few pieces of kindling and logs stacked next to the stove – making a note to replenish the wood stocks before I leave in the morning – and as the pasta bubbles, I poke around the rest of the bothy, making sure I'm familiar with the layout before the light fades and I'm plunged into the deep darkness of a wilderness night.

As I examine the wooden sleeping platform, I see the metallic glow of hinges caught in the flicker of the firelight. It's not just a platform, it's a storage cabinet.

I lift it up and gasp in shock.

A waterproof survival bag stuffed full of sleeping bags and camping packs. Someone has been here and they've left their stuff. All of it. They're coming back. I won't be alone for long.

## 52

I drop the survival bag without looking too closely, and close the lid of the sleeping platform. The survival bag isn't familiar, so this stuff must belong to strangers. Of course, I understand that bothies are shared spaces – you can't book a bothy so there's always the possibility you'll be sharing – but I just hadn't anticipated sharing this space with anyone except my own family.

I consider leaving, sloping off into the night in the hope I'll find somewhere else to sleep. But that would be stupid. These people are hikers. They might have seen Callum and the kids. They might have a spare sleeping bag I could borrow, or at least a jumper.

But what I don't want is for them to enter the bothy and find me rooting through their stuff. That's one way to make enemies really fast.

The pasta done, I spoon it into a bowl and mix in tomato sauce. It's a plain, simple dinner but I shove it into my mouth like it's the best thing I've ever tasted.

When I finish the bowl, I lean back, gasping with relief like a shipwreck survivor coming to shore. I hadn't realised how much of my despair had been fuelled by hunger.

But the post-dinner euphoria doesn't last long. The bothy descends into darkness as the sun finally sets behind the horizon, and as I huddle into myself, a creeping sense of dread appears with the darkness.

Ella was once my friend. We were friends for years, and saw each other every week without fail, both at self-defence classes and socially: dinner, drinks, barbecues, parties... Ella was the life and soul of each event. I'd offered her a shoulder to cry on after disastrous dates or difficult break-ups, I'd set her up on dates, taken her for coffee for debriefs the next morning... And in turn she'd helped with ideas for my wedding to Robert, accompanied me to the theatre and gigs, and given valuable feedback on how I could grow my self-defence school.

And yet, all that time she was pretending to be someone else. She knew Simon and blamed me for his death years before. She sought me out and befriended me, and everything I remember of our friendship was a lie. She was lying in wait, biding her time until she could exact what she felt was the perfect revenge.

If I can be tricked by one person who masqueraded their intentions, it could happen again.

I'm not upset by Ella's betrayal. I haven't seen her in a decade, after all. But I am terrified by what it might mean for my life now. The long game she's been playing has no limits when she's as unhinged as she is, believing that Simon's suicide was my fault.

No, what causes my blood to turn to ice in my veins tonight is the fear for what poison she's planted within my family. With Callum.

I wonder how long she has been infiltrating my relationship, and what she might be planning. What has she told him? What does he believe?

And, consequently, what is Callum capable of?

If Ella could trick me, pretend to be my friend for years... I can't tell if it's possible that Callum has been tricking me too. And if so, for how long?

Does he really love me? Did he ever?

These questions peck at my brain like a flock of crows over carrion, pecking and pecking at my sanity until I'm curled in a ball on the bare wooden platform again, shivering uncontrollably.

Callum has kidnapped my children. I'm convinced of it.

And that's the thought that's whirring through my brain when I hear footsteps approaching the bothy door, and the door swings open, torchlight blinding me.

## 53

I bring my shaking hands to my face, shielding my eyes from the piercing torchlight.

What if it's Ella? What if she's found me?

I scramble to my knees and shuffle away, my back pressing against the cold stone wall of the bothy. I mentally scan the room, assessing what I remember could be used as a weapon, as a shield... there's not much here except pans and plates. The only knife is blunt. I checked.

'Ooops, sorry,' a male voice says, and the torch drops, aiming at the floor. At his mud-covered walking boots that he's unfastening on the mat by the door. 'Didn't expect anyone else to be in here. I hope I didn't wake you.'

My eyes start to adjust to the dull light, and my stomach twists. I recognise that voice.

'Callum?'

The figure freezes midway through removing his boots. He stands up, the light still trained on the floor. I can only see his silhouette as he straightens, but I know from his build and height that it's my husband.

Alone.

'Gilly?' he says, his tone uncertain. 'What are you doing here? Is everything OK?'

I listen carefully to the way he speaks, trying to discern his thoughts. Is he happy to see me? Or have I thwarted some of his plans? And *where are Jake and Polly?*

'I thought you'd gone. The place was empty.'

'We went for a hike and then were collecting firewood.'

I scramble to my feet and fly at him, unable to contain my fear and frustration. I grab his fleece jacket in my fists. 'Where are they?'

'Whoa, what's going on?' He steps back, pushing a hand onto my chest to get me away. 'They're fine. We've made a campfire on the other side of the river. They're toasting bread and cooking baked beans. Covered in midge bites and moaning a lot, but secretly having the best time.'

He strides to the sideboard and sets the torch on its end so the beam illuminates the ceiling and fills the bothy with a milky light. He's frowning, a mix of concern and frustration. He has no idea the hell I've been through in my mind for the past few hours, thinking all sorts of things. And I still have so many questions. So much I can't trust.

'Show me,' I demand, crossing to the door and holding it open.

He gives me another look, this one slightly resentful, and slides his feet back into his boots without tying the laces. He walks through the open door without looking at me, and heads out into the night.

I follow him as he rounds the bothy towards the river which runs behind, and there on the opposite bank I see the glow of a campfire, and two small figures perched on logs alongside, huddled into the warmth as they reach out to toast bread on sticks. My children.

The air rushes from my lungs in a whoosh of relief, and I sink into the grass, dew soaking my hands and knees in seconds.

Callum's by my side immediately, a hand on my back, rubbing. 'Hey. Hey,' he mumbles in a soothing tone. 'What's happening? Tell me, G. This isn't like you.'

I shake my head, unable to speak. Instead, I hear the chirp of my children talking to each other, a rare, momentary accord between the two rivals. No arguments, no bickering. Just two siblings around a campfire. Just like Callum had planned. And I came here thinking he might have kidnapped them. Maybe even... I can barely think it. But I did, somewhere in my consciousness. Maybe even killed them.

Ella would do that. And for a moment, subconsciously, I had wondered if she'd managed to enlist Callum into the same goal.

I retch into the grass, emptying my stomach of the pasta I stuffed into my mouth earlier this evening.

Callum crouches next to me, a steady hand on my back.

When my breathing slows and the vomiting subsides, I raise up onto my knees and pull him into a hug, smelling the woodsmoke and outdoors on his fleece and in his beard. His skin is warm against my cold, clammy cheek. I thought I'd lost him. I thought he'd betrayed me.

'Who were you talking to outside our cottage this morning?' I ask, releasing him from the hug.

He leans back, and in the half-light I can see a frown of confusion cross his brow. 'This morning?'

*He's buying time*, an evil voice hisses in my head. I shake my head to rid myself of the thought.

'Before you got in the car. I saw you. Shaking hands with someone.'

He lifts his head in recognition. 'Ohhh. You didn't see her?'

'What?'

'That was Sarah. She introduced herself. She said she was popping into the cottage to see how everything was. I was just thanking her for letting us stay.'

My stomach curdles again and I swallow through another retch, but there's nothing left inside me to expel. Ella told him she was Sarah.

'What's up, Gill?' He squeezes my shoulder. 'Did she not come in to say hi? I thought you'd spend the morning having a coffee with your old friend. But you didn't see her in the end? I'm really confused about what's going on.'

I shake my head.

'That wasn't Sarah.'

He opens his mouth in an 'O' shape and closes it again, baffled.

I can't mask the urgency and fear in my voice. 'Did you tell her where you were going today? Does she know we're here?'

And also, a little niggling voice asks in the back of my mind: *How does Ella know Sarah?*

54

---

'There are some things about me that you don't know,' I say, my words shuddering with fear. I step back, knowing what I'm about to say will push Callum away from me for ever. I take in his kind eyes, his weathered skin, the half-smile which always plays around the corners of his mouth, and I almost can't say it. But it needs to be now. It's time to tell him everything, and as soon as Callum had confirmed he didn't tell Ella their destination, the truth pours out of me. 'My real name isn't Gilly. I'm Maeve Ross.'

I scan his face for recognition at the sound of the name of a wanted criminal, but there's nothing but confusion and concern on his face, his eyes scanning my own, trying to understand.

My knees still planted in the grass, the chill slowly creeping up my body to match the fear in my heart, I tell Callum everything. The words come out in a whoosh and he doesn't move, barely breathes as I recount it all: my rape, the trial, the verdict, my travels and training... and then we come to Robert.

My cheeks flush and I grab handfuls of grass as I talk, tugging the strands from the earth and feeding them through my fingers, feeling the tug at my skin as their sharp edges threaten to slice.

'His name was Robert McAuley.'

He cocks his head then, recognising the name that was splashed across the newspapers.

'He was murdered.' I tell him of that morning, of waking up next to his lifeless body, covered in blood and a knife in our bed. Of the certainty that I'd been set up.

His breath falters and he drops to the ground to sit in the grass next to me, his forearms resting on his knees.

'Callum, I need you to know that I didn't do it.' Aside from Sarah, he is the first person I've said this to. The first person I've told everything to, right from the start. And the next bit needs to come out, too, even if admitting it makes me want to run away and never come back. Tears of relief roll down my face as I realise I was always holding on to a little doubt. Even years later. 'For a while I thought it possible that I'd done it myself. In my sleep.'

He draws in breath through his teeth in a sharp inhale. 'While sleepwalking?'

I nod, glancing up at the kids on the other side of the narrow stream. They have eaten their toast and are now poking at the fire and cheering when they send sparks up into the sky.

Callum shakes his head and lays a hand on my shoulder. 'I've seen your sleepwalking, Gill—' He stops himself, and his shoulders slump. 'Maeve? Gilly? What should I call you?'

I lean on his shoulder, feeling the warmth of his body. 'I don't know. Gilly, I guess. I'll always be Gilly to you.'

He lifts his head in acknowledgement and carries on, but I know he'll hesitate before using my name every time now. A little barrier between us. A barrier I put there.

'It always happens when you're stressed. It makes sense you'd sleepwalk the night before your wedding. But I've seen your sleepwalking. You're slow, you're meticulous. You wander around the house touching things with your fingertips. Sometimes you sit at the kitchen table for a minute. Sometimes you look in on the kids. And then you get back into bed. You're not a killer. I don't believe it.'

'Nor do I, now. But at the time, when I was in that cottage... I didn't know what to believe. I'd been plunged into this world which was so unbelievable, so horrific. Anything could be true, I felt at the time. But now, encountering Ella...' My voice cracks as I tell him about the Safeline calls, Ella's resentment and blame for Simon's death.

'So she knew Simon, back when you were at university?'

I shrug. 'It sounds like it.'

'What I don't understand is why now? She was friends with you for so long before Robert was killed. Why wait, if you want to kill someone and frame their partner? And has she been looking for you all this time, since you disappeared? Or did she know where you were and was biding her time? And again, why wait?'

I shake my head, wrapping my arms around myself to suppress a shiver. Callum notices and removes his fleece, laying it over my shoulders and tugging it around my body. It smells of him; his soap and his skin. It's so comforting that tears spring to my eyes.

'I wish you'd been able to talk to me about this earlier. I feel like I've never been allowed to really know you.'

'I'm sorry. I never wanted it to be this way.'

He pulls me to him and kisses the top of my head. 'You didn't deserve any of this.'

I freeze, letting his words sink in. Ella believed I deserved that. She believed that I deserved my fiancé to be brutally taken away from me before we could be married. And more.

*I want what you took from me.*

Suddenly, I know why she did this.

## 55

I close my eyes, reliving the courtroom once again, as I have many times since the Safeline caller revealed themselves to be part of my life. Part of that time.

I remember sitting in the dock, facing the advocate depute with his grey wig, and the barristers sitting at the table in front of him. Defence and prosecution. Their eyes on me. The jury's eyes on me. Simon's eyes on me from the dock. And, behind him, his friends and family filling the seats in the public gallery. Glaring at me.

If looks could kill, I'd be dead. I remember thinking that. Feeling their wrath and resentment.

Now that I'm years away, now that my sheer panic and fear are gone from being in proximity to my attacker, I think back to that girl in the public gallery who was there for my entire testimony, and I remember her in a new light. I didn't attend the whole trial after I'd given my testimony; I couldn't bear the idea of sitting in that gallery amongst people who hated me and my existence. But every day that I was there, so was she – and I assumed she attended the whole thing.

She sat next to Simon's mum. They held hands.

I assumed she was his sister. Maybe a cousin. But now, when I close my eyes and block out the vision of my children huddled around a campfire, I can conjure the image of the courtroom, burned into my memory by sheer adrenaline and fear, and I know it was Ella. A younger version than the one I became friends with years later – with a rounder face and different hair – but Ella nonetheless. And if anyone knows how unrecognisable a few facial changes and a new haircut can make a person, it's me.

'She was his fiancée,' I say to Callum, the weight of the realisation rendering my voice breathless and quiet.

'Hm?' he mumbles, his mouth pressed into my hair.

'It's the answer to your question: "why now?"' I say, shifting away from him so I can see his face. 'She told me she wanted to take from me what she believes I took from her. She never got to marry him, because he ended his own life. So she befriended me and waited until the night before my wedding. She never got to get married, so she wanted to take that from me, too.'

He shakes his head. 'That's unhinged.'

'She *is* unhinged, Callum. Think about everything she's done. She's not going to stop.' I suddenly feel lightheaded with fear, and I glance up to our kids on the opposite bank of the stream. The kids she believes I should never have had, produced with the husband I managed to marry without Ella's knowledge. I swallow the saliva pooling in my mouth. 'She believed Simon was innocent of rape. She had to, I'm sure of it. She stood by him through all of it. And even though he wasn't found guilty, he was harassed after the trial. Many people – rightly – still believed he was guilty. He was attacked, his house vandalised. The papers at the time speculated that the hate campaign against him was what drove him to suicide. In her eyes, he was punished for a crime he didn't commit.'

Callum nods slowly, listening carefully to my theory. His

expression is non-committal, but that's him: he hears all the facts and makes up his own mind.

'She won't stop, Callum. Not until I'm as alone as her. Until my family is gone and I'm in prison for Robert's murder, paying the price for a crime I didn't commit just like she believes Simon had to.'

## 56

I wake up standing in the middle of the foggy dawn, my feet aching with cold, wet grass sticking to my chilled skin. I'm shivering, my bare legs covered in midges feeding at my flesh.

I'm not supposed to be here, I know immediately. I'm meant to be snuggled up next to my husband and two children, in a warm bothy surrounded by sleeping bags. Where we all drifted off to sleep together last night, after chats around the campfire until late, once Callum and I finished talking.

But I'm alone. Cold on the riverbank, the sky above me tinged a deep blue with a light pink close to the ground as the sun starts to creep up the horizon. A crow calls into the silence, a haunting cry.

I've been sleepwalking again.

The realisation strikes fear into my soul.

We'd barricaded the door of the bothy last night, before we all went to sleep. We told the kids it was to keep animals from scavenging our food. But really, even though Callum and I agreed that it would be incredibly unlikely that Ella would find us, we didn't want to take any risks.

I must have somehow moved the heavy wooden table to get

out of the door, and Callum and the kids likely slept through the noise – they're heavy sleepers. As I felt decades ago, horror fills my soul at how much I can do without being consciously aware of it. No wonder I feared I'd killed Robert myself. I have no idea what I'm capable of while I'm sleepwalking. There are no limits. No rules. It's terrifying.

I run back to the bothy, my feet catching on the grass and thistles scraping at my raw shins.

As I approach the bothy I freeze, listening. I can hear the murmur of a car engine somewhere nearby.

But there are no roads. Only gravel-strewn tracks for off-roaders. How is there a car, and this early? What are they doing?

And then the utter terror dawns upon me. I led her to them. I led Ella here and then I left them defenceless, sleeping with the door open and all protection removed. My stomach caves in on itself and I suddenly want to destroy myself. If there was a weapon or a blade nearby I'd maim myself, inflicting blow after blow on my own skull or carving marks into my skin. I did this. I brought this here.

My steps speed up, pushing through the waist-high grass and scraping by gorse and heather. My skin is raw and scratched but I don't care.

The bothy door stands open when I finally reach it.

I scramble inside, my footsteps echoing off the bare stone walls.

The bothy is empty.

My family is gone.

She found us. She's taken them.

## 57

Even though I know the truth, I can't quite grasp it straight away. I run to the sleeping platform, where our sleeping bags are still piled up, and I shift them around, as if I'd somehow find one of my family hiding underneath their clumped fabric. But there's nothing there except an empty medical vial, with the label reading *scopolamine hydrobromide: CONCENTRATE.*

I pick it up before I realise what I'm doing, and drop it back down as soon as I see the label.

She's been here. And she's drugged my family.

I grab some trousers and a pair of shoes, not pausing even when I realise I'm wearing my son's trainers which are two sizes too small. It doesn't matter. Nothing matters except catching up with Ella and stopping her before she does whatever she's planning to do.

I know about scopolamine. It's the drug that the police suspected Simon had given me to make me disorientated and biddable.

Ella's a nurse. She has access to things like this.

I rush from the bothy and freeze, listening. The rumble of

the engine is still nearby, and I splash through the shallow river and sprint up the hill.

The sun is almost risen now, and the top of the hill is dyed pink by the rising sun as I crest the summit. Not far away I can see the cliff edge and the sea, the cliffs dark and spiky. And further out, the sea is rough as it breaks on the jagged rocks below. I hadn't realised we were so close to the coast.

My lungs are burning, but from up here I can see for miles: the mountains in the distance, a column of smoke from someone's chimney a few miles away. And down on the other face of the hill, far below and small: a little winding track with an old Land Rover Defender parked up and the engine running, the exhaust spluttering out clouds of fumes into the cold morning air.

And Ella, her hood pulled up over her head, shoving my children's floppy, barely alive bodies into the open rear door of the truck.

It takes everything I have not to call out, not to yell at the top of my voice at her to stop. To leave them alone. *Take me*, I want to shout. *It's me you want.*

But it's not. She wants me to be alone, bereft. Blamed.

I have no doubt that whatever she has planned has included putting pieces in place to make it look like I did this. Like I followed my family out here into the wilderness to hurt them as she is about to. She wants my family taken from me, as she believes hers was with the death of her fiancé. And she wants me in prison for a crime of which I am innocent, just as she believes happened to Simon.

My fingerprints are all over that bothy. And now the drug she administered.

I descend the hill, slipping and sliding down the dew-covered grasses, almost tumbling head-first over myself many times. I don't take my eyes off the Land Rover as I run, and I watch as Ella finishes loading my family into her stolen car, slams the back door and runs around to the driver's seat on the opposite side.

Then I hear the car kick into gear, the accelerator bursts to life and the wheels spin on the slick grass.

'No,' I scream, and I try to pick up my pace but like I'm in a nightmare I can't move faster, can't stop what's about to happen. My legs feel heavy, the fabric of my jeans constraining my movements like I'm dragging my legs through mud. My lungs burn, and my blood surges through my body, causing a roaring in my ears, beneath which I can almost hear the desperate screams of my children, even though I know it's all in my mind.

The tyres get a grip on the grass and the Land Rover lurches forward, towards the cliff at speed.

I scream again, my voice filling the dawn air until it cracks and splinters, fading away.

Time slows down, and all I can do is watch as the car containing my entire family – my everything – all I have in the world – plunges off the cliff.

Then I hear the sickening, mechanical crunch of it hitting the rocks a hundred feet below, where the waves smash against the headland.

She's taken everything. Just as she wanted.

I drop to my knees and don't stop screaming until my throat is hoarse.

## 58

I rush towards the cliff edge, desperately searching for a way down. If one of them is still alive, I can get to them before the car fills with water. Before they're dashed against the rocks.

Another howl of anguish escapes my lips and it's whisked away by the wind before it reaches my ears.

My whole body is shaking and I can't find a way down from here. If I stand here any longer I'll fall too.

But maybe that's OK. Maybe that's what I want: my body smashed up on the rocks, dashed against the cliffs by the waves. At least then I'd be with my family. And then Ella would never get what she wanted: me, alone, in prison.

I let the wind buffet me, swaying as I'm pushed towards the edge with every gust.

I dig my toes into the dirt and look down at the smashed-up Land Rover on the rocks below, the exposed underbelly pointing up to the sky. The wheels are still spinning, pressure still on the accelerator from inside the vehicle. There's liquid pouring from a tank somewhere, whether that's diesel or water or something else, I don't know.

I sway, readying myself to jump.

There's a sound from behind me and I whirl, nearly over-balancing in the process.

'You.' The voice emerges from my throat like a gravelly hiss.

It's Ella, a triumphant smirk on her face as she advances towards me. She must have set the accelerator before darting away from the moving car. She let it go over the cliff without her. Well, of course she did. She wouldn't kill herself. Not when she could enjoy her revenge from a front-row seat.

I tear my eyes away from her vengeful face, staring back down at the waves smashing on the rocks below. Ella doesn't matter. My family are the only ones who matter.

'I hope you're not thinking of jumping,' she whispers, and I force my gaze away from the sea and back to Ella. Her arms swing loosely by her sides. Outwardly she looks relaxed, but one scan of her body and I can see that she's primed, ready for me to attack. Her arms are by her sides, yes, but they're hovering like someone about to duel with pistols, ready to grab and fight. 'Not when I'm so close to getting you where I want you.'

I swallow my grief, my fighting instincts taking over like I'm on autopilot. I clench my fists and grit my teeth. 'You got what you wanted,' I grind out. 'Killing Robert was your revenge. You wanted me to suff—'

'Maeve.'

I stop, nonplussed.

'I wanted *Maeve* to suffer. But you're Gilly, aren't you?' She cocks her head, mock-innocent. 'I don't think we've met.'

I shake my head, dismissing whatever madness she's driving at. It doesn't matter. *She* doesn't matter.

Slowly, almost imperceptibly, I move myself away from the cliff edge, stepping sideways so I maintain the distance between us while putting space between me and the sheer drop behind me. In my mind, an hourglass is running, each grain of sand trickling away is a moment of potential and hope for saving my family's lives as they lie drugged and unconscious in the upturned Land Rover below.

'It didn't work, then, did it?' I ask as I move, trying to keep the urgency from my voice. *Keep her talking. Distract her until you have a plan.* 'You'll never win.'

Ella's face clouds with confusion.

'Maeve got away, didn't she? She lived a long life and got what you didn't want her to have. No matter what you do now, you can never take away those years of happiness. I got to see my kids grow up—' I swallow the crack in my voice and force myself not to rush back to the cliff edge, force myself to carry on. 'I got the true love and the wedding. Even if you kill them'— my voice breaks again as I say it—'I still got to love them and hold them. I got things you never had before you shoved them off the cliff.'

As I say the last words, I finally ease myself far enough away from the cliff edge that I can launch myself at her. I throw my whole body weight against her and shove her to the ground, just as I did yesterday outside the cottage. I pin her to the grass, my face inches from hers.

'I didn't shove anyone off the cliff. What are you talking about?' Her breath is warm against my cheek.

I roll my eyes. 'Stop, Ella. I saw the drug vial in the bothy. I saw the Land Rover. I saw you loading my kids inside. I'm sure Callum was already in there, drugged out of his mind. And then I watched you set it to accelerate off the cliff.'

Her face is so baffled that I loosen my grip on her wrists for a second. She doesn't move, doesn't make to take advantage of my momentary inattention. I'm so confused. What have I missed?

'I didn't come here in a Land Rover, Maeve. I have an air tag in my own car – the one that you stole – so I stole a car and traced the tracker. I followed the footpath from where you parked. I didn't take your family. I didn't kill them. I wouldn't kill children.'

All smugness and malice have disappeared from her face and for a moment it strikes me as absurd that a murderer would have standards, a hierarchy of who they would and wouldn't kill. So she'll kill my fiancé in our bed as I sleep, but she wouldn't load children into a car and push it off a cliff.

It's such a ridiculous standard that I actually believe her. Ella didn't do this.

'I wanted to take them from you, to show you what it felt like to have that taken away. I wanted to show them the truth, to tell them what you did to my life. I wanted you to lose them, yes, but because they chose to leave you, not because I took their lives. I thought it would be more painful if they didn't want you any more because of all your lies and your past. Not because they're dead.' She pauses, and her next words are so quiet she's almost talking to herself: 'Where's the fun in that?'

She slips from my loosened grasp and crawls to the cliff edge, staring down at the wreckage.

I watch, frozen in grief and shock. If Ella didn't do this, who did? Could there be someone else out there who knows about my past, who hates me so much that they'd kill my family? Or is this unconnected with me?

Unless... my throat constricts. Unless it was Callum I saw, loading our children into the Land Rover and driving it over the cliff. It happens, doesn't it: one parent taking the children and killing themselves alongside. Every parent's nightmare. And Callum's a dentist: maybe dentists use scopolamine as a sedative. He'd probably have access to a drug like that through his surgery. In concentrated form, too.

A chill creeps across my skin.

I shake my head hard. No. He wouldn't. He couldn't. We talked it all out last night and I believed everything he said. He heard me when I bared everything to him. He still loved me after learning all my secrets. He held me while I slept.

Until I stood up and walked away and left them all defence-less, the bothy door wide open.

Perhaps that was the last straw for him.

I hate myself.

Enough. Think about this from another angle, I tell myself.

Perhaps someone was after Callum all along, not me. But the absurdity of this hits me immediately. Not only is Callum the most clean-cut man I've ever met – a man with no secrets – there's also so little likelihood that someone would be after Callum at the same time as Ella was stalking me. No. No, this must be someone Ella knows, even if she doesn't realise it yet. She recruited an accomplice and they've gone rogue. They've taken her instructions and gone off-plan.

Before I can do anything, before I can stop her, Ella shuffles around until her legs are dangling over the cliff edge, with nothing but one hundred feet of air between her and my family.

She's going to fall.

'What are you doing?' I yell, rushing forward to stop her. I can't have another death on my hands. Especially not in the eyes of the police. Plus, she must have a phone. Mine's at the bothy, its screen black and unresponsive due to lack of battery. I can't call the coastguard to rescue my family if Ella's phone is at the bottom of the cliff in her pocket. 'Wait,' I shout, but she doesn't respond.

She inches back, concentrating hard as she finds a foothold and then moves her hands down to cling to the roots and stones emerging from the cliff face. I lean over, barely breathing. The cliff face is raw and exposed, fresh dirt betraying where recent cliff falls have exposed the inner bowels of the cliff. It's not secure.

'This isn't safe. Get back up here. We'll find another way.' I scramble to my feet, scanning the cliff edge along the coast to find a path to the rocks. There must be one.

But maybe I should just let her go. If she gets down there in one piece, she might be able to help my family. But do I trust her? If she gets down there and I made a mistake in believing her to be innocent of putting them in the car, then she's down there with them and I'm up here. What's to stop her killing them if they even survived the fall? That'd be one way to get rid of any surviving witnesses so she can effectively continue to frame me.

I don't know what to believe and I need to save my family. If it's not already too late.

I'm paralysed. Lost.

Below us, the Land Rover wheels still spin, although there's smoke emanating from the smashed-up engine now, and fuel dripping from somewhere. It's not long until the entire vehicle will ignite. And I'm sure the inside is filling up with water every time a wave hits. The tide is coming in. There's no time.

'Go call for help.' Ella's mind is clearly following the same trajectory as mine. She glances down with renewed determination, lowering herself further down the face of the cliff. 'I'm climbing down. We need to save th—'

A look of shock and terror crosses her face as she loses her grip. Her hands flail, grabbing onto handfuls of grass which release from the soft earth, leaving her with nothing. I hear the clatter below as stones fall, bouncing off the cliff and landing on the rocks below.

I throw myself down to the ground and reach forward, anchoring myself and reaching out for her hands.

I manage to get hold of her fingers but I'm too late. I can't hold on. Her fingertips slip from my grasp before she gets a good grip, and her piercing scream fills the air.

I let her go.

Without consciously deciding to, I close my eyes and cover my ears, blocking out the sight and sound of her fall.

Then there's nothing except for the pounding of the waves on the rocks below, and the unearthly whining of the strained Land Rover engine, still toiling, wheels still spinning.

# 59

I can't look. For the second time in my life, there's a corpse and I know it seems like I'm a killer. Below me, I hear the waves lick at Ella's broken body on the rocks below. Even without peering over the cliff, I know there'll be no life left in her body after a fall from that height.

For a moment, I get a quick perspective shift, my awareness zooming out as if I'm looking down on this situation from a great height, like an out-of-body experience. For almost a decade, Robert's murderer has loomed large in my mind as an evil, one-dimensional being with no nuance except evil. Now, that all has to change. Yes, Ella was the one who killed Robert. And now, ten years later, she also intended to save my children. She died trying to get to them.

I shake my head, ridding myself of the confusion and complexity. There's no time to contemplate any of that. I need to save my family.

Having seen Ella fall to her death, I know I can't take that same risk myself. Not when there's a chance I could save them. So, my job is to get help. And I need to move: whoever shoved the Land Rover off the cliff might be still around, and if they're willing to kill children to get what they want then they'll stop at nothing. They're dangerous and violent, and they have no limits.

I start to run.


Back at the bothy, I turn everything upside down, looking for Callum's phone as my breath comes in short, panicked gasps. I empty the backpacks, I shake out the sleeping bags, but nothing. He must have it with him. Even if the drugs wear off long enough for him to be aware of what's happened, it's unlikely his phone will be working if it's soaked in seawater.

I curse myself for not letting the kids have mobiles; for thinking I was protecting them. Protecting us. If I hadn't done that there would be something here, something with connection where I could call for help.

Tears pour down my cheeks as I kneel on the bare stone floor of the bothy, surrounded by my family's camping equipment. Is this it? Is this how they die? Because I'm too pathetic to work out how to save them from the sea?

I'm pathetic.

Over my shuddering breaths and pathetic self-pity, I hear a little chirp, from a pocket of Jake's backpack. A low-battery notification. *The tablet.*

Swiping the tears from my eyes, I tear at his bag until I finally find the tablet, its screen dark on its last 5 per cent of battery power. My heart pounds as I swipe through the menus. Is there a way to get this thing online? To somehow call for help?

As I scroll and click, my fingers fumbling in my panic and rush, I click on a recent Snapchat notification and suddenly Jake's message thread with TheMagician opens up, along with a picture that's been recently sent and the caption: 'Recognise anyone?'

Sarah's face fills the screen, a little countdown timer ticking off the seconds before the image will disappear. She's a little younger, her smile a little wider, her face framed with unfamiliar blonde highlights. A jaunty red fascinator perched in her coiffed hair – the same one she wore to Robert's wedding. The same dress, too. And next to her, with an arm slung around Sarah's shoulders and smiling just as wide, is a much-younger Ella.

The tablet screen goes dark as the battery dies and it drops from my hands, back into the pile of bags and clothes.

Sarah and Ella were friends. Ella went to Robert's wedding. They've known each other for years.

What does this mean?

My thoughts are interrupted by the creak of the bothy door opening and closing and I freeze, listening. Someone has entered the little cabin with me.

A hiker? Or Ella's accomplice, here to finish their attack?

I slowly turn to face the doorway, and at the sight of the figure standing in the middle of the dark cabin, my voice pours out before I can control it.

'Oh my God, it's you.'

## 60

'Hello, Maeve,' she says in her once-familiar voice. Memories flood back at the sound. Good memories. Happy ones. 'Or do you prefer Gilly now?'

I shake my head. It doesn't matter.

Part of me wants to rush to her, to wrap my arms around her. I wish we were reuniting in better circumstances. I wish we could see each other like normal people, for a drink or a coffee or dinner. Laughing. A kiss on the cheek. Her perfume in my nostrils. My brain hasn't caught up yet and I want to be close to her, like the friendships I've never been able to maintain since I became Gilly.

I'm frozen. The sound of her voice makes memories flood back to me, but I can't forget what I've just seen. Her bright smile, cuddling up with Ella. Robert's murderer. Their faces shining out from Jake's tablet.

*Jake.* There's no time.

'Call the police,' I shout. 'The coastguard. Ambulance.' I scramble to my feet.

She doesn't move.

'They went over the cliff. Into the water. The car, it's upside down.'

I'm babbling, but she doesn't move. She barely flinches at what I'm saying.

I stand up, start opening and closing cupboards. 'Help me find a rope. Or anything.'

She just stands silently and watches me, her eyes narrowed.

'You have a mobile, right? Get it out, please. Call for help.'

She gazes at me with a fixed smile, as if she's pleased to see me. She doesn't look any different from how she looked when I last saw her, that day nearly ten years ago. The auburn shine of her hair is slightly duller, perhaps, and the lines around her eyes are more pronounced. Other than that, she could be the same person who drank with me in university bars until we were kicked out at 2 a.m., who compared notes on our respective crushes, who consoled me in the aftermath of Simon's trial...

Those mostly happy memories are quickly supplanted with dread. What is she doing here? What does she want? Even though her face is familiar, I realise I have no idea who she is.

And then fear strikes me in my chest. She was the one who led my family into the Land Rover.

She's not responding because she already knows. Because she did this.

She has been there for almost everything that formed me into who I am today. And for all that time, presumably she's just been biding her time, waiting until she can smash everything up into smithereens.

Sarah. My best friend. And Robert's sister.

She killed my family.

How did she know Ella? When did she shift from being my champion and protector, from helping me get a new identity and sending money to my bank account, to this person who wants to destroy my family? Who drugs them and leads them into a Land Rover which she then pushes over a cliff?

Based on that wedding photo, Sarah and Ella must have been friends long before Sarah and I met. Since the first years of university, back when Ella's fiancé raped me. Perhaps it was easy for Ella to persuade Sarah that I lied about the rape. After all, Sarah didn't know me back then, didn't see the damage to me first-hand. But she did know Ella.

And Ella believed that I was responsible for her fiancé's death. She was adamant. Heck, I've even felt responsible at times.

Perhaps they got back in touch recently. Maybe Ella even managed to convince Sarah that I killed Robert after all. I'm sure it would be an attractive prospect to finally know who was responsible for her brother's death. To assign blame. To provide justice.

Hope is a strong drug. And so is the hunt for justice.

Slowly, Sarah closes the bothy door and we're alone, just the two of us plunged into a dim light, only the tiny windows letting in the meagre, milky daylight.

'Where's Ella?' she asks, looking around for her collaborator.

I wonder how long they've been planning this; how involved Sarah has been. Did Sarah know about Ella's Safeline calls? Perhaps she fed Ella information, exploiting my confidences from years before when I cried to her in our student house, sobbing and rocking and hating myself because of what Simon had done to me. Comforting me in the aftermath of the failed trial and then again when I blamed myself for his suicide. She must have told Ella everything. Perhaps she even helped Ella infiltrate Jake's tablet to gather more information – I'd never given Sarah my address, after all. But unlike Ella she had enough details about me to be able to find me if she looked.

Because I trusted her.

'How could you, Sarah? They are children. Jake is Robert's son. Your nephew.'

Suddenly, every muscle in my body loses strength and I slump to the bare stone floor, the cold seeping into my bones. I don't care about anything except my family. None of it matters. Yes, perhaps Ella didn't get what she wanted – she didn't destroy Maeve's life permanently like she intended – but in this moment I know that Sarah has achieved her twisted goals. She's taken everything I've ever had and she's smashed it up. My husband, my son, my daughter... dead because of her.

And now, the person I thought was my best friend. She's gone too.

She can kill me if she likes. She can do whatever she wants. I have nothing to lose any more.

## 61

But, like a little green shoot emerging from the soil after the depths of winter, a small part of me still has hope that my family might be saved. And, with nothing to lose, I have nothing holding me back from getting what I need to save them.

I shove my despair deep, deep down and I straighten, getting up from the floor and raising myself to my full height. I stand facing Sarah, her eyes inches from my own.

I glance around the bothy for a weapon, for anything I could threaten her with, but there's nothing. And that doesn't matter: I'm the weapon. And Sarah knows it.

Before she can back away, I reach forward and wrap my fingers around her throat. I don't squeeze, just hold a firm grip so she can't wriggle away or run. I don't want to hurt her. Not yet.

The colour drains from her face and her pupils dilate. Her breath emerges from her nose in distressed puffs of air.

'Wh-what are you doing?' she stammers, her eyes flicking from side to side as she attempts to find an escape.

'Why did you wait so long, Sarah? A decade. Why?'

She closes her eyes and turns her head away from me.

'You lost your brother. Robert died because of me. That's what you believe, isn't it?'

She shakes her head, still flinching away from me. She reaches up and wraps her hands around my wrists, trying to prise herself from my grip but it's no use. She knows how much training I went through after university. She's attended some of my self-defence classes. And I've told her about the stuff I learned back then that I can never teach anyone else: the killing techniques. The scary stuff. I can see it all flashing behind her eyes as she scans my face, desperation all over her own.

She knows she's made a big mistake.

'No. I know it wasn't your fault. I've never blamed you.' She grits her teeth and asks me for the second time: 'Where's Ella?'

I ignore her. I don't need her to know yet that Ella is dead. I need information first. I need to understand.

'Of course you blame me, Sarah. Ella killed Robert as revenge on me. And yes, she took him from me but she also took him from you in the process. Why wouldn't you blame me? If I had never met him or got engaged to him, Robert would still be here. Alive.'

'No. Ella's unhinged,' she croaks out, scrabbling at my arms. 'Don't do this. You've got it all wrong. *Where is she?*' She asks that last question with desperation.

I ignore her again.

'Even if you believe it's my fault that Robert's dead, don't take it out on Callum and the kids. Let me get them help, Sarah. Give me your phone. Come with me to the cliff. We need to save them before the tide comes in and—' I can't continue. There's still hope. But not if the Land Rover is swept out to sea. 'Help me.'

But Sarah just shakes her head, and I see her lips forming the question yet again: 'Where's Ella?'

I tighten my grip around her neck. 'She's dead,' I hiss.

'What?' she whispers. 'What?'

'Ella. Your accomplice. Your partner in crime. Whatever she was to you. She's dead.'

She seems to deflate, some colour returning to her cheeks.

I watch her, confused. My grip slackens while I try to understand what's happening. What have I missed?

'She's dead?' Her voice shakes and I wonder if she'll grieve Ella like she grieved Robert. 'Really?'

Then I realise that this is my way to get her to help save my family, if it's not too late already. I turn her around and shove her towards the door.

## 62

I push Sarah towards the cliffs, following close behind her and keeping a grip on her upper arm so she can't break away. I need her. And I need her phone.

I don't really know what I'm planning, all I know is that I need to be close to that cliff. I need to do something to save my family from the water, if there's still hope that they've survived the crash.

We stumble down the hill and I shove Sarah towards the cliff edge. She's cautious, taking small steps and testing her weight as she gets closer to the edge. I increase the pressure on her back. If she falls, she falls. Once, I would have protected Sarah as much as I'd protect a member of my own family. Once, she *was* a member of my family. My almost-sister-in-law. But now she's my enemy, and I'll treat her as such until I can get my family to safety and then get her to a police station to tell them everything.

My world is down there at the bottom of the cliffs in that car. My whole world. And she put them there. I'll stop at nothing to save them.

As we get to the edge, Sarah reaches back to me and in a

confusing echo of the friendship we once had, holds her hand out to mine. As if powered by memory, I reach for her and grip her fingers, holding on tight as she leans forward over the edge of the cliff.

Within seconds, she draws back with a gasp, her face pale once more. 'She's dead,' she whispers, her eyes wide. 'I saw her body in the water. She's not moving.'

I nod and let go of her hand. I wonder what it feels like to lose someone with whom you shared such unhinged beliefs. The belief that I deserved so much loss. That I needed to pay for Simon's suicide and Robert's murder. There's something deeply wrong with Sarah if she believed that uniting with her brother's murderer against me was somehow the right choice. What has happened to her in recent years to make such a wild psychological path? Or was Ella just that persuasive?

'Ella *is* dead,' she says again, and her voice cracks.

I don't have time for this. Ella deserves no grieving after what she did to me and my family.

Sarah sinks to the grass, her head in her hands. She lifts her face up to the sky, a manic glint in her eyes, and then she looks at me and shouts. A sentence; something. But the wind whips it away before it reaches me.

I cross to her, ready to shake her into submission, to rip her phone from her pocket, to push her down the cliff myself if that's what will get my family to safety faster. But then she looks up, and I freeze.

She's not crying. She's laughing.

And then she gets to her feet and starts to run.

## 63

I swear and dart after her. She's not going to get away.

She runs inland, towards the woods and the river. Away from the cliffs.

She's faster than me. I'm still strong but I'm not as fast as Sarah any more. The stress and adrenaline of the last few days have caught up with me, and it's like dragging my legs through treacle.

A sob rises in my throat as I realise that my window for saving my family is closing, and Sarah was my one hope for getting to them.

My breath catches in my lungs and I can feel my throat tightening with panic. I'm going the wrong way. I'm running away from my family, from Callum and Jake and Polly.

I stop running, my chest heaving.

Sarah disappears into the trees, not looking back. Still believing I'm right behind her.

Screw it. I'll climb down the cliff myself.

It killed Ella, yes, but I have nothing to lose. If I can get down there, there's still a chance. I've wasted too much time as it is.

But Sarah must have noticed my hesitation and she re-emerges from the trees, a manic smile on her face. I have no idea why she's behaving like this or what she wants, but I don't care. I'm exhausted. I'm done. She's deranged, just like Ella. And I'm not putting up with it.

'Come with me, Maeve,' she calls, and something in her voice forces me to stop. It's something about the tone, the use of my name – I'm transported back twenty years and we're best friends again, hanging out every day, each others' ride or die. 'Just trust me. One last time.'

She holds out a hand as if inviting me to join her on a stroll through the woods, and I shake my head in disgust. 'I'm not going anywhere with you.'

Her smile disappears, replaced with frustration. 'You don't understand. I have something to show you. Now that Ella's dead I can—'

'I don't care.' I turn away and run back to the cliff edge, dropping down onto my stomach once more and gazing down at the upturned Land Rover, which is still mercifully out of the water, the tide not quite high enough yet to drown its occupants. But if they're alive, why haven't they climbed out?

I scan the cliff face, looking for a better way down than the one Ella chose.

I get up and walk along the edge for twenty feet in each direction, assessing the risk and measuring the drop. Every direction looks treacherous, and no matter what route I choose I'm risking ending up just like Ella, a crumpled, broken heap on the rocks below. But it doesn't matter.

Finally, I find a place with what looks like an underground stream emerging from midway down the cliff, which has eroded a rocky outcrop where the water pours out. It's a gamble, but if I lose my footing here there's a chance I can slow my fall with the outcrop and only injure myself instead of falling to my death.

I'm concentrating so hard on making the plan, readying myself for the cliff descent, that I don't notice Sarah has disappeared until I look up, prepared and ready to lower myself legs first over the cliff side. She's gone. I don't care.

I begin my descent down the cliff face.

## 64

This is a terrible mistake. I've been rock climbing and bouldering before, but always with safety equipment and during a time in my life when my upper body strength was much more advanced. This is a new level of challenging and I'm one small slip away from turning back and climbing to the top again.

Jake's shoes – two sizes too small with worn grips on the soles – scrabble for purchase on the crumbling cliff face, dirt and rocks dislodging and skittering onto the jagged stones below with every movement. My fingers are already raw and scraped from clinging hard to every root and solid piece of earth I can find.

My heart pounds so hard that it feels like that alone is enough to loosen my grip and send me tumbling to my death. I inch downwards so slowly that it's as if I'm just clinging to the same spot, frozen in place. One inch at a time. Slowly. Carefully.

I try not to think about dying with my corpse shattered on top of Ella's, and Sarah living to tell her own twisted version of events to the police.

Ella. Her body must be directly below me.

And then I look down.

A terrible mistake. The ground seems to rise up to meet me, the whole world tipping upside down as vertigo attacks my balance and sends my brain spinning. I cling harder to the cliff face and straighten up, pressing my forehead into the dirt and squeezing my eyes shut.

*I'm going to die. I'm going to die.*

Dredging strength from inside, motivated only by the need to save my family, I shift my weight and start to descend once more, even slower now.

A wall of heat hits my back. I freeze, clinging to the cliff face once again as I realise what's happened: fire. With the engine leaking fuel and the accelerator jammed on, it was only a matter of time. I knew that. And time ran out.

Above my head, seagulls squawk and circle, filling the air as their nests were disturbed by the heat from the fire.

A sob escapes my lips, and my eyes fill with tears. I look down, and all I see is the smoking, burning carcass of the car. The Land Rover is engulfed in flames.

My family are dead.

I've lost everything.

## 65

My family are dead. My beautiful daughter, with her perpetually tangled hair, her still-rounded cheeks. I'll never again feel her curl up in my lap to read a bedtime story, her weight just right on my thighs. My kind son, who feels everything deeply and cares so much for others. Who'll offer his last cheese puff just because he wants to be generous to a friend. And my honourable, sensible husband, who only wanted to love me for exactly who I was, even though I could never show him the full me. He deserved better. They all did.

The loss feels like a hole has been ripped in my chest. I can barely breathe. My vision is black. There's nothing left.

Time passes; it could be minutes, it could be hours. My hands grip the crumbling cliff, the dirt embedding beneath my fingernails. I glance over my shoulder to see the smoke dwindling as the tide rises and begins to douse the flames and swallow up the remains of my family.

I wail, a deep moan that comes from deep in my chest. The wind whips it from my lips and sends it out to sea, where the seagulls whirl as they wait for the smoke to dissipate before returning to their nests.

I could let go right now. I could just lean back, release my grip on the rocks and lean into the wind. I don't even have to look down to know that the jagged rocks below would claim my life in seconds, just like they did to Ella.

No more pain. No more loss. I'd be with them all again: Robert, Callum, Jake, Polly. My parents. Everyone I've lost.

There's certainly nothing left to live for here. Even if there's no afterlife, there's no world up there above this cliff that I want to return to. I've lost it all.

I'll just let go.

Then I hear a noise from above. A rustling.

A pebble hits me on the head. Someone is above me, watching my struggle.

'Are you OK? Let me help you.'

Sarah.

I resist the urge to shout and swear at her to back off, to go away, to leave me alone. I'm a frightened wild animal in a cage, ready to lash out at anyone who comes near.

'Step back from the edge, please,' I shout with my last crumb of energy. 'You're going to push earth onto me.' Not that it matters any more.

'Gilly? Maeve? I'm not sure what to call you.' She lets out a nervous giggle, and for once I'm not sure how to read her – is she laughing because she's panicking, or because she wants me to fall?

'I don't care. I don't care what you call me. Just back the hell off.'

She reaches for me, her hand buffeted by the wind. 'But—'

I grit my teeth. 'Get back from the edge,' I yell, as loud as I can.

There's a silence, and I wonder if she's heard me. But then there's another sound. One more movement. I'm again pelted with falling debris: dirt and little rocks scatter on my head and in my hair. I freeze, every muscle rigid. Even if I don't let go, I don't know whether to continue my descent; to see what's left after the fire, or whether to give up and climb back up. Whatever decision I make, I need to keep moving, before this stupid insane woman causes the whole cliff to slide. I'm only a couple of metres down and there's still so many to go.

'I said—'

'Mum?'

I inhale sharply and open my eyes, immediately turning my gaze upwards to the sky. There, peering over the edge of the cliff are two faces, looks of concern across their brows. Jake and Polly. Tears blur my vision and I almost let go of the cliff face in shock.

Then there's another face, a bearded, smiling, friendly bear of a face. The face of home. I let out a sob.

They're alive. They're alive and I need to get up there to them and pull them into my arms and bury my nose into their hair and hug them and hug them and hug them and never let them go. My family is alive.

'Get away from the cliff edge, all of you,' I shout. 'No one else gets hurt today.' And with a renewed strength, I begin to climb up towards them.

## 66

I've got tea. Hot and sugary, cradled in both hands. There's a sleeping bag around my shoulders and it smells of Callum, a comforting, homey scent. In front of me, the campfire Jake built is roaring, and my beautiful son is leaning forward to poke at the embers with a stick, sending sparks up into the air.

Callum reaches out a stern hand and gives a little shake of his head to Jake. Be safe, his face says. He doesn't need to speak. Jake nods and drops the stick into the fire.

Polly's sitting on the log next to me, leaning her head against my shoulder. On her other side is Sarah. My best friend. She's toasting a marshmallow, occasionally bringing it out of the flame and dabbing it with her fingertip to test whether it's done. As soon as she's satisfied, she hands it to Polly who takes it with a delighted grin, blows on it a couple of times and pops it into her mouth.

My two worlds are clashing: my best friend from the old world and my family from the new.

Despite the warmth of the fire and the heat of the early July day, I can't stop shivering. Callum keeps giving me concerned looks. There's so much he doesn't know. In his mind, I'm acting

strange: the impromptu trip, the nervous demeanour, the cliff
climb... but he doesn't know even half of it. Mercifully, he's
been sheltered from most of the events of the last few days.
Although I know I'm going to have to tell him. No more secrets.
No more lies. He deserves to know everything.

He doesn't understand why I was scaling the cliff. Why I
was so afraid that 'someone else' might fall off the cliff. Because
when I finally made it back to the flat grassy ground at the top
of the cliff and turned back around to show them, Ella's body
was gone. Washed away to sea. And the water had risen enough
to almost obscure the still-smoking Land Rover against the
rocks. Evidence of my nightmare swallowed up by the water.

As if it never happened.

Soon, the fire loses its novelty and Callum leads the children away for a game of football, using two stumps as goalposts.
They're close enough that I can see them – I never want to take
my eyes off them – but far enough away to be out of earshot.

Now I need answers.

'What happened, Sarah? There's so much I don't
understand.'

She grabs another marshmallow and skewers it onto the end
of her stick. 'I'll start at the beginning, when I got your text
asking for help. I set off straight away and I got to the cottage in
time to see Ella breaking into one of the parked cars just outside
the village. You must have just left with Ella's car. I followed
her until she pulled over in a layby to sleep. I got lucky: when I
checked the map I could see that at a certain point this part of
Scotland becomes so remote that the only possible place she
could have been heading was the bothy. Other than this little
cabin it's all farmland, hills and then the sea. There was nothing
else. I managed to overtake her while she slept and I got here as
the sun was rising. I found you wandering around outside. I
knew it's dangerous to wake a sleepwalker so—'

'Actually that's a myth,' I muttered through chattering teeth.

She pauses, a grin on her face. 'Well, I know now.' She raises her eyebrows at me in a faux-exasperated look and suddenly it's like no time has passed. She keeps her voice low. 'I woke the kids, and Callum and I took them to a little fishing burn further in the woods.'

'You didn't drug them?'

She looks at me with wide eyes, a baffled expression on her face. 'Drug them? What?'

'There was a bottle of scopolamine in the bothy.'

She raises both hands to her forehead and smooths out the skin, as if trying to help her mind process what I've said. 'Scopola-what?'

I sigh. I believe her. 'A drug. It can be used to control people. I thought Ella had given it to them to get them in the car. And then when I thought it was you...' I shake my head. 'It can be a party drug, I think. I guess it might have just been some other campers left it behind. Out in the wilderness for a good time.'

She shakes her head. 'I didn't drug anyone. I got your family out of the bothy – undrugged – because I knew Ella was looking for you and I wanted them out of the way for whatever insanity she was about to create.'

I nod, trying not to interject that Sarah had also contributed a significant amount of insanity. 'Why not just tell me what you were planning?'

She twists her mouth and looks skywards, thinking. 'Ella and I met in freshers' week, long before you and I were friends. She was... extreme, even then. The kind of girl who would throw her boyfriend's clothes out of her window if he received a text from another girl. Or who'd empty her drink on someone in the bar if they looked at her funny. We stuck together for a while until I realised she wasn't my type of person, and that's when I started finding friends who suited me a bit more. Friends like you.'

'Why didn't you warn me? I was friends with her in Glasgow, after university. She was in my self-defence classes for years.'

'When you and I became friends, your court case was already done, so I didn't make the connection between Ella's fiancé and the trial.' She shakes her head, baffled. 'You and Ella met after we graduated. I was in law school and we barely saw each other, remember? So I never met your Ella to link everything together. I didn't know she was the same person until you called me the other day and told me what had been happening with Safeline. It had to be someone who knew you right from the court case and through your relationship with Robert. And as far as I knew, there wasn't anyone. We hung up the phone two nights ago and I went back through all my files until I found the photos from your rehearsal dinner, and there she was. Ella. My old friend, and your new one.'

I close my eyes and process this. The butterfly effect in action again: if I'd had just one get-together that Sarah could have attended in those few years after university, she'd have been able to warn me about Ella before any of this happened. If Sarah had made it to the rehearsal dinner and seen Ella again, maybe Robert would still be alive. I wouldn't have married Callum. Polly wouldn't exist.

'I had my suspicions that it was her who killed Robert, but – as you know – the justice system needs proof. It was too early to involve the police. They'd just arrest you. So I got in the car and headed straight to the cottage, then I got your family to safety.'

I open my eyes again and gaze at the fire. 'Why didn't you tell me they were alive? I was accusing you of all sorts. I thought you'd murdered them. I could have killed you.'

She shakes her head. 'Even though you hated me, you wouldn't have killed me. You had too many questions, for one thing. You've spent years waiting for answers, if you thought I had some you wouldn't have done anything that stopped you getting them.'

She's right. And with Ella's death there are so many things I can't ask her. Things I'll never know.

She holds out her stick to offer me the toasted marshmallow on the end. I shake my head. My stomach is still churning after everything that's happened. She shrugs and takes a sticky bite before continuing. 'She needed to believe that your family were dead so she'd leave you all alone. Your reactions needed to look real.'

I exhale, momentarily reliving the way I felt in the moment I watched that Land Rover plummet over the edge of the cliff, with what I thought was my family inside. And then the horrifying finality of the flames. But no, they were just a couple of Sarah's spare outfits stuffed with whatever she could find in her Land Rover, anything to trick Ella – and me – from a distance. And it worked. I nearly fell down the cliff trying to save them. And Ella did fall. To her death.

'I can't help but think this was all so pointless.' I pause to sip the sweet tea and feel the hot liquid trickling down and warming me from the inside. 'Ella needed help years ago. After Simon died. A therapist. A psychiatrist. Anything to help her process that grief instead of letting it fester inside into something ugly.'

Sarah nods. 'I can't imagine how it must feel to have your fiancé accused of rape. And then his suicide...' Her voice trails off and she shudders. 'Of course Ella needed therapy. Anyone would.'

'We should call the police,' I say, my hands shaking even as I make the suggestion.

Sarah's eyes widen. 'Are you ready for that? To face everything? You'll have to tell Callum first.'

I give her a sad smile. 'I've got a few choices. I could stay living as Gilly for now. We could leave and do nothing. Wait for someone to discover the wreck and call it in. But we'll be traced and questioned as soon as the police look into who was in the area around these dates. Or we could report your wrecked car and Ella's death. As far as anyone will know, we're just a family on holiday who saw a tragic car accident after someone tried to steal your Land Rover. Either way risks them looking into my past, my identity. You could be implicated, as you helped with the paperwork.'

She purses her lips. 'I don't regret it. No matter what happens.'

'Or we come clean on everything straight away. I contact the police about Ella's accident and Robert's death, try to clear my name now we know the truth.'

She reaches out and takes my hand. 'I'll be here for you, every step of the way until your name is cleared. That day at the cottage, I told you I'd find out who killed Robert. I've been working on a case file, full of stuff about the murder. And now we can add everything we know about Ella. Tangible evidence.'

I swallow a tearful giggle. *Of course* she's got a case file. How very... Sarah. 'Then maybe it's time to say goodbye to Gilly. Reintroduce Maeve to the world. I don't want to hide any more. I don't want to be afraid.' A hysterical giggle emerges from my throat. 'I want to run my own self-defence classes again. And drive thirty-five miles per hour in a thirty zone without freaking out about being pulled over. And make proper friends I can talk to without holding back; people who'll laugh when I make weird jokes. Like you.'

She squeezes my hand and lets out a low chuckle.

'And yes, I'll tell Callum the rest,' I say, mentally cataloguing the extra details that have emerged since I poured everything out to him last night. Everything except what's happened since. 'I should have told him everything years ago.' I shake my head at the wasted closeness we could have had, at how much of myself I was holding back from him, the man I love.

'Should have told me what?'

I took up to see Callum and the children approaching, their faces flushed and happy from their football game. He's holding hands with Polly, and as I watch Jake reaches out and takes Callum's other hand. Jake's trousers are muddy, the knees covered in grass stains. His hair falls over one eye just like Robert's used to. And Polly is the spit of Callum with her piercing brown eyes. My world, all three of them, with a little piece of Robert living on in Jake.

Sarah gives me a nod, her approval for our plan to come clean, move forward with our lives and finally put Robert's memory to rest.

'There's a lot to tell you. Later.' I nod towards the kids, who are already bickering over who gets the next marshmallow. 'For now, I just want you to know—' A laugh bubbles from my throat; what feels like the first genuine, unfettered laugh I've expelled since the night of my rehearsal dinner ten years ago.

Callum sits down on my other side, his shoulder warm next to mine. 'Mm?' he prompts, his expression amused while he waits for my laughter to subside. He's never seen me like this, happy and carefree, laughing with a friend. 'You want me to know what?'

I take a shaky breath, and when I start to speak my laughter bubbles under my words. 'I've decided to start taking self-defence classes. I might be quite good at it.'

Sarah guffaws, and cuffs me on the shoulder just like she used to.

Suddenly, I feel a rush of peace. A deep calm washes over my body as I know that my fight is over and one day soon I won't have to hide any more. I can be myself, whether I'm named Gilly or Maeve, I don't know.

All I do know is that today is the first day of the rest of my life.

# EPILOGUE

I crouch down and trace my fingers over the carved letters, dug deep into the grey granite of his headstone: Robert Angus McAuley, aged 38 years. Above my head, the wind rustles through the leaves of a giant oak tree which casts shade across the grave on this otherwise sunny afternoon.

He would have liked it here. He loved being outdoors, feeling the wind and the sun on his skin. His parents chose a good gravesite: on a sloping grassy hill with Glasgow's majestic skyline in the distance; houses, blocks of flats, church spires, and then in the distance the hills.

I wish I could talk to him.

*I miss you,* I'd say. *I'm sorry.*

I open my mouth to speak, but no sound comes out.

Now that the police have been able to close his case, I can finally visit him without worrying about leaving in handcuffs. For more than ten years I've imagined this moment – yearned for it – and wondered what it would feel like to stand at Robert's grave, his body underneath the earth I stand on. I thought I would feel close to him; that I would feel able to finally say goodbye in a way I wasn't able to back then. I imagined it would feel painful to be so close to him without being able to hold his hand, to wrap my arms around his tall, thin frame.

But he's not here, I tell myself as I stare at the damp grass under my feet. I can't feel his presence like I imagined I would. His spirit and warmth and life left this world long ago, while I slept a drugged sleep next to his body and his last breath left his lips. Nothing of Robert remains here. If I want to be close to Robert now, I can look at his paintings on my walls, trace my hand along the ridges of the dried oils where his brushes once swept across the canvases. Sarah kindly gave me some of the collection from the cottage, and Callum likes having them around, says Robert was a true talent. Instead of needing a grave to visit, I carry Robert with me everywhere, his name written on my heart alongside my other loves: Callum, Jake, Polly, Sarah.

But I'm glad to be here today, to finally run my fingers along the carved lettering that mark the beginning and end of the life of a beautiful person, cut short by misplaced hate and bitterness. I'm grateful I can now leave my own offering: the picture of Robert and me at that barbecue years ago, Robert kissing my hand, my cheeks flushed with happiness and love. Sarah saved it for me when she renovated the cottage, and now it's in a waterproof frame ready to leave by his grave.

In front of his gravestone are three hand-tied wildflower bouquets in varying stages of decay. His parents visit every week, Sarah told me, so I suspect this is three weeks' worth of offerings. To make space for the picture I move the oldest bouquet, its petals browning around the edges. Underneath, there's a round, flat pebble about the size of the palm of my hand, painted with a windswept seaside scene: a steep cliff face dropping down to a narrow beach and then a rough sea, breakers easing up the sand. One of Robert's artist friends must have left it here for him. I smile and pick it up to admire it closer, feeling its weight in my hand.

Just then, the wind picks up and blows something away from the grave – the pebble must have been weighing down a note or a card or something. It snags in the grass a few metres away and I hurry over to collect it, ready to place it right back where it came from under the painted stone.

But as I bend to collect it, my breath snags in my throat and the pebble tumbles from my grasp. It's a note, dry and clean as if it's only just been placed at the grave. The writing is familiar, but the ink even more so: it's an acid green, vibrant and poisonous. The same acid green that scrawled a warning on a wedding 'congratulations' card over ten years ago.

My heart rate speeds up further and the hair on my arms raises in goosebumps despite the warmth of the afternoon sun. I glance over my shoulder, scanning the graves and the trees, checking if I'm being watched. Nothing moves except the grass shifting in the summer breeze.

In one hand I hold the pebble, in the other is the note.

I bring the pebble closer to my face, squinting to see the detail painted on the stone. They're so small that at first they blended into the cliff. But now I'm out of the shade of the oak tree, I can see the detail: there, on the beach below the familiar cliff, with the waves lapping, is an upturned Land Rover. And standing beside it on the beach is a waving figure.

My guts churn and I turn my attention to the note, its wicked green ink dancing on the page in front of my eyes.

*'I know what you did. You'll never be free.'*

# A LETTER FROM ROSIE WALKER

Dear reader,

Thank you so much for choosing to read *The Bride's Secret*. I hope you enjoyed reading it as much as I enjoyed writing it. If you did, please spread the word: write a review, tell a friend, buy a copy as a gift, or post on social media. Word of mouth and positive reviews make a huge impact, and the more successful a book is, the more new ones the author can write!

You can also stay up to date with all my latest releases; just sign up at the following link. Your email address will never be shared and you can unsubscribe at any time.

*www.bookouture.com/rosie-walker*

Like many books, *The Bride's Secret* started as a couple of distinct ideas that weren't quite right until I worked out how to join them together into one really robust and exciting plot. Often these ideas are things I want to understand at a deeper level, and by writing about them I can get inside and explore them from as many angles as possible.

For a long time, I'd been fascinated by news stories about sleepwalkers accused of murder, and especially those who were acquitted because the jury accepted they were asleep when the crime took place. There are many cases and legal defences like this – some more believable than others – and when they came up on the news I'd pore over them with interest, imagining the nightmare that the accused woke up in that morning, and the emotional struggles their family underwent in the aftermath of a loved one's death and the subsequent trial. Like many issues that fascinate me, I took the murder-while-sleepwalking accusation and wrote it into this book so I could look at it closer and consider it through the eyes of Maeve, who fears that maybe she killed her fiancé in her sleep.

Like Gilly, I volunteered on a phone helpline while I was a student, and it was one of the most rewarding things I've ever done. I loved it (mostly), and was lucky enough to meet some of my oldest, closest friends in my fellow volunteers. Unlike other university clubs where we would share a hobby or interest with other members, on that helpline we shared something bigger: a desire to help other people – just like Gilly experiences with Safeline. I talked to some amazing people and hopefully made a difference for some who needed help.

While volunteering on that helpline, I did experience a couple of the challenges that Gilly encounters, and some wormed their way into my brain and lived there for the past two decades until I could process fictionalised versions of them during the writing of this book. I've wondered a lot about the psychology of regular callers to helplines; not the ones who genuinely need help, but the ones who abuse these services and their policies and manipulate the call handlers. And that's how Gilly's thread was born.

I love hearing from readers, and I'd love to hear your reactions to *The Bride's Secret*. Did you believe that Maeve could have killed Robert? Have you ever received a phone call that chilled you to the bone? Do you think someone who kills in their sleep is innocent or guilty? Did you guess the midpoint twist about Gilly and Maeve, or was it a complete surprise?

You can contact me through Facebook, Bluesky, Instagram, or my website.

Thank you again for reading, and I can't wait to hear what you think of this book!

Love,

Rosie Walker

www.rosiejanewalker.com

 facebook.com/rosiewalkerauthor

instagram.com/rosiejanewalker

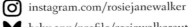 bsky.app/profile/rosiewalkerauthor.bsky.social

# ACKNOWLEDGEMENTS

First, I'd like to thank my literary agent, Charlotte Robertson, who has supported my writing career since its very beginnings back when I queried her agency on the day it opened. Charlotte taught me so much about writing, genre, structure, and the publishing industry as a whole, and she was always at the end of an email to offer support, advice and help. Without Charlotte I wouldn't be writing these acknowledgements for my fifth book, with a sixth in the works and countless more ideas for future novels in the pipeline. Thank you so much for everything, Charlotte, and good luck on your next adventures!

Next, I'd like to thank another person without whom I wouldn't be a published novelist today: Suzy Pope. She's always the person I bounce my first ideas off or inflict an early draft upon, and her suggestions and encouragement are invaluable. My books wouldn't exist without Suzy.

Writers are notoriously solitary creatures, but we like to occasionally crawl out of our burrows and share our woes or celebrate our wins with friends who stop us getting cabin fever. First a special thanks to three strangers: Keith, Carlos and John. You did a good deed to help a stranger one snowy night and I promised I'd thank you in my next book! And thank you to all my writer- and reader-friends who lend an ear, who ask how it's going, who pre-order the latest release, who wander into book-shops and libraries to ask them to stock copies, and who spread the word. This also applies to my family in the UK, Switzerland

and the US – who are hugely supportive even after now five books. You all keep me sane and I'm massively lucky.

Thanks to my husband Kevin, who understands that I'm happiest (and easiest to be married to) when I've got time and space to write a book, and who, like Callum in this novel, also always offers that I can wake him up in the middle of the night when I'm being an insomniac. I rarely do, but it matters a lot that the offer's there. And thank you to Elsie, who is now four years old and has learned to tell people, 'My mummy writes books,' which is so adorable and probably sells many more copies than my own publicity efforts can.

Thank you also to Maisie Lawrence, my former editor at Bookouture, who was brilliant with my previous two novels, *The Baby Monitor* and *My Husband's Ex*, and who helped shape the initial idea for *The Bride's Secret* before heading off on her next publishing adventure. She was a pleasure to work with and I wish her the best of luck in her publishing career.

And finally, thank you so much to the Bookouture team, whose names are listed in the credits on the next page. Special thanks go to my editor Ruth Jones, whose insightful and supportive guidance and suggestions helped shape *The Bride's Secret* into the novel you hold in your hands today, and who is a pleasure to work with on this and my next book. I'm delighted to work with such a great bunch of talented, inspiring and knowledgeable people, and I hope to continue being a Bookouture author for a very long time if they'll have me.

Last but definitely not least: thanks to *you*, dear reader, for choosing to read *The Bride's Secret*. I hope you enjoyed Maeve and Gilly's tale as their stories wove together. If this is your first book by Rosie Walker, I hope you loved it and are inspired to read another in the future. If you've read all five, thank you so much. My readers are massively important – your feedback and encouragement keep me writing, so please get in touch, or tell your friends, or write a review.

# PUBLISHING TEAM

**Turning a manuscript into a book requires the efforts of many people. The publishing team at Bookouture would like to acknowledge everyone who contributed to this publication.**

### Commercial
Lauren Morrissette
Hannah Richmond
Imogen Allport

### Cover design
The Brewster Project

### Data and analysis
Mark Alder
Mohamed Bussuri

### Editorial
Ruth Jones
Charlotte Hegley

### Copyeditor
Jane Eastgate

### Proofreader
Liz Hatherell

## Marketing

Alex Crow
Melanie Price
Occy Carr
Cíara Rosney
Martyna Młynarska

## Operations and distribution

Marina Valles
Stephanie Straub
Joe Morris

## Production

Hannah Snetsinger
Mandy Kullar
Ria Clare
Nadia Michael

## Publicity

Kim Nash
Noelle Holten
Jess Readett
Sarah Hardy

## Rights and contracts

Peta Nightingale
Richard King
Saidah Graham

Printed in Dunstable, United Kingdom

65265867R00180